GOODNIGHT, JOHN-BOY

PAT MILLS

MILLSVERSE
BOOKS

Read Em and Weep Book Two

Goodnight, John-boy

This first edition published in 2017

Copyright © 2017 Pat Mills

Based on the Read Em and Weep story Copyright © 2017 Pat Mills and Kevin O'Neill

All rights reserved.

ISBN 978-0-9956612-6-4

Published by Millsverse Books 2017

Published in the United Kingdom

Cover illustration by Alex Ronald

http://alexronald68.blogspot.co.uk/

Cover design by Lisa Mills

Edited by Lisa Mills

First Printing, 2017

The authors greatly appreciate you taking the time to read our work. Please consider telling your friends about this story to help us spread the word. Thank you for supporting us!

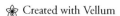 Created with Vellum

To the late Joe Colquhoun,
Artist-Creator of Charley's War

PART I

_____

MARCH TO MAY 1976

'Only I can do this and survive.'

CHAPTER ONE

METROPOLITAN POLICE COLD CASE UNIT NOVEMBER
3RD 2016
Detective Inspector Mary Read
REPORT INTO THE MURDER OF MRS JEAN MAUDLING
Summary

1. On 2nd August 2016 a body was found in a secret room in the basement of 10, Mordle Street, Stoke Basing, by the current homeowner, John Trigger. It has been identified as Mrs Jean Maudling, 32, who lived at 2, Mordle Street, and was reported missing in March 1957. She lived there with her husband Peter, daughter Annie, 12, and son David, 8.

2. Forensic examination confirmed she had been strangled with her fur boa, which was found beside the corpse. A knuckleduster in Mrs Maudling's shopping basket had blood on it and it is thought that Mrs Maudling may have used the weapon to defend herself against the murderer. However, there is no match for the murderer's blood on the national DNA database.

3. A copy of the comic *The Fourpenny One* was found at the crime scene and, according to Mrs Maudling's daughter, Mrs Annie Ryan, now aged 71, her mother would have purchased the comic for her son

from Mr Cooper, a local newsagent, on the Saturday, shortly before she was killed.

4. The comic is dated Saturday 9th March 1957. Three days later, on Tuesday 12th March 1957, Peter Maudling reported his wife was missing. Therefore, her likely time of death was between these two dates.

5. 10 Mordle Street was a derelict, bombed-out house for many years before it was renovated. The upper floor was illegally used by Peter Maudling to produce 'moonshine' alcohol. He died in the premises on November 6th 1970 after sampling his latest 40% bockbier that he called 'From Here to Eternity'.

6. Mrs Ryan has provided valuable information on her mother's life, enabling us to put together a profile of Mrs Maudling and persons of interest in this case.

7. Despite extensive enquiries, we have been unable to trace Mrs Maudling's son, David, now aged 67, and we have little information on his life. During the 1970s, he worked for Fleetpit Publications in Farringdon Street, London EC4, and was editor of a number of comics such as *The Spanker* and *Aaagh!*

8. Judging by statements obtained from witnesses who knew David when he worked for Fleetpit Publications, he appears, in my view, to be mentally unbalanced.

CHAPTER TWO

IT WAS FEBRUARY 1957 AND, once again, the doorbell jingled as eight-year old Dave Maudling nervously entered the newsagent's shop in search of his favourite comic: *The Fourpenny One.*

Inside, to his huge relief, there was no sign of Mr Cooper; it was Mrs Cooper who was standing behind the counter. This was his lucky day. He could quickly find his comic, pay her and run out of the shop.

Once more, he searched the racks for the comic every boy must have, or be a pariah in the playground. He cast his anxious eyes past *Basher, Scarper, Blimey!, Pinafore, Radio-Active, Goggle Box, Spunky* and *Homework.* He knew exactly where *The Fourpenny One* should be, but – to his horror – it was missing.

Mrs Cooper saw the boy desperately looking through the rows of comics. She realised what was on his mind and what could happen. 'Stan drank too much tea last night. He's sleeping it off. Run while you've got the chance, Dave.'

The boy looked up at her with his troubled Bambi-like eyes.

'But he'll *know,* Mrs Cooper.'

Mrs Cooper did her best to protect the youngster. 'I won't say anything. Forget about your comic. Run, Dave. Please. He's in a terrible mood.'

Dave was about to make a bolt for it when he heard the all-too familiar rustling of the beaded curtain that separated the shop from the back room. The hungover and unshaven newsagent, dressed in striped pyjamas and brown jacket, entered and cast a black look at his wife: 'Private deals? You dirty cow.'

'Don't be silly, Stan,' said Mrs Cooper lightly. 'He's just a lad.'

'He'll be a big lad soon enough. I'll deal with you later. Now get back there.' She reluctantly disappeared into the back room. Mr Cooper turned to Dave, who was frozen to the spot with fear. To calm himself, he repeated the words on a box of *Sherlock's Liquorice Pipes*. 'He chews *Sherlock's*. We choose *Sherlock's*. Everyone chooses *Sherlock's*. He chews *Sherlock's*…'

Mr Cooper scowled down at him. 'And I'll deal with you now. You get your own tarts.'

He held up a copy of *The Fourpenny One* that he'd kept hidden under the counter. 'Is this what you're looking for?' Dave said nothing; he was too scared to speak.

'Well, come on then. I haven't got all day. Tell me what you want, young man.' Mr Cooper grinned and clenched his fist in anticipation.

There was no way out. No escape. Just as there had been no escape for endless past Saturdays. Dave took a deep breath.

'Please, sir, I'd like a *Fourpenny One*.'

The newsagent's fist headed towards his face…

CHAPTER THREE

DAVE STROKED his chin as he relived that punch in the face. It was 1976 and he was now the editor of *The Spanker*, which incorporated *The Fourpenny One*, the legendary comic of his boyhood. But the bitter memories of youth still remained. Particularly as Mr Cooper was now a storeman working in the vaults of Fleetpit Publications, so they would sometimes bump into each other. Even though only a month ago he had finally stood up to him and given his tormentor the fourpenny one he so richly deserved. Maybe the memories would never entirely fade, and some part of him would always remain marooned in 1957 as an eight-year-old boy, endlessly entering Mr Cooper's shop, asking him for *The Fourpenny One,* and being punched in the face, in an eternal time loop.

Best to think of something else, he decided. Best to think of something cheerful to distract him.

And there was plenty to be cheerful about. Dave's new comic *Aaagh!* was a huge success. 'Geiger counters at max! We're radioactive!' it had announced to kids living in the shadow of nuclear destruction. 'Great free gift with issue one: The Super Nuker. The Red Terror from the skies.' Actually, it was a made-in-Hong-Kong, elastic band-propelled, delta-winged piece of red plastic. With its ballsy, kick-arse, anti-authority stories about killer white sharks, car thieves, good German soldiers, black footballers, mutant families, working-class heroes, futuristic death games and gun-toting rebellious kids, *Aaagh!* was filling a void in the marketplace, and selling a record 180,000 copies a week.

Dave looked at the empty seat opposite him that belonged to his assistant editor, Greg, and wondered if he'd ever return. After all, he had just sent him into the lion's cage at London Zoo.

It was one of the *Aaagh!* dares the readers had suggested for "Aaagh Man".

'Why do I have to be "Aaagh Man"? Why can't you be "Aaagh Man"?' Greg had protested. Dave had patiently explained he was too old himself (he was one year older) and Greg, with his cool Man in Black image, was more photogenic and handsome.

The appeal to Greg's vanity worked and so every week Dave sent "Aaagh Man" up London's highest crane, or driving on the London bus skid pan, or through an army assault course. That last dare had been problematic; Greg had taken considerable persuading because he was a pad's brat, the son of a soldier, and wanted nothing more to do with the army.

His father had been discharged from his regiment, but could not go home to Northern Ireland because of the Troubles. The experience had made Greg bitter and resentful.

'You don't actually sound Irish to me, Greg,' Dave said suspiciously. 'Are you sure you're not a terrorist in disguise?'

'If you must know, I have a Heinz accent: 57 varieties from our travels,' said Greg sullenly.

'I'm envious,' said Dave insincerely.

'Oh, sure. Living with military issue furniture: orange-brown, and green and yellow in weird patterns, all bearing the Nato stock mark: the crow's foot, like we're convicts.'

'Sounds psychedelic to me, Greg. Quite groovy, in fact.'

'If you ever needed to hide in a lava lamp factory, they'd be perfect camouflage. The answer is no, Dave.'

'But the assault course would give you brilliant material for your novel.'

'I've given up on it. Forty-eight rejections from publishers was enough.'

'It could also toughen you up.'

'The army's already toughened me up, Dave. Seven schools and I never spent more than three years at any of them. So I had to fight seven school bullies when they picked on the new kid.'

'That explains your detachment, Greg. You're always moving on. Never settling down. It's why you never really made a go of it with Joy.'

'Who? Oh, yeah.'

'And possibly your interest in writing about German soldiers. The enemy. You haven't got a secret Nazi temple back home in Churchill Way, have you?'

'No,' said Greg defensively. I just happen to like the uniforms. A bit. Without the swastikas, of course,' he added hastily.

'Hence your Rommel look-a-like, leather trenchcoat,' agreed Dave. 'But you were saying your dad always wanted you to "man up" and follow in his footsteps. This is your chance to show him what you can do.'

'Not after what the army did to him,' said Greg bitterly. 'Poor bastard's all washed-up. He's a barman in the officers' mess.'

'So you can get in touch with your negativity when you're on the assault course and write about it afterwards.'

Greg suddenly brightened up. 'You mean I get to slag the army off?'

'And get paid for it. It's the perfect catharsis for you, Greg.' Dave thought it all went rather well. Apart from Greg twisting his neck and meeting rats on the tube crawl; crushing his testicles when his foot fell through the scramble net; slipping and smashing his chest on a concrete stepping stone; hanging by his helmet chin strap on the cargo net; then landing on his head after clambering over a nine foot wall. Otherwise, it was a walk in the park.

Dave looked again at the empty seat opposite. He was rather pleased that he'd convinced Greg to go into the lion's cage. But maybe he should have insisted on him putting his head in a lion's mouth, too? And maybe done the boa constrictor dare while he was there?

Greg was currently in good spirits, which needed taking advantage of. His obsession with all things German had resulted in him dating Leni, the new German-Californian publisher.

'No more writing novels,' he announced to Dave. 'Shagging Leni is now my road to fame and fortune.'

'You're her gigolo? Her William Holden in *Sunset Boulevard?*'

'She's only ten years older than me. You know what she calls me? Promise you won't laugh?'

Dave nodded. Greg grinned. 'Her schnookie. Her schnookieputz.'

Dave swallowed a laugh, keeping it back to share with Joy later. 'So she has … nookie with her schnookie?'

'I'll tell her,' chuckled Greg. 'Germans. They need a little guidance where humour is concerned.'

It was because Leni was unsure about what was acceptable and what was not acceptable in British comics that Dave had got away with quite a lot on both *Aaagh!* and *The Spanker*.

At first, she had scrutinised his comics carefully, wanting to cut down on the usual violence, smoking and xenophobic attitudes towards Germans.

She looked at an episode of *The Caning Commando* where the teacher and his young assistant, Alf Mast, have emerged from an unlikely fish and chip shop in Hamburg before they begin their secret mission.

'The Caning Commando says this boy is as thick as a plank, but he knows his way around Hamburg.' Leni looked at Dave suspiciously. 'What does this mean?'

'It means Alf learnt all about Hamburg in his Geography lesson,' explained Dave smoothly.

'And this line where the Caning Commando says, "How can I give the sausage noshers …" ' She broke off, 'Sausage noshers …?'

'Nickname for Germans,' said Dave. 'The writer has lots of them: Dresden dustmen; Frankfurt fire-raisers; Munich mutton munchers; pudding-headed Prussians.'

Leni's eyes widened.

'I'm sorry about the racial stereotyping,' said Dave.

'Hmm,' said Leni thoughtfully. 'He's probably right about the Prussians.'

She returned to the strip, ' "How can I give the sausage noshers six on the bare if I haven't got vinegar on my cane? The little monkey has used it all on his fish and chips." ' Leni looked coldly at Dave. 'This is offensive violence. You must get rid of this terrible story.'

'But it's the most popular serial in *The Spanker*,' Dave protested.

'The readers love the Caning Commando. "It's time to Carpet Bum the Hun!" is the number one chant in school playgrounds.'

A puzzled Leni looked up at Dave. 'The readers want to "carpet bum" us?'

'Not you personally,' said Dave hastily. 'I'm sure you would never be carpet-bummed. Or not in that way. I'm sure you'd be carpet-bummed in a good way. You know, like you and Greg. Maybe?'

'They want to arse-fuck us?' smiled Leni. 'Now I understand.'

'No. No. It's perfectly innocent. No. It's a meaningless joke, see? It's our British sense of humour.'

Leni frowned disapprovingly. 'I want no more such caning scenes. Is that understood?'

Dave 'misunderstood' and took her instructions literally. So in the next story, he had the Caning Commando's cane whitened out of all the pictures. Therefore it looked as if the Commando, minus his cane, was constantly 'fisting' German soldiers, especially when they were bent over his knee with their trousers down. Particularly as he was snarling his famous catchphrase, 'It's time to Carpet Bum the Hun.'

This amused Dave greatly, especially when there were complaints from church groups about the 'fisting' and the Commando was quickly allowed his cane again.

Similarly, Leni required a ban on comic characters smoking, such as the chain-smoking secret agent *Force Major,* 'the storm that destroys everything in his path.' So, once again, Dave took Leni's instructions literally and had the secret agent's cigarette whitened out of the artwork. Without a cigarette in his hand, it looked as if Force Major was constantly giving readers the V-sign, which, once again, delighted Dave. It echoed his own feelings about the readers.

Leni was also not happy with the story *Gas Mask.* This featured a hero who breathed in gas to make himself invisible. Yet his domino mask somehow remained visible, which somewhat defeated the purpose of being invisible.

'Parents are complaining about Gas Mask sucking on a gas pipe,' she said.

'To be fair, Leni,' Dave reassured her, 'Gas Mask *does* say in every episode, when he sticks his head in the oven, or puts the hose from a

Bunsen burner in his mouth, "This would kill an ordinary human. Only I can do this and survive." So it should be all right.'

Leni looked coldly at Dave. She read on. 'This is so bad.'

'It gets better once you get into it,' Dave said encouragingly. 'You see, despite Gas Mask's super-power, he still has his kryptonite. He's allergic to propane, which makes him *more* visible, so he glows in the dark.'

Leni read a page where Gas Mask's enemies were guarding three sources of gas in a house, so he could not get to the source of his invisibility and he slowly became visible. The villains were guarding the New World cooker, the coal-effect gas fire and the Ascot gas heater in the bathroom. One of them warned the others: 'Keep him away from the Ascot!'

But Gas Mask knew how to outsmart them. 'My gassy senses tell me there's a mains pipe under the lawn. It's risky, but I've got to do it.' His enemies saw him digging up the garden like a mole. 'Stop him reaching the mains. But don't fire, you fools!' But they were too late. Gas Mask broke into the pipe and filled his lungs with North Sea gas as he gave his health and safety warning to the readers, 'Only I can do this and survive.'

Leni cancelled *Gas Mask* immediately. But she had no time to look at further examples of Dave's editorship. She had been primarily hired by Fleetpit Publications to adapt their teenage magazines for sale in the States. So she was busy working on new American versions of *Megahits, Good Vibes, Sassy Girl, Smash Stars* and *LBD (Little Black Dress)* for Fleetpit's 'American invasion'.

Dave wasn't bothered that *Gas Mask* was scrapped. The important thing was Leni hadn't looked too closely at *The Caning Commando*. This was just as well. Because Dave was secretly adding dangerous ideas to the Caning Commando that his readers could try at home with potentially lethal results. He was literally getting away with murder.

He wrote serials and he was a serial killer.

CHAPTER FOUR

WHAT WAS the matter with the cop, thought Sam Morgan bitterly. He was just standing there, emotionless, in front of them. This was not how a 'death message' visit was meant to go. His robotic manner distracted the twelve-year-old from the success of his plan: the ingenious 'accident' he'd carefully planned and executed after reading *The Caning Commando* in *The Spanker*.

The cop should have been like the ones on TV, the boy felt. Like in *Barlow; New Scotland Yard; Z Cars*; or *Dixon of Dock Green*. The bereavement visit with the kindly and pretty WPC in attendance. It was a familiar scene to millions of viewers, and certainly to Sam. With a sad and sincere expression on his face, the cop should have said softly to his mum, 'Mrs. Morgan, I'm sorry to tell you, I have some very bad news. Perhaps you'd like to sit down…?'

And then he would carefully break the terrible news that her husband had accidentally electrocuted himself. Meanwhile, the WPC would make his mum a cup of tea with plenty of sugar. And gently ask her if she was all right. And was there someone she could call? A neighbour? A close friend or relative? That's how all the telly cops did it. It's certainly how doddery old Dixon of Dock Green would have done it. That's why he was so popular, with his cosy, kindly, 'Evening All' manner. Everyone felt safe knowing George Dixon was out there patrolling the streets, even if he was doing it in a bathchair these days.

But then, 1976 was the final year for octogenarian George Dixon. It was the end of an era, Sam had to remind himself, and *The Sweeney* was now the face of modern policing. So perhaps it was not actually surprising that this unsympathetic prick had turned up on his own with no WPC and no 'I'm very sorry…' by way of introduction.

He didn't suggest his mum sat down before he told her the bad news. He just stood there, rattling off how her husband, Giles, had used a faulty power drill while working on their Summer cottage, with fatal consequences. And because he stood there, his mum also stood – in a state of shock – and Sam felt he had to stand, too. So they all stood there as the cop told her the graphic details in an emotionless, flat voice, like a robot. Far more information than his mum really needed to know. How his dad had been standing on a stepladder at the time, fell when he was electrocuted, and the drill bit cut through his throat and right up into his skull, killing him. And you couldn't make the excuse he was a young, nervous, inexperienced cop on his first bereavement; he was a middle-aged sergeant.

So Sam sat his mother down and made her a cup of tea with plenty of sugar and put his arm around her and told her it was okay, she was going to be okay, everything was okay. The cop never even asked how his mother got her black eye and perhaps that was just as well because his mum wasn't a good liar and no one would have believed she walked into a door. Again.

Sam had begged her to leave his dad and take shelter in a women's refuge. But she was far too middle class to go into a battered wives hostel. And too afraid that Giles would come after her. There was madness in his family: his brother, Tristan, had been sectioned after he had set fire to a deserted house. Protecting their five-bedroom, double-garage, detached property standing in its own landscaped grounds was far more important to Mrs Morgan than Giles breaking half the bones in her body.

Her solution to his violence was to jam the vacuum cleaner across the bedroom window and run the cable down to the garden. She was desperate enough to abseil down it and run across the lawn and escape the next time he went into one of his rages. Only he beat her to it and that was how she ended up with the black eye. 'You're dumber than dog shit,' he snarled before he started.

That was when Sam decided enough was enough, and his dad had to go.

Still without a trace of compassion, the robot cop gave Mrs Morgan an incident number and explained the procedure: what would happen next, the coroner, the inquest and so on. Not that she was paying any attention. It hadn't yet sunk in: that she was free of the monster who had made her life a living hell. The same was true for Sam. He had long ago lost any feelings of love for his father, who was violent with him as well. And everything had gone just as he planned. This cop seemed to think the inquest would be just a formality. Defective drill. Open and shut case. A tragic accident with no suspicious circumstances.

Sam had got the idea from a Caning Commando story where the hero, Victor Grabham, once more meets his deadly enemy, the Oberspankerfuhrer, leader of the feared Wackem SS. He was also known as the Blue Man, because his backside was frozen solid on the Russian front so he was invulnerable in caning duels. The story seemed pretty stupid, but there was a surprising amount of detailed instructions on how Grabham secretly sabotaged the Oberspankerfuhrer's lethal electric cane, taken from an authentic commando manual.

It was easy enough for Sam to adapt the instructions to sabotage a power drill and, when his dad switched it on, the result was lethal.

The cop had barely been in the house ten minutes and, satisfied that he'd carried out his orders, was making a prompt exit, without so much as a 'so sorry for your loss, Mrs Morgan.' But that was all right, because Sam would take care of his mother. He might only be twelve years old, but he was the Man of the House now.

Sam opened the front door, ushered the cop out and watched as he got into his pale blue and white panda car and drove away. The boy resisted the temptation to call after him, 'Evening All.'

* * *

Detective Inspector 'Fiddy' Ferguson believed he was a good cop, although his superiors would have disagreed. That's why they had insisted he take early retirement, and he'd ended up living on the Costa

Del Crime, alongside many of the villains he'd done business with during his time on the Flying Squad. He was certainly a smart cop, his bosses never found his secret bank account, no matter how hard they looked. It was tucked away in Gibraltar, safe as the rock itself. He could see Gibraltar from his room in the Sol Tower Hotel, near Estepona, and it made him feel good to think that all that lovely money was only an hour's drive away.

He was also a persistent cop, because he wouldn't let that business of the Caning Commando go. When he'd seen his grandson's comics with detailed instructions on how to construct a pipe bomb and administer a lethal poison, he knew he was onto something serious. It had taken him longer than expected to get to the bottom of it, though. And by the time he had, his daughter, son-in-law and grandson, Tim, were back in the UK. He blamed the delays on the Spanish phones. To make an international call, he had to book a slot through the Malaga operator and it took forever. Fiddy was a great admirer of Franco, but the Generalísimo really needed to do something about his bloody telephone system.

Eventually, he got through to his old mate on the squad, Harry Peters, and asked him to do some digging. Harry owed him big-time: when Fiddy was being investigated by A10, he'd made sure Harry's name was kept out of the frame. It turned out that Harry knew the art editor on *The Spanker*, one Steve Barclay, and he went for a drink with him in the Hoop and Grapes, the pub over the road from Fleetpit Publications where the comic was produced.

'He's nicknamed "Deep Throat" Barclay for some reason,' said Harry. 'Kind of appropriate as he dished the dirt on that comic book character you wanted to know all about.'

According to Deep Throat, Harry revealed, the Caning Commando stories were scripted by a freelance writer known as The Major, but they were edited by a Dave Maudling. Maudling seemed to have a pathological dislike of his readers. Deep Throat's studio was next door and he had overheard Maudling chatting to his assistant editor. He'd talk about *The Spanker* surviving a nuclear holocaust, but 'We'll have to chisel the comic out on a rock. We'll have two-headed readers coming to buy it. We'll be able to sell the little bastards two copies at once.'

Deep Throat said Dave was strange: he'd once disguised himself as the tea lady; there were rumours he was living in the attic at the top of the Fleetpit building, and something about him wearing a gorilla suit, only it was turned inside out. Fiddy decided Harry must have got that bit wrong. Why would anyone in their right mind wear an inside-out gorilla suit?

Harry reported that the teacher who had 'mistakenly' swallowed the tasteless and odourless poison had a criminal record for violence. And a priest had been 'accidentally' blown up by a pipe bomb: a chemistry experiment by his altar boys that had gone tragically wrong. Boys 'messing about' with their chemistry sets and blowing themselves or adults up were so commonplace, the story hadn't made the nationals, but, as it involved explosives, it had still come to the attention of the Yard.

The dates fitted, all right. The altar boys could have read how to construct their bomb from the story in *The Caning Commando*. Apparently, the priest had moved parishes six times in the last eight years, and the cops knew what that meant.

Maudling was a wrong 'un, that much was certain. Even though they hadn't yet met, Fiddy could just smell it. But what was his game? Was he trying to kill kids or save them? There was a contradiction there. Either way, he was playing with fire.

Fiddy looked at his calendar. Time was running out and he knew he would have to act fast. He got hotel reception to book him a taxi, then braved the journey on the lethal two-lane coast road, known as the 'Highway of Death', to Malaga airport.

He was on the next plane back to Blighty.

CHAPTER FIVE

CHEWING HIS LIQUORICE PIPE, Dave sat down to watch *The Awful Truth* on TV. He was dressed appropriately in his inside-out gorilla suit, ostensibly because it kept him warm, but really because he wanted the comfort of fur next to his skin. He watched in awe as Irene Dunne sashayed across the screen, a divine apparition enveloped in a white fox fur, surrounded by a female entourage also wearing furs. What a treat. What a coat. He was in fur Heaven.

Then a bullet thudded into the wall of his turret home at the top of Fleetpit House. The shock caused Dave to bite through his pipe. He turned to see Mr Cooper standing there, in a raincoat, gun in hand, like a character out of one of the noir movies Dave was so fond of. Cooper pointed the Webley at his head. It had taken several whiskies, but Cooper was deadly serious. He wasn't afraid to use it. He had used it once before, when he'd had to get rid of his wife. Buried her on his allotment.

No one was going to get away with treating him like that. Least of all Dave Maudling, the kid he used to enjoy punching in the face every Saturday when he came in for his *Fourpenny One*.

Maudling, who he'd met all these years later when he was a storeman at Fleetpit Publications and discovered he was secretly living in the building. He had got himself a nice little earner there to keep schtum. Then came that night in the Hoop and Grapes when Maudling had finally stood up to him. He'd refused to pay anymore, beaten him up and humiliated him in front of his lady friend.

'What do you want?' asked the pink gorilla.

'What you owe me. Plus interest.'

'I don't have it.'

'Get it or I'll give it to you.'

'I'm not taking this,' the ape said defiantly.

'You'll take it and like it,' warned Cooper, waving the gun. His vocabulary was limited, so he would sometimes supplement it with lines from gangster movies.

'All right.' Maudling went to a cupboard and rummaged inside.

'Thought you could get the better of me, huh?' Cooper gloated. 'What you don't realise is, I improve with age.'

In response, the gorilla turned round and punched him savagely in the face. As he staggered back, the beast grabbed for the gun and ripped it out of his hand. Then pointed it at the ex-newsagent's head. His twisted face contorted with fear.

'No. Don't, Davey. Please. No.'

Dave regarded him long and hard as *The Awful Truth* continued with Cary Grant and Irene Dunne, holding a white fur muff, arguing over who got custody of Mr Smith, their dog. But such an exquisite fur was lost on Dave as he considered shooting Cooper. His new-found courage had been hard-earned and there was no way he would ever 'take it' again. He enjoyed Cooper's fear, but it was enough. Nothing was to be gained from putting a bullet in his brain and there was everything to lose, including an excellent scene in the movie where Irene's aunt appears draped in the most fabulous fur.

He was about to lower the gun when Jean Maudling appeared beside Cooper. At first he thought she had emerged from the TV screen and he glanced over at the movie's progress. But there was only a stout, elderly matriarch with a fur boa, disapproving of Irene. Whereas his mother was young and beautiful, as she was in the 1940s when she was a hostess: her Lauren Bacall-style costume finished off with a gorgeous fur stole.

He realised he must be hallucinating, so he took off his mask to see if that made a difference. It didn't. She was still there: a femme fatale to compete with any screen siren and she urged him now to pull the trigger. Dave felt that familiar surge of violence as she possessed him again.

Whatever she was, a soul from the other side returned from the dead, dedicated to turning her cowardly son into a hero, or an elaborate construct of his subconscious, she was in deadly earnest and he had to obey her.

He felt a surge of hatred and pressed the revolver into the trembling storeman's forehead. 'Get ready to die, Cooper.'

Wherever Dave's homicidal desire came from, it was understandable. Cooper's punch in the face every Saturday was the primary reason he was so screwed up. Doubly understandable if the ex-newsagent had murdered his mother, which was possible, as she visited his shop just before she disappeared.

'Kill him, son,' she ordered. There was blood lust in her lustrous dark eyes now and a cruel smile on her lips as she drew heavily on a cigarette.

But the murderous look on her face brought him to his senses and made him aware of the consequences if he pulled the trigger. He would be the one doing twenty years for murder, not her. 'I can't. I just can't,' he whispered and backed away. Cooper breathed a sigh of relief.

'Trust me,' said Jean. 'You'll get away with it, just like you always do.'

This was true. He was aware how often his inner demons seemed to protect him. He called them his Gadarene swine, and they were Legion. But could he really get away with shooting Cooper in cold blood?

'How would I dispose of the body?' he asked out loud.

'Good point,' said Cooper, aware Dave was still training the gun on him. 'It's not easy getting rid of a stiff. Believe me, I know.'

'What about that sewer pipe in the basement?' Jean whispered to her son. 'It leads straight out to the Thames.'

'Problem solved,' smiled Dave.

'Do it!' she exhorted him.

A trembling Cooper saw the new resolve in Dave's face and his heart sank again. 'No! You can't kill me, Davey,' he pleaded desperately.

'Why not?'

'Cos I'm your dad.'

'Yeah, right,' jeered Dave.

'It's true.'

'You? You? You think I'm crazy enough to believe a low-life like you could possibly be my father?'

'I'm not lying,' said Cooper, 'I am your father.' There was real conviction in his face and in his voice.

'How?' Dave asked contemptuously.

'How d'you think?' replied Cooper truculently.

'I meant, why would my mother go with you?'

'She was miserable, looking for someone to make her happy, and I was there.'

'No. It's impossible.' Dave shook his head.

He looked towards his mother for the reassurance of an outraged denial at such a ludicrous lie.

But she blushed and looked away from him, and he feared it might, just might, be true. The possible revelation hit him with the savagery of a sledgehammer blow to his stomach.

'Not that any man could ever make your mum happy,' Cooper continued. 'I'd say to her, "Jean, you'll never be happy as long as you've got a hole in your arse." '

'But … I don't look like you,' Dave protested.

'Not now. But think back to when I was younger and you came into the shop.' Dave remembered.

It was possible Cooper was right. Okay, there was a certain resemblance. And he had never looked anything like Peter Maudling, his legal father, or anyone on his side of the family, which had always puzzled him, whenever he gave it any thought, which was not often.

But so what? There were plenty of other possible explanations. It didn't mean anything. It didn't prove anything. It didn't prove a thing!

He looked over at his mother once again for answers. For her to tell him that this was all a terrible mistake, a horrible lie, dreamed up by Cooper to save his skin.

Their eyes met and locked.

She looked defiantly at him at first, angry that her son was in a position of power over her, and was daring to question his own mother about her lovers. But he held her gaze.

Finally, she nodded her head sullenly.

'Yes, it's true,' she whispered and swiftly looked away again.

Stunned, he lowered the gun.

But deep down, in some remote corner of his subconscious mind, where family secrets were meant to remain hidden forever, he already knew it was true. He had always known Cooper was his father. It was a truth that was best locked away.

Now it was out in the open, consciously, it started to make a horrible sense.

Maybe that was why Cooper had gone out of his way to humiliate him. Why he'd played sick games at his expense. Tormenting him was a way of keeping his son at a distance, making sure they would never bond. So he would never have to acknowledge him as his own.

Dave felt sick to his stomach. He was lost for words. Maybe *that* was why he was drawn into going back to the shop every Saturday, because, on some deep subconscious level, he sensed the newsagent was his real dad.

'Cheer up, Dave,' Cooper grinned. 'It was only a bit of "How's your Father?" if you'll pardon the pun. And everyone was rutting like stoats in them days. That's why there were all you baby boomers.'

Cooper smiled triumphantly at him, aware he had the upper hand once again. 'I told her to flush you while she had the chance.' He grinned at his son. 'I'd flush you now if you weren't so big.' And with that, he left the turret.

Dave put the gun down and sat with his head in his hands. He knew that his mother had affairs. But Cooper? *Cooper?* He looked across at her for an explanation as she nervously lit another cigarette.

'Why, mum? Why?'

She looked sheepish and avoided his eyes. 'I was confused. I didn't know what I was doing.'

'But Cooper?'

'I … I've got to go,' she said hastily and faded away into the darkness, leaving Dave alone with *The Awful Truth*.

CHAPTER SIX

VERA WAS wary of bringing teas into *The Spanker* office since Dave had hijacked her tea trolley and pretended he was the tea lady. So she had positioned the trolley outside the *Shandy* office and was chatting to Joy as Dave lumbered down the corridor to join them.

'Leni didn't want proper tea,' she explained to Joy. 'Said she only drank Celestial Seasonings peppermint tea.'

'Better for her health?' Joy asked.

'She needs something,' said Vera. 'When I went in there just now she was groaning and panting heavily.'

'Is she all right?' asked a concerned Joy.

'I don't know, dearie,' said a puzzled Vera. 'I think she could be having a funny turn.'

Greg emerged from Leni's office and swaggered over to join them at the trolley.

'Is Leni okay?' asked Dave.

'She is now,' Greg smirked.

Vera looked at him strangely. 'I didn't see you in her office. Where were you hiding?'

The only possible place was behind the modesty panel fitted to the front of all female staff's desks to put a stop to the unwanted attention of male pen-droppers.

'So how was the casting desk, Greg?' Joy asked sweetly.

'Coming up for air?' Dave grinned.

'So it's inglenookie with your schnookie now?' Joy suggested. Greg shrugged off their jibes. 'I think you can safely say you're looking at the next managing editor,' he said confidently.

He'd lost his punk look and was wearing a poncho, which somehow managed to look both Clint Eastwood and New Age at the same time. He had nearly got Ron's job before, but for his fashion *faux pas* at the eminently conservative restaurant, Rules, when he had turned up for the interview looking like a cross between Engelbert Humperdinck and Peter Wyngarde. Clearly, he was making progress with Leni.

'I'm worried about Ron,' said Joy. 'He just sits there in his office, day after day, with the door locked. Maybe you should take him in a cup of tea, Vera?'

'He hasn't drunk tea for weeks, dearie,' sighed Vera. 'He's on the hard stuff now.'

'Drowning his sorrows,' nodded Greg. 'Ah, well, it was time for a new generation to take over.'

'Law of the jungle.' agreed Dave, having no sympathy for his soon-to-be-redundant boss.

'He could be having some kind of nervous breakdown in there,' insisted Joy

'If he's feeling suicidal, he's got a direct line to Cross Line,' said Greg.

'Don't you two care?'

'It's a dog-eat-dog world,' shrugged Dave indifferently.

'And he is a bit long in the tooth,' added Greg.

'Time he was put out to pasture,' confirmed Dave.

'Yes,' said Greg, 'If he doesn't take the hint and give in his notice, they'll just keep moving him into smaller and smaller offices, until he ends up in the lift.'

'Then you know the only way is down,' said Dave sagely. They smugly collected their teas.

'You two really are a couple of shits,' observed Joy.

'On the subject of failures,' said Dave, 'Are we all still on for the Hoop and Grapes tonight? To celebrate the death of *Everlasting Love*?'

'Oh, you bet,' said Joy.

'It must be kinda like a beautiful dream for you, eh?'

'It is, now I've got shot of it,' she agreed.

Everlasting Love had lasted just eight weeks – something of a record in Fleetpit's history of comic disasters. Joy was delighted: it meant no more stupid stories from the Major about *Wedding Belle*, the supermarket checkout girl who yearned to go from shopping aisle to wedding aisle. Science fiction was what Joy yearned for and hence why she had already opened *Time Machine*, her comics and movie memorabilia shop, in Covent Garden.

'It just wasn't gear,' said Dave.

'But I can see you are these days,' said Joy looking appreciatively in his direction before she disappeared back into her office. It was a signal even Dave couldn't fail to recognise. Jean had made him adopt a whole new cool look, insisting on him buying new clothes every month, and it was clearly paying off.

Dave had been down for a few days after learning that Cooper was his father, but he'd picked himself up now. He had decided that rekindling his relationship with Joy was the answer to his problems. She was beautiful: the only woman remotely in his mother's league, and she would help him forget his awful past. He was in the middle of finalising plans that would definitely win her heart.

Back in his office, 'Deep Throat' Barclay came through from the studio with the latest original art pages of *Black Hammer*, Dave's favourite strip in *Aaagh!*, inspired by the West Ham player Clyde Best and his mum's former lover Ernie Gambo. Dave looked them over. 'The football action and the crowd booing from the terraces are great, but Bob's still got to improve his depiction of the Hammer.'

'It's difficult,' sighed Barclay. 'He's never had to draw black people before, you see?'

'Well, it's time he learnt,' Dave snapped, 'or we'll replace him with another artist.'

'Not so easy,' said Barclay. 'I doubt you'll find any artist at Fleetpit or Angus, Angus and Angus, who knows how to draw black heroes.'

'Can't you alter the artwork?'

'Not my thing. Sue's the artist and she's still away on maternity leave. Does it really matter?'

'It matters. See if another art assistant can make the changes. Find a way.'

It mattered to Dave: it rekindled fond memories of Ernie, who had worked on the docks and taught him to play football. He would tell him stories of his old life in Nigeria, where he had first met Jean Maudling when he'd been her houseboy. How he used to snake-charm cobras and puff adders. And how he once walked safely past a man-eating lion because he was wearing a charm of invisibility.

'But you must never turn your head, Davey, or you'll break the spell, and then the lion will eat you!'

Dave was definitely invisible. His was the perfect crime. He was completely under the police radar. No one had any idea what he was doing on *The Caning Commando*: giving kids ideas so they could wreak their revenge on adults, just as he had wanted to wreak revenge on Mr Cooper. He saw himself now as their secret leader, a kind of super hero, helping them to fight injustice. Except he didn't actually have to do anything. Just make sure he didn't turn his head.

Dave was torn away from his thoughts by Deep Throat talking to Greg about his assistant, Sue. 'I was the first to realise she was pregnant,' Barclay recalled. 'I could see how her breasts were swelling.'

'Well, you are the pen dropper-in-chief,' said Greg, 'so I suppose you would notice.'

Oblivious to the insult, Barclay persisted. 'I wonder if she and her husband have resumed marital relations? It was a very large baby. She's probably quite sore. Probably needed a couple of stitches.'

'What the hell has it got to do with you?' shuddered Greg, clicking his pen. 'It's none of your business.'

'Just wondering…' mused Deep Throat, a far away look on his face. '… And do you think she's using formula or breast feeding? Formula might be best. You can get very sore nipples, apparently.'

'Oh, give it a rest,' grimaced Greg.

'Pervert,' muttered Dave, as he reached over to answer his phone. 'Maudling.'

'This is reception. There's a Detective Inspector Ferguson here to see you.'

'What does he want?'

'It's about *The Caning Commando*.'

CHAPTER SEVEN

FIDDY CHUCKLED TO HIMSELF. He was loving every minute of this. His wolf-like, piercing blue eyes drank in Dave's performance. It was a little rehearsed, true, but it was not bad for an amateur. Not bad at all. Lacked a little of the conviction a professional villain would have given it, but credit where credit was due, the lad was trying hard.

They had arranged to meet in Ye Olde Cock Tavern across the road from the Royal Courts of Justice in the Strand. Dave had to cancel his drink with the others in the Hoop and Grapes to celebrate the death of *Everlasting Love*. He couldn't risk the others overhearing.

'Oh, my God,' said Dave. 'I had no idea what the Major was up to, Inspector. I blame myself, I really should have paid more attention.'

'Very good,' grinned Fiddy.

'And you say that two adults – a priest and a teacher – were killed? By kids using these methods the Major had sneaked into his Caning Commando story?'

'Two we know of. There could well be others.'

A shocked Dave shook his head sorrowfully. 'That's … that's just awful. What … what can I say, Inspector?'

'Yes, Dave,' smirked Fiddy. 'What can you say?'

'What was the Major thinking of?' ruminated Dave, continuing his performance of a lifetime. 'He can't be right in the head. You know he was a prisoner of the Japanese? Worked on that railroad. Must have suffered terribly. D'you think he maybe took one beating too many?' Dave looked inspired. 'Yes, maybe *that's* why he did it, Inspector. It affected his mind. He had to get back at the world for all the terrible things that were done to him.'

The cop leaned purposefully forward. 'We know about the Major, Dave. "The Major" – aka Battle of Britain fighter pilot 'Tiger' Thomson, aka Desert Rat Lieutenant 'Nobby Clarke', real name John Taylor, private in the army catering corps. Following the fall of Singapore, he was indeed a POW on the Thai-Burma railway.'

'So he's a fantasist? And he's been acting out his fantasies in a kid's comic?' A shocked Dave took in this information. 'I see ... yes ... it's all starting to make sense now.'

'When he returned to Britain he used forged papers to take up the post of housemaster at St Swithin's College for boys. Before leaving under a considerable cloud, along with the school fees.'

'I had no idea,' said Dave sorrowfully. 'So you can't trust a word he says? If he was, for example, to deny that he was encouraging his readers to kill adults, you couldn't believe him. Could you?'

'From his court appearances,' Fiddy continued impassively, 'we know The Major was also a bus conductor, a door-to-door vacuum cleaner salesman, and a tally man, collecting hire purchase debts, but forgetting to pass on the money to his employers. He was guilty of similar absent-mindedness as a bus conductor, not just living out of his own bag, but other conductors' bags as well. And when he vacuumed a lady's carpet, he claimed her jewellery got sucked into the dust bag by mistake.'

'A man like that is capable of anything,' sighed Dave. 'And then he finally hit rock bottom and became a comic book writer.'

Dave started to relax. With the Major's long record of dishonesty, his denials of any wrongdoing would cut no ice with the police. He was the perfect patsy.

'Now, I did some checking,' continued Fiddy. 'I went right through my grandson's collection of *The Spanker*. I read every single Caning Commando story.'

'So you saw his whole descent into insanity? Tragic. Tragic.' Dave shook his head sadly.

'It was enlightening. Because, you see, Dave, the homicidal

incidents in question only start appearing in the Caning Commando when *you* took over as editor.'

'Me? I guess that's just coincidence,' shrugged Dave.

'Showing the readers how to make a Molotov cocktail, a pipe bomb, an undetectable poison, potassium nitrate rocket missiles, electrocute people, and so on.'

'The Major's name *is* on the scripts,' Dave said defensively.

'But I've got hold of one, and I can see where there's an addition made with your typewriter.'

Fiddy showed Dave the document that Deep Throat had given to Harry.

'You see …? Just there. You've added the bit where the Oberspankerfuhrer holds the Commando down in a bath of water and he survives by breathing air through the plughole.' The detective chuckled. 'Bet there were a few kids lost their teeth on that one.'

'I don't remember. I'm sure there's an explanation,' said Dave, stroking his chin.

'And you just need a bit of time to think what it could be?' prompted Fiddy sympathetically.

'Yes, please,' said Dave.

Fiddy grinned triumphantly at him and waved the incriminating script in his face. 'I've got you, Dave. Bang to rights.'

The guilt was written right across Dave's face.

A judge, who spent most of his time in the Tavern when he wasn't on the bench, staggered drunkenly past them on his way to the exit. He was Dave's personal Nemesis and, once before, had observed his guilty expression and accused him of unspecified but undoubtedly heinous crimes.

'Detective Inspector! Good to see you,' boomed the florid-faced judge.

'And you, My Lord,' responded Fiddy. 'You're not at the Bailey now?'

The judge's face dropped. 'Appeals. Boring. Need to get back there. Criminals getting away with it. We need longer sentences: bring back national service; birching; the rope.'

'I couldn't agree more, My Lord.'

'The cat. A good flogging is all the cosh-boys understand.'

'Absolutely, My Lord.'

The judge's eyes rested on Dave. 'You! I know you!'

Dave squirmed. 'Me?'

'Yes. *You.*' His eyes lit up as he remembered their previous encounter and smiled knowingly. He turned to Fiddy. 'So you finally got him. Good work, Inspector. He eyed Dave up and down. 'I knew from just one look at you, you were guilty of some revolting and callous crimes, some despicable and depraved malefactions, some heartless and inhuman acts that would appal even such as myself, who is inured to acts of evil. I shall look forward to seeing you in my court, young man.'

'I'll do my best to arrange it, My Lord,' said Fiddy.

The judge prodded Dave in the chest. 'Guilty. Guilty. *Guilty.*' Then he lurched off out into the Strand.

Dave realised it was all over. When the truth came out how he was leading kids astray, he would be vilified as a complete animal, a heartless brute, the beast of Fleetpit. They wouldn't send him to a psychiatrist, they'd send him to a vet.

He decided there was nothing for it but to play the insanity card. 'It's because of my childhood, Inspector. What happened to me every Saturday when I went to get my weekly comic. I'm not right in the head, you see? I tock when I should tick.'

'Now, Dave…' said the cop, lighting a cigarette.

'I'm nuts, Inspector. It wouldn't be fair to send me to prison. If you do, I'll build a spaceship from fruit tins and escape. I'll make a paste that will dissolve the bars of my cell.'

'Let me explain …' continued the cop.

'He chews *Sherlock's.* We choose *Sherlock's.* Everyone chooses *Sherlock's.* He chews *Sherlock's.* We choose *Sherlock's …*' Dave muttered fearfully.

'You're not going to prison,' explained the cop.

'You've got a padded cell for me instead?' Dave breathed a sigh of relief. 'This is a victory for human rights. For democracy. Thank God we're living in the enlightened nineteen-seventies.'

The Inspector stared at him. 'Calm down.' He stood up. 'I'll get us some more drinks.'

Dave was even more hyper when he finally returned from the busy bar with two more pints. 'I'm not a number, I'm a free man,' said Dave, laughing triumphantly.

'That remains to be seen,' said Fiddy coldly. 'We haven't much time. That's why I flew over from Spain especially.'

'I don't understand.'

'It's my grandson Timmy's birthday in seven weeks. I want him to appear in a Caning Commando story. It'll be the best birthday surprise he's ever had: to open his favourite comic and see himself alongside his hero, Carpet Bumming the Hun.'

Fiddy handed over some photos. 'Here's some recent photos of the boy. And me, too, if you can fit me into the story.'

'Oh, definitely,' agreed Dave. 'It will be a story to treasure. This is such a relief, Inspector. 'Cos you know, I really thought I was fucked back there. I was sweating worse than Lonely, the tramp in *Callan.'*

'I noticed,' said Fiddy, stubbing out his cigarette.

'But wait! Seven weeks?' said Dave, 'that's not enough time. There are print schedules and artists to consider and I don't know if I can write a kid into a story that easily.'

The cop looked solemnly at him. 'I think you can, Dave.'

'Actually, I think I can.'

'I really think you should, Dave.'

'I really think I should.'

Fiddy got up and slapped Dave on the back. 'Good man. Me and the wife will be over again for Timmy's birthday, of course.' He looked warningly at him. 'So make sure it's a good story. Know what I'm saying …?'

'It will be a masterpiece, Inspector.'

Fiddy smiled happily to himself, 'I can't wait to see his little face light up.'

'And that other business?' Dave asked nervously. 'The – er – you know, those … changes I made to *The Caning Commando*?'

'I don't give a fuck about them,' said Fiddy.

Dave struggled to comprehend. 'No … of course not,' he said uncertainly

Fiddy looked at Dave for a long moment with his husky-blue, cold, hard eyes.

'You see, Dave, I hate nonces. Just the thought of one of them messing with my grandson makes my blood boil. They deserve to die, Dave. Slowly.'

'Oh, absolutely. Nail their heads to the floor, Krays-style, right?' said Dave.

'That was the Richardsons,' said Fiddy flatly. 'And I actually had something else in mind.'

'Oh, sorry. Yes, of course. Nailing their heads to the floor would really be letting them off lightly.'

'So if kids decide to get their own back on some nonce, why not?'

The detective turned to leave, pushing his way through the evening heavy drinkers as he headed for the door. He looked back expressively at Dave.

'Mind how you go, son.'

CHAPTER EIGHT

DAVE HAD the luck of the devils. His inner demons, his Gadarene Swine, somehow always seemed to get him out of trouble. The fear of exposure of his criminal activities caused him to move fast. He took an existing Caning Commando script and quickly adapted it to feature Fiddy's grandson, showing him in the co-starring role, rather than Alf Mast, Victor Grabham's regular sidekick. Raised from his usual creative torpor, he made a supreme effort, knowing the consequences if the story was not to the detective's liking.

The setting for the story was Mafeking and Jones: the Caning Commando's official cane-makers, who actually existed. The Major had bought his canes from the emporium when he taught at St Swithins and the cane-makers rather appreciated Victor Grabham being their poster boy. In fact, whenever the Major featured them in a story, they would send a bottle of malt whisky to Fleetpit for the comic writer.

Dave and Greg had just had a most unfortunate run-in with Mafeking and Jones[1], with painful results, so he had plenty of information about the legendary caning emporium to inspire him. More than he cared for, in fact. The experience was one he would not care to repeat. Neither would Greg.

But Dave was happy with his story starring Tim, and he was pretty certain Fiddy would be, too.

It was as ridiculous and frenetic as usual and the picture strip story began with the regular introductory caption:

'Because of his legendary caning skills, the War Office recruited schoolmaster Victor Grabham to be – *THE CANING COMMANDO.*'

The episode was entitled:

The Bottom Line

Wearing a sinister black teacher's cape over his army uniform, the Caning Commando scanned the racks of canes arranged along the walls of his cane-makers, Mafeking and Jones of St James's. There were hundreds of canes on display, along with leather tawses for Scottish teachers, wooden spanking paddles for American teachers and birch rods for use in prisons. Victor Grabham was tall and gaunt, but he had the strength of ten gym masters. A Military Cross medal from a grateful nation hung down from the mortarboard on his head. He had a widow's peak, a hawk-like nose, a cruel mouth and beetle brows which were furrowed in concentration as he went about selecting the best and most punitive canes to use on enemy backsides.

He gave each cane the circle test. A good cane should bend into a complete circle with the tip touching the handle. These were perfect for sending the Boche back to Berlin with red rears. As he picked his canes, he saw the owner, Mr Jones, was showing another gowned teacher and his young grandson around his shop.

Jones held up a rattan with knobbly segments along its length. 'How about this one, Mr Ferguson? "*The Holler!*", an unprocessed rattan ranging in colour from pale yellow to a mottled brown. A pliant, reliable weapon for 20 shillings a dozen.'

'Very reasonable,' commented the teacher approvingly as his grandson wandered off around the shop.

'Gosh! You're the Caning Commando!' the boy exclaimed, spotting Grabham's army uniform under the cape. He was a plucky little chap, the kind that Grabham thoroughly approved of.

'I trust you can keep my secret, young man?' asked the Caning Commando.

'Oh, you bet, sir,' said the boy, looking up at him in awe. 'I'm Tim and I'm your biggest fan. Are you here to "Carpet Bum the Hun"?'

Suddenly, Grabham's attention was caught by a sinister smell emanating from the basement. A smell of pure evil. 'Yes, Tim, I rather think I am,' he murmured grimly. 'Stay up here with your grandfather.'

His favourite cane in hand, a *Windsor Chastiser*, Grabham slipped away down the dark stairs, merging with the shadows, an almost invisible figure in his black cloak. 'I've got to get to the bottom of this,' he growled.

Meanwhile, the boy's grandfather had picked up a sturdy cane and was flexing it for size. He turned to Mr Jones. 'I rather like the feel of this one. *The Persuade*r, eh?'

'Half an inch in diameter,' explained the owner. 'It's heavier and thicker than the official canes approved by the Home Office. But sometimes this is the only cane that will *persuade* boys to mend their ways.'

'Yes. It looks like the perfect instrument to instil ethics in boys through violence,' agreed the teacher.

'How long does a cane last?' asked his grandson Tim curiously.

'The life of a cane depends on how often it's used, young man,' said Mr Jones. 'I guarantee them not to break with fair wear, but, should they fail to give satisfaction, I will exchange them. I have repeat orders from schools all over the world. My canes warm white, black and brown seats equally.'

Meanwhile, following his nose, the Caning Commando had entered the shadowy basement of the caning emporium. Suddenly, he saw an all-too familiar, black-clad figure emerge from the darkness. It couldn't be! But it was! His greatest foe: Moriarsey, the leader of the British Union of Fascists! His ominous emblem: a bundle of fasces, canes, with a crook cane on one side, emblazoned in a circle on his chest.

'Moriarsey!' exclaimed the shocked Commando.

'So we meet again, Caning Commando,' scowled the teacher's evil Nemesis.

'But I thought you were dead!' said Grabham. 'You had to be after our legendary caning duel on the Reichenbutt Falls in "The Final Thrashing".'

Moriarsey sneered: 'When you thrashed me over the edge of the waterfall? And I, seemingly, fell screaming to my death? Think again, Caning Commando!' And he lunged at him with his cane and the two great enemies began a furious duel.

'Allow me to introduce my 36-inch *Dragon Smoking Malacca*,' Moriarsey smiled. 'I adapted it from an opium pipe.'

'You fiend,' snarled Grabham turning his head away from the fumes, leaving his rear unguarded to a succession of rapid blows from the malacca. 'It was the opium I smelt, pouring from your hollow cane.'

'Correct,' laughed Moriarsey. 'A drug I am immune to, after years of abuse.'

'A dope fiend and a traitor to your country!' barked the Commando covering his mouth with his gown as he retaliated and striped Moriarsey's rear.

'Under fascism, Britain will relive the glories of the Roman Empire,' retorted Moriarsey, wincing from the cuts. 'The days of the Emperor Gluteus Maximus, the great caning Caesar.'

The two men locked canes and glared into each other's faces. 'Let's see how much punishment your gluteus maximus can take, Moriarsey!'

Grabham used his legendary flexible wrist action to deadly effect, getting in three vicious stripes in rapid succession without having to raise his arm. 'Here's three off the wrist,' he proclaimed.

'Aah! Aah! Aah!' screamed Moriarsey.

With his *Chastiser*, Grabham should have got the better of his enemy, but the *Dragon Smoking Malacca* was now filling the basement with its foul fumes and Grabham's cloak could no longer protect him from its effects; he started to choke on the drug.

'I'm not blowing smoke up your arse, but you're good,

Grabham,' acknowledged Moriarsey as the hero staggered back under its effects then slumped to the ground in a narcotic stupor.

The mastermind looked down at the prone figure and smiled, 'You're just not good enough.' And snapped the *Chastiser* over his knee.

When the Caning Commando recovered consciousness, the smoke had cleared and he found he was bent over and tied to a flogging block as Moriarsey wheeled a caning machine into position

'Your arse is grass and I'm the lawnmower,' Moriarsey taunted him. 'Meet … *The Spinmeister*!'

'You swine!' growled Grabham as he slowly regained his wits.

The electric machine was fitted with three revolving canes, each 36 inches long. The speed knob controlled the motion from slow to rapid movement: one, two, three or more strokes every five seconds. Moriarsey turned the machine even higher. So it inflicted one stroke a second! *Sixty strokes* a minute!

He was going to cane Grabham to death!

'The Emperor Gluteus Maximus,' Moriarsey gloated, 'had revolving canes fitted to the wheels of his chariot, to thrash his enemies to death, just like the *Spinmeister*. Now it's time to kiss your arse goodbye, too.'

Moriarsey switched on the caning machine. 'The machine is now live. It cannot be switched off. Anyone who tries to do so will be electrocuted. I leave you to your fate, Caning Commando.'

The Spinmeister delivered an endless series of cruel blows on Grabham's posterior. He almost lost his mind from the pain. Whenever he caned his boys, he always urged them to avoid 'girlitis' and not cry out. Now he, too, had to bite his lip not to scream. But he gritted his teeth and took it. The Caning Commando would never blub.

Then he saw – through a haze of pain – the boy Tim, from upstairs, approaching the machine. 'Don't worry, Caning Commando. I'll save you!'

'No, Tim! No! Get back! It's electrified!'

But the courageous boy took no notice. At great personal risk, he crawled under the revolving canes and pulled the plug out from the wall. Then, as *The Spinmeister* came to a halt, he ran in search of Moriarsey.

'Come back, Tim!' Grabham called after him. 'Leave Moriarsey to me! He's too dangerous!' But the boy hero was gone.

Moriarsey was preparing to escape, loading his van with valuable canes for his gang. As he was about to go up the stairs with a final consignment, Tim used the crook of a cane to trip up the fascist, and he tumbled back down into the basement.

Grabham picked a cane from a rack and brandished it at his old enemy.

'Now let me introduce you to *The Germicidal*, Moriarsey. It's an antiseptic, sterilised cane that enables teachers to still cane boys on the bare during contagious school epidemics. So they can't get out of a beating with namby-pamby excuses like having measles, mumps or scarlet fever. Your arse will have scarlet fever after I've finished!'

Moriarsey looked horrified. 'No! Please! *No!* Not…*The Germicidal!*'

'Yes,' leered Grabham with great relish. '*The Germicidal.* An appropriate name for a cane to punish a Nazi-lover. But no need for trousers down, Moriarsey. The cane will cut them to shreds. Into him, Tim! It's time to Carpet Bum the Hun!'

Tim and the Commando, both wielding their canes, attacked and soundly thrashed the cringing arch-villain.

'Here's some heat for your seat,' laughed the intrepid boy. They were still caning him when a Black Maria arrived to take him off to prison.

Then Grabham turned to congratulate the boy and told him he made a far better companion for him than the gormless idiot, Alf Mast. 'You've done well, Tim, my boy. I'd never have survived without you. You're a true hero.'

Tim explained that he and his grandfather were in London for his birthday and invited the Caning Commando to join them for a slap-up meal. Grabham was delighted to accept and meet the boy's kindly grandfather, Mr 'Fiddy' Ferguson.

'Happy Birthday, Tim,' said the Caning Commando.

'Together, we Carpet Bummed the Hun!'

* * *

Dave was taking no chances. He ensured the artist draw a large flattering image of the Caning Commando and Tim together as the boy was presented by Grabham with his very own special cane. A souvenir of the day when he had saved Britain's greatest hero from Moriarsey.

And saved Dave's arse, too.

[1] See bonus story 'Relieving Mr Mafeking' for an account of what happened when Dave and Greg visited Mafeking and Jones. Details at end of book.

CHAPTER NINE

'MY LATEST MOVIE PROP,' Joy explained. She took out a packet of *Embassy* and used the miniature guillotine on her desk to slice off a filter tip. 'It's from *A Shot in the Dark.*' She used the tobacco to roll herself a joint.

Dave briefly admired the cigar-cutter. 'One of my favourite films.' He tried an Inspector Clouseau voice 'And I submit, Inspector Ballon, that you killed Miguel in a rit of fealous jage!'

'You're nothing like him,' laughed Joy, opening the window.

'I'm not?'

'No,' she looked at him meaningfully as she lit the joint. 'You're far too romantic.'

'I am? You know, I don't think anyone's ever said that to me before, Joy. Weird, yes, romantic, no.'

'Maybe it's possible to be both?' suggested Joy.

'Yeah, I had a girlfriend once who said, "You're so weird, Dave, you make me seem normal and sane. So when you're being a fucking idiot, which is most of the time, no one notices me and I can relax."'

'I can see how that would work,' considered Joy.

'I was like a "beard" for her,' continued Dave, 'so no one would know how boring she was.'

'What happened?'

'She caught me two-timing her with her fur rug. That was too weird for her.'

'Actually, Dave,' smiled Joy, drawing on her joint. 'I've been thinking about all those wonderful little notes you've been sending me.'

'What notes?' asked a puzzled Dave.

'Don't tease. Don't pretend you don't know,' Joy looked coyly at him. 'You know.'

'Invoices …? But you haven't accepted any of my stories yet. Unless you bought *Penny never saw the Pitch,* about a blind hockey player? Or *Paula Never Saw The Pool,* about a blind high diver?'

'No, Dave,' said Joy patiently. 'I haven't. Let's not spoil this.'

'For some reason I'm really fond of the name Paula,' Dave reflected. 'I remember you also rejected *Paula's Fit for the Poorhouse.*'

'Every morning, I come in and find another little message waiting for me on my desk. I'm really touched, Dave.'

Dave hadn't the faintest idea what she was talking about. But his mother had drummed it into him that he needed to be more romantic if he was going to get off with Joy again, so he went along with it. 'Okay,' he grinned. 'You got me.'

She brought out a small pile of 'Love Is …' cartoons from a drawer. 'I'm really looked forward to a new one from you every day.'

Dave read one out, 'Love is … what makes everything right with your world.' He resisted coming out with any number of cynical responses. He had no idea who was sending her the 'Love Is …' cartoons, but he was more than happy to take the credit for them.

'Love is … when you're lost for words,' he ad-libbed. He couldn't actually think of anything else to say.

'It's very sweet, Dave. In fact, too sweet for my taste. I don't usually like this kind of drippy shit. It's a bit like Wedding Belle in *Everlasting Love.*'

'Yeah, unfortunately, I couldn't find any that said, 'Love is … being rogered hard over a desk,' Dave suggested hopefully.

'But my friend Sophie really recommends starting off with the old-fashioned slush. She says you've got to fake it to make it. And then … we do something absolutely disgusting!' Joy's eyes lit up. 'She said it gave her the most incredible orgasms.'

'You know, that's exactly why I did it, Joy,' Dave lied. 'We start off with all the sugary sweet stuff and then we get into some indescribable and shameful filth. Preferably involving fur.'

'I'm glad we're on the same page, Dave. I knew it was you when you started leaving a Fry's *Turkish Delight* beside the messages.'

'Oh, you know me, Joy. I'm full of Eastern promise.'

'I'm hoping so. You know, Sophie said if you were freeballing, like the Arabs, it would enlarge your penis. You could end up with a fire hose, Dave.'

'Do thank Sophie for her interest and concern, Joy.'

'And today, you left me ... *this.*' With a flourish, she produced a Cadbury's *Flake* chocolate bar.

Whoever Joy's mystery admirer was, he was putting a considerable amount of effort into romancing her and Dave was delighted to take advantage of him. It saved him having to make the effort, and anyway, he only had five-year-old free gift sweets in his confectionery box. He suspected that *Yo Ho Ho* liquorice chewing tobacco or *Kojak* lollies wouldn't have quite the same effect on Joy.

'Only the crumbliest, flakiest ...' he began.

She put down her joint and started to undo the wrapper.

Looking deep into Dave's eyes, she slowly, sensually, peeled it back. Then he took the flake from her as she opened her lips and parted her teeth. He gradually slid the bar inside her mouth and, closing her eyes, she gently moved her head up and down, then nibbled off the end.

He was going to take it slowly this time. Not rush things. Thanks to his mother's advice and the secret Cadbury's *Flake* donor, he was finally pulling the woman of his dreams.

And with her eyes closed, she wouldn't be aware he was actually focusing his attention not on her, but on her vintage fox fur hanging by the door. Oh, yes, that really hit the spot.

Then Greg swaggered in and it felt like a brick being thrown through a furriers' window.

'Thought I could smell dope.'

'Haven't you got work to do?'

'Ah!' said Greg, as Joy took the flake out of her mouth. 'I see you've got your present from Deep Throat.'

'What?' gasped Joy.

'Cadbury's *Flake*. That's from Barclay.'

'You mean,' said Joy slowly, 'I've had something from Deep Throat...*in my mouth?*'

'Yeah,' said Greg casually. 'He knows all the models in the adverts, their names, vital statistics, addresses. He's got this thing about one model in particular. Keeps sending her long, passionate love letters, wanting to meet her. I think she had to take out a restraining order against him in the end.'

'No. It's – it's just coincidence that we share the same taste in sweets,' said Dave hastily. He turned to Joy. 'I was going to bring you a *Yorkie* bar tomorrow.'

'It was definitely Barclay,' said Greg. 'He's been cutting those cartoons out of the paper for you as well.'

'That pervert has been sending me "Love Is ..." messages?'

Joy looked revolted. I think I'm going to puke.' She looked down at the half eaten bar. 'It's disgusting.'

'Sorry,' grinned Greg. 'Have I said something I shouldn't have?'

'But you kept it in the wrapper, so you didn't actually touch it,' Dave reassured her. 'So it's okay: it acted like, you know, a condom?'

'That's an even more disgusting thought. And you are disgusting, lying to me.'

'But I thought you liked disgusting?' protested Dave. 'You know? Start off sugary sweet and then get into something really offensive? I mean, what could be more offensive than Deep Throat? He's the ultimate perversion. That's why I went along with it.'

By way of response, she inserted the flake into the guillotine and sliced it in half in a way that made both Dave and Greg wince.

She was suddenly distracted by Greg's new outfit. 'And what the fuck are you wearing. Greg? That's disgusting, too.'

Greg was no longer The Man in Black. He was The Man in Green. A pale viridian trouser suit, to be precise. 'What's wrong with it?' he complained.

Joy noted the shapeless trousers and pursed her mouth. 'It's got an elasticated waist, Greg.'

'So?'

'An *elasticated* waist. Greg, those are the kind of trousers mothers buy for their little boys and lead to them getting beaten up in the playground as sissies. And rightly so.'

'I'm no aficionado of fashion, Greg,' said Dave, pleased his assistant editor was taking the heat off him, 'But even I can see that's a serious fashion *faux pas.*'

'Leni bought it for me,' Greg said defensively. 'It's part of my new look. She's grooming me to be managing editor again.'

'She's grooming you for Crufts,' Joy snapped. 'What are you? Her fucking dog? You can't let her humiliate you like that.'

'Yeah,' agreed Dave. 'Just how much green snot can you eat, Greg?'

'If you mean the super food spirulina,' said Greg, 'it's a blue-green algae that Leni says has unbelievable health benefits.'

'It's green snot, Greg,' insisted Dave. 'Would you like a couple of my bogies as well?'

'I'd just come in here for a quiet spliff,' said Greg plaintively, 'but if you're going to be like that, I shall have one of my herbal cigarettes instead. They're better for you,' he revealed, as he lit one up.

'You could fool me,' said Joy, coughing on the bonfire-fumes as she wrote something down on a piece of paper.

'Leni says the Hopi Indians use it in their rituals. The smoke carried their prayers to the Gods.'

'Yeah,' said Joy, *'Save us from this fucking mad woman.'* She got up from her desk 'Go on, get the fuck out of here. Both of you. I've got work to do. And tell Barclay I'm onto him and there will be *consequences …'* she looked down at her guillotine, '… if I find anymore "romantic confectionery" on my desk.'

She escorted them from her office and pinned a notice on her door: 'Love is … Lies perpetuated by the advertising industry to maintain the patriarchal consumerist society.' It was this, but, more likely, her guillotine, which had the necessary deterrent effect on Deep Throat.

It was a setback for Dave, but he didn't give up so easily. His serial for Joy had come together. His plan to enter Fabulous Keen's apartment and borrow his Grand Master costume had come together. It was so much more sinister than Mrs Thatcher's witch's cloak that Greg had gotten hold of. The story and the robes would definitely impress Joy.

He had ignored his mother's remonstrations about Keen being a hard man, a dangerous man who you don't mess with. That might well be the case, but he was only borrowing the Torquemada look-alike outfit. He'd put it back afterwards.

Keen would never know. Dave had been perusing *The Radio Times* for when Fab would be off on his travels for *It's a Fabulous World*, but the series was scheduled for the Summer, unfortunately.

However, he was currently presenting *Tomorrow's Britain* live, so he knew exactly when he would be away.

CHAPTER TEN

TWO DAYS LATER, Dave let himself into Fabulous Keen's apartment. He had a large collection of keys from his days when he had been an errand boy for M&R Pell, Seed Merchants, and the key he'd had cut still fitted. He had thought of everything: he was wearing a smart suit and tie in case any of the neighbours observed him entering, so they would assume he was 'respectable'.

The spacious penthouse apartment, in a luxury block overlooking the Thames, had changed somewhat since Dave had last visited it as a fifteen-year-old. It still looked like the lair of a James Bond villain, but the dazzling white had been replaced with groovy, green-patterned wallpaper and vast, hideous, orange psychedelic paintings, relieved only by a Rolling Stones Rock and Roll Circus poster. The long white sofa had gone and there was an equally-long black leather sofa encased in a white plastic surround escorted by two uncomfortable-looking Bauhaus leather-and-chrome chairs. There were further chairs in the form of a pop-art, giant yellow hand, and a 'matching' one-man, open, yellow submarine, which the sitter climbed into. It was the ultimate in 1970s décor.

The bar remained the same, with its awesome collection of alcohol that he had previously sampled and had made him violently sick. In fact, the whole room was making him feel queasy, all over again.

Perhaps it was because the 'conversation pit' was now converted into a sunken Jacuzzi, in the shape of a love heart.

Even Dave's poor sense of taste felt affronted by it.

The dramatic, futuristic, Picassoesque TV cabinet was gone and, in its place there was a white 'flying saucer' shaped colour TV that looked like a giant eyeball and seemed straight off the set of the film *2001: A Space Odyssey*. One of the new Betamax video recorders was underneath it.

There were still the religious paintings and statues of Mary Magdalene, clothed and unclothed, and a dais with an impressive gold bust of her head, its beauty marred by that ancient skull in the middle. Taking pride of place, alongside his endless awards, were framed messages from the Pope and a relic of the True Cross, with its certificate of authenticity.

Dave turned the eyeball on and watched Fab presenting *Tomorrow's Britain* live so he could keep an eye on the time. Fab was putting a futuristic electric car, an Enfield, through its paces, driving it out of the White City car park, down the heavily-polluted road to Shepherd's Bush. He emerged from the little orange runabout to announce, 'Only 103 of the *Thunderbolts* have been built. They cost nearly three thousand pounds! But in ten years time, we will all be driving one of these super-size "spangles".' He coughed on the fumes pouring from the congested traffic in Wood Lane.

'Because the infernal combustion engine is finished. Its time is up.'

Dave moved onto the bedroom. The black leather waterbed was also gone. In its place was a giant 'medieval' four-poster bed, fit for a Knight of St Pancras, and, Dave assumed, it was Keen's heraldic coat of arms proudly attached to the top horizontal beam. To one side was a large writing desk, with what Dave recognised as a comptometer: an old-school, enormous, electro-mechanical calculator.

But it was Keen's wardrobe that Dave was interested in, and the reason he was here. He slid one of the doors back and, just as before, inside there was a range of Keen's trademark Nehru suits with their distinctive collars.

As a teenager, he was awed by Keen's distinctive fashion style and tried in vain to imitate it. One year, with his Christmas money, he'd actually ordered a made-to-measure Nehru suit just like them. He'd described the jacket collar to the baffled Co-op tailor very clearly. 'No. No. *Not* a Beatles jacket collar. It's got to *stand up*. Like Fabulous Keen's jackets. Like Manfred Mann's!' Unfortunately, the Co-op had still got it wrong. It had come back as an ordinary jacket with the bottom half of the lapels sliced off; the top half still lay there, flat on the garment. The suit, with its 'sawn-off' flat lapels, looked horrible, and he had only worn it once. There was only so much humiliation he could take from his mates.

And there it was: Keen's ceremonial white robe with its *four-feet-high* purple hood, now with an accompanying purple robe, too. It was the most scary uniform imaginable. Was that why the Knights wore them at their secret ceremonies, Dave wondered. To induce fear? But in whom, and why?

Or maybe, simply because they were part of a Spanish Holy Week tradition that inspired their founder, Father Faber-Knox, when he was living in Seville, to found his order of Knights? It was a tradition that went back to the Inquisition and flagellants who, either voluntarily or as a punishment, were flogged as penance for their sins, and were required to hide their faces.

Certainly, he knew the Knights were connected with his family. His mother had been a Virgin Soldier, an organisation closely associated with the Knights. Mr Pell, the seed merchant, his boss and his father's boss, was a Knight. He remembered how his father had furiously smashed in their TV screen with a cricket bat when he was watching a drama about the Spanish Inquisition.

He carefully folded the garments in their transparent dry-cleaning bag into the sports bag he had brought with him. He was only borrowing them. He'd bring them back next week, and Keen would be none the wiser.

Joy had loved it when Greg had appeared in a witch's cloak, possibly once worn by a young Mrs Thatcher, to present his new serial *Slaves of War Orphan School,* featuring a sinister witch headmistress clearly based on Maggie.

Well, the Spanish Inquisition robes would definitely trump Mrs Thatcher's cloak. And Joy would be crazy about the story he had to go with them. He'd finally cracked it.

His mother appeared beside him. 'You just had to do it, didn't you?'

she sighed. She drew heavily on a Park Drive. 'Just don't leave any sign that you were here, okay? Because this man is seriously dangerous.'

'What do you mean "don't leave any sign"?' he protested. 'What about you smoking? That'll tell him someone's been in his apartment.'

'It's etheric smoke. It doesn't leave any trace.'

'So everyone thinks you're just a figment of my imagination? How very convenient.'

'Well, now you're here,' she grimaced, 'you'd better check that desk for clues, too.'

'Clues?'

'To find out who murdered me, Mr Detective. Or had you forgotten that's the reason I came back?'

'What exactly am I looking for, Mum?' he asked, as began rummaging through the drawers of the desk. "Evidence that he was the Blackout Strangler? The Soho serial killer who strangled four women?'

'Evidence that will shove his halo down his throat,' she growled.

'Like a scrapbook of newspaper clippings about women he murdered?' Dave speculated.

'He's too smart to leave any incriminating evidence.'

'Maybe something on the other suspects?' Dave pondered. 'The Canon. Mr Czar the coroner. Mr Peat. They're all Knights of St Pancras. Or *Mrs* Czar? She was a Virgin Soldier with you. Or Mr Cooper? Or how about dad? My legal dad, I mean.'

'Why would evidence about Cooper or Peter be here?' she arched a perfect eyebrow. 'Just keep looking, Inspector Clouseau.'

Her sharp manner reminded Dave of Joy, which he realised was why he was so comfortable around the editor of *Shandy*.

'Although I'm not convinced Keen can be a murderer, mum,' pondered Dave. 'I mean, he's a national treasure.'

'That's part of his camouflage, son. And be careful going through those things. When your hand is in the hound's mouth, withdraw it gently.'

'Good advice.'

'Irish expression. We give a lot of advice.'

'I've noticed.'

He had gone through all the left-hand drawers of the desk now, and in the bottom one, he found several copies of typed information about the Knights. He remembered it from when he was an errand boy and used to deliver packages to Keen. It was exactly the same document: 'Knights of St Pancras. Opening Ceremony. Closing Ceremony. Diagram of Lodge Room. Report of the Secretary. Order of Service.'

'Better take one,' said Jean. 'Could be useful.'

It looked just as boring as when he first read it as a fifteen-year-old, but Dave didn't want to argue with her, so he put the papers in his sports bag.

Then he checked the right-hand drawers of the desk. In the top one he found *The Enchiridion of Indulgences*, a book that meant nothing to him. It had a list of 'norms and grants', works and prayers for indulgences and explanations, none of which he understood.

He chewed on a liquorice pipe to help him concentrate. Something to do with time off in Purgatory, yet it also said there *was* no time in Purgatory.

There was also a ledger in the same drawer with daily entries and figures in the credit and debit columns. Dave could just about make out Keen's spidery handwriting: Charity walk 500 credit. Donation to the blind 100 credit. Lourdes Pilgrimage 5,000 credit. Hospital visit 1000 debit.

A further search of the remaining drawers revealed nothing else of any significance.

'Look, mum,' he sighed. 'I'm a comic book editor. Editor of *Aaagh!* and *The Spanker* – You can't expect me to solve your murder.'

'You promised.'

'I'm not smart enough.'

'You come up with ingenious ideas for crazy kids to copy.'

'That's different and, actually, kids are using my ideas to wreak their revenge on *adults*.'

'Now.'

'I used to hate kids. But not anymore. I'm not sure why,' pondered Dave. 'Maybe it was standing up to Cooper?'

'Because he used to love playing games on kids and you were subconsciously imitating him?

'I guess.'

Dave turned his attention to the grey, gunmetal comptometer.

'Adding and calculating machine. These things are on the way out now. They're almost antiques.'

'I remember them from the war,' agreed Jean. 'I didn't want to be stuck in an office behind a mechanical abacus. That's why I went to work at The Eight Veils.'

'You know, I've always wanted to have a go on one.' said Dave. 'It's like something out of Bletchley Park.'

He turned it on. It was a massive, heavy machine, with a moving carriage and endless rows of numbers that clattered and whirred around as he got it to add and subtract. Gaining in confidence, he set it multiplication and division tests. He watched enthralled as the carriage rolled noisily backwards and forwards, making a thunderous sound like a cross between an underground train and a machine gun.

'This is brilliant,' he said. 'But what's Keen doing with it? Hey – I'm going to set it a really tough task. Divide a figure by zero. That should, theoretically, keep it going for infinity.'

'That's what he's concerned about: infinity,' said Jean. 'What's going to happen in the afterlife. That's why he keeps a credit and debit ledger of his crimes and his good deeds.'

As Dave set the machine its new task, his mother sneered to herself. 'But he can climb Croagh Patrick in his bare feet, it still won't save him.

To Dave's delight, the comptometer thundered noisily backwards and forwards, then began growling and heaving, 'overflowing' with the calculating challenge. It came to a standstill, the numbers going crazy as it went into an *infinite* loop.

Disappointed the carriage wasn't moving any more, he went round to the back of the over-revving machine and leant over it to investigate what was wrong.

'Do you realise, Mum?' he said excitedly, 'If I can get this to keep working, I could solve the mystery of infinity?' His tie dangled down and the comptometer seized hold of it, sucked it into its innards and began strangling him.

'I warned him,' his mother continued. 'When Jenny was found strangled, I told him, "You can dress a goat in silk, and he still remains a goat. But your day will come, Johnny boy. Live horse and you'll get grass." ' She rasped out the words with a dark Celtic menace.

'Guuhhhh!' said Dave as the tie was sucked deeper inside the comptometer, tightening around his neck. His strangulated cry was drowned out by the coughing and wheezing of the machine in infinity mode.

'I said to him, "The lamb of God will stir his hoof through the roof of Heaven and kick you in the arse down to Hell",' recalled Dave's mother. 'And he knew it. Oh, yes. He was afraid I had The Sight. That's why he stopped.' She took a long draw on her cigarette. 'There were no more stranglings after Jenny.'

Positioned round the back of the machine, Dave couldn't see where the 'stop' button was, so it continued to strangle him as he tried blindly pressing random buttons without success. It just seemed to make it worse, judging by its groaning and heaving and straining sounds.

'Have a look at the ledger, Dave,' she said, flicking through the book.

'And, by the way, could I really do this if I was a product of your imagination? Although,' she reflected, 'I suppose you could still be imagining me doing this.'

But Dave, desperately trying to free himself, was too distracted to hear her.

'Yuuuggh!' he said, flailing helplessly.

'So every time he does something good, like a charity walk, or raising money for a hospital, he awards himself time off in Purgatory. That goes in the credit column, so he can be sure he's always in the black. Wonder how he calculates the bad stuff? Probably with that book of indulgences.'

Dave's head was pulled down close to the carriage, as the ever-changing numbers spun on their relentless journey to infinity. His ear mere inches from the machine, the noise was thunderous. He was trapped there until the end of time, or until the machine caught fire, burned out, or Keen returned – whichever came first. Probably Keen returning, although the machine was becoming unbearably hot and starting to smoke ominously now.

As best he could, he desperately twisted his head to look around him, but there was nothing to cut his tie off with, to stop the strangulation.

Jean continued to leaf through page after page of the ledger, with all its complex calculations. 'But I'm not sure St Peter would accept these figures. Even if Keen did threaten to kick his teeth in.'

With his vision starting to darken around the edges, he realised he would have to turn off the power at the wall socket. The cable led from the back of the machine, across the desk and disappeared over the side, hopefully to a socket below.

The comptometer was heavy, especially so when crouched over and half-strangled by it, so Dave began to drag it across the desk.

He reached the edge and, unable to turn his head to look, blindly reached out his arm, feeling a surge of relief as his hand found the plug. He yanked it from the socket, finally switching off his tormentor. The blood rushing in his ears and his choking wheeze were loud in the sudden silence of the apartment.

'Hrrrrrgh!' said Dave, finally able to breathe again.

'What are you doing down there?' asked his mother irritably.

'Are you listening to me?'

'I need to get my tie out of the machine,' he said, still intimately connected to the comptometer. With no power, the mechanical calculator refused to release its prize. So he had to switch it on and off again a few times, starting and stopping it, and, after a few unsuccessful attempts, it finally, grudgingly, released the garment and he was able to stand up. His tie was mangled and smeared with oil as he shifted the comptometer back into the centre of the desk and breathed a sigh of relief.

'So you understood about indulgences?' she asked irritably.

'Absolutely. It's like pre-paid sin. Buy one, get one free.' Suddenly, he and Jean both heard the sound of a footstep outside the bedroom door and they exchanged apprehensive glances.

'It can't be Keen,' whispered Jean. 'Not yet. *Tomorrow's Britain* is only just over.'

'So who's out there?'

CHAPTER ELEVEN

DAVE GUESSED what was going on the moment he stepped back into the lounge and he saw who was standing there.

He barely noticed his mother fading away as his mind immediately flashed back to a scene in *The Caning Commando*, when Grabham replaced the evil scientist Von Vroom's schnapps with thallium, a colourless, odourless, tasteless – and fatal poison.

Because the kid standing by the bar was pouring a colourless liquid into a bottle of Keen's vodka. He was a boy with a man in his eyes. Fresh-faced, youthful, yet somehow – imperceptibly – old before his time.

Imperceptible, except to predators and other prey. Just as stoners, public school boys, swingers, soldiers, cops and villains often recognise each other – even before even a word is said – by body language, clothes, hair and, above all, by the expression in the eyes, so Dave and the kid recognised each other as kindred spirits.

So he knew what the kid was doing and why, but he still had to ask: 'Why?'

'Why do you think?' said the boy. He was a handsome lad, about fourteen, a young David Essex. He wore a white hat, like Dylan on the cover of his latest album, *Desire*. And a similar knotted scarf.

'I have no idea,' lied Dave.

'The parties. The gifts. The visits from "Uncle" Fab to Castle Ramparts.' The boy loaded his words with bitter sarcasm.

'Castle Ramparts?'

'An approved school for gifted but "problem" boys. Uncle Fab takes his favourites out for "treats". As well as the girls from Mildencroft down the road from us.'

'You did something wrong?'

'We're sent there for drugs, going on the game, trying to top ourselves, that kind of shit.'

Dave nodded at the vodka bottle. 'So this is the only way to stop him?'

The boy gritted his teeth. 'We're a family. We look out for each other, especially the young ones.'

Dave said nothing, but the boy answered his unasked question. 'You think the cops would believe approved school kids rather than Saint Fab?' He shook his head. 'Nope. *We've* got to take him down. It's got to be done. No more bullshit. No more skullduggery.'

'Don't you mean skullbuggery?'

'That's not funny.'

'I'm sorry,' Dave sighed. 'I say stupid things when I'm nervous. Actually, I say stupid things when I'm not nervous, My name's Dave Maudling, and–'

'I know who you are. I heard you talking to yourself in there. The editor of *Aaagh!* and *The Spanker*. I'm Scott.'

'Hi, Scott.' They shook hands.

'What the hell was that noise?'

'The comptometer.'

'What's a comptometer?'

'You don't want to know.' Dave gently felt his neck. He changed the subject. 'A *Spanker* and *Aaagh*! fan, eh?'

'They're better than the shit comics they give us.' Scott frowned 'Old *Homework* annuals and *Davy Crockett Picture Libraries*.'

'They are shit,' agreed Dave.

'Those old geezers have no idea.'

'You mean, for services rendered? I'm shocked.'

'We were, too.'

'And you know what? *Homework* annuals don't even smell as good as good as the other annuals. I love the smell of an Angus, Angus and Angus annual. *The Corker, The Bazooka* or *The Tosser*. Reminds me of Christmas. I could sniff them all day. I think it's something they put in the ink. Much better than Fleetpit annuals. But the *Homework* annuals smell kinda ... posh. Horrible.'

Scott was looking at him coldly.

'Sorry, Scott. There I go again. Me and my stupid mouth. I don't know what's the matter with me.'

'We get other stuff as well. But the wardens get the serious money.'

'Wardens?'

'They're in charge of us. They supply Fab's parties.' Scott glowered. 'It's why I fucking hate cowboy comics. *Kit Carson. Buffalo Bill. Davy Crockett.*' He spat out the names.

'Yes,' admitted Dave. 'We usually put our worst writers on *Davy Crockett Picture Library*. I myself have written several. But you've got to admit they smell pretty good? They've got that nice, fusty letterpress smell? That's 'cos the paper's already starting to decay, you see?'

Dave realised Scott was still looking at him coldly.

'Anyway, I'm glad you like *The Spanker,*' Dave added lamely.

'No, actually, *The Spanker's* a bit shit, too,' said Scott. 'We only read it for *The Caning Commando.*'

''Cos it's so ridiculous, it's actually pretty funny, right?'

'It's okay. But we get it 'cos it tells us how to kill people.'

Dave looked taken aback. Scott grinned at him. 'What? You didn't think we'd notice?'

Dave's face gave nothing away. Or rather, he thought it didn't. If he had checked in the mirror, he would have seen he looked guilty as hell.

'*Aaagh!* is better,' Scott continued. 'We all read it – especially the girls.' He looked enthusiastic. 'They love *White Death*. Oh, man – we loved that scene where Airforce One crash lands in the Pacific!'

'And the shark bursts in through the cockpit?'

'He swims down the aisle ...'

'And eats the President of the United States!' Dave laughed.

'And he's screaming, "No! Not ... the jaws!",' whooped Scott. 'I've got to congratulate you, Dave. That was seriously sublime.'

'Thanks. But actually, Joy writes *White Death.*'

Scott grinned 'You are really fucking with our heads, you know? *Carjacks*. Wicked! You know your cars, man.'

'That was Greg.'

'And *Black Hammer*! A *black* hero in comics. Too much!'

'That was me,' said Dave, pleased to finally take some credit.

'So cool. For the first time a comic is telling kids not to look up to people in authority, like *Homework*. All the people *Homework* approves of: magistrates, MPs, titled geezers, bishops, they're the bastards who are at Fab's parties.' Scott clenched his fists at the thought.

'Pillars of the community,' said Dave. 'I bet they're all tweedy and suited and booted.'

'They ask how we're getting on at school. Are we doing our homework?' said Scott sarcastically. 'Like they're such good, such kind people. "Terribly decent people",' he said with a mock refined accent. 'Like they actually give a shit.'

'Party chat-up lines,' explained Dave. 'They can't really ask, "Have you come far?" or "What's your star sign?" or "I just love your jacket." '

'Oh, they come out with some of that crap, too. It's just like a normal party. And they talk about maybe adopting us if we're good. What they mean is, if we do what they want,' said Scott. Then added darkly as an afterthought: 'And if we pretend to be enjoying it.'

'Evil fuckers,' said Dave, finally losing his facetious armour.

'And *Aaagh!* is telling us to fight back against these evil fuckers. You do know that's what you're telling us to do, Dave?' said Scott looking seriously at him. 'To fight back?'

Dave hesitated. He knew that's what he was telling kids, but it had always been a very distant knowledge. Now it was hitting him right between the eyes. He inhaled, enjoying the free transit of air straight down his windpipe. 'I know.'

'But not like this, Scott,' he added, taking the bottle of vodka, tearing himself away from being a man-child and reluctantly playing the adult. It was an unfamiliar feeling, but he felt he had to, more because of his seniority of years, rather than from any genuine adult feeling of responsibility. 'I mean … anyone could drink it.'

He pursed his lips, nodded his head, and looked seriously at Scott, the way he imagined adults looked reprovingly at kids. That typical teacher or policeman look, which comes so easily to most adults, but somehow came out weirdly when Dave did it.

'Are you all right?' asked Scott anxiously.

'What do you mean?'

'Your face … you look like you're about to throw up.'

'I'm fine.'

Dave was also conscious of the time. *Nationwide* was nearly over and Fabulous Keen would be home soon. They had to get out of there.

'I'm a "gifted kid", remember?' continued Scott. 'Vodka and tonic is what Keen always drinks. I'm not going to put the poison in the Babycham, am I?'

Dave couldn't let Scott do it, even though, via *The Caning Commando*, he had been encouraging kids to kill. But brought face to face with it, he couldn't let it happen. Not because the kid would get into serious trouble, but because he would be complicit in the crime.

Dave took the bottle over to the Jacuzzi. 'It's just too risky.' He poured the poison down the plughole, filling up the vodka bottle with tap water. 'We'll find another way to deal with him, Scott.'

'Like what?'

'I don't know yet, but we'll find it.'

'Are you sure?' Scott looked at him skeptically. 'You're not just saying that because you don't want to be involved in his murder?'

'Course not. Not at all. No way.'

'*Three* negatives,' observed Scott shrewdly, looking carefully at Dave's face. 'That makes me doubt you.'

'Why would three negatives be wrong?' asked Dave guiltily.

'It's like when people come out with three excuses why they can't do something. One excuse is genuine. Three excuses, you know they're always lying.'

'I didn't know that,' mused Dave. 'I'll watch out for it. But no, I'm not just saying that.'

'Okay,' said a satisfied Scott. 'Because you know you're already responsible, Dave. Because the idea for the poison came from you in the first place.'

Dave nodded uneasily. 'I know.'

'And Keen needs to die. You do know that?'

'You and I are on the same page, Scott. Trust me.'

'Okay. But when he drinks water instead of vodka,' pondered Scott, 'he'll know someone knows where he keeps his key, and has been helping themselves to his drinks.'

'He'll think it's the cleaner,' Dave reassured him. He nodded towards the window. 'Watch out for his car. I'm going to have a good look around and make sure we haven't left any clues we've been here.'

He scanned everywhere with eagle eyes to ensure there was no incriminating evidence. The unfamiliar adult behaviour actually felt good to Dave.

Scott looked out the window overlooking the car park. 'They never tell us their names when they come here. I recognise one or two from TV. But usually, I know them by their cars: Reliant Scimitar, Marcos Mantis. AC Cobra, Vanden Plas Princess. I'd say the more expensive the car, the bigger the bastard.'

'That's an interesting theory,' said Dave. 'James Bond is licensed to kill and he's got an Aston Martin. What's Fab's?'

'Jensen Interceptor. He'd drive me home sometimes.' Scott's face grimaced with rage. 'You know what I really hate, Dave? More than anything in the whole world? I really hate the dashboard of a Jensen Interceptor.'

Dave was now thinking of his exit strategy, how he could best extricate himself from the situation, without it making it look too obvious, especially as Scott was so clearly intelligent. 'Apart from the cops, you never considered asking anyone else for help?' he asked casually as he switched off the TV and took a final look around.

'No. Because I'm asking you.'

'I meant – someone official.'

'Like who?'

'Oh, you know: Cross Line? "Whatever your cross, we'll help you carry it".' Scott turned away from the window. 'How do we know they're not in league with Keen? Every other fucker is.'

'Teachers?'

'Yeah, right.'

'Social services?'

'Those jobsworths?'

'Your own social worker?'

'You mean the one Keen supplies with heroin? Who jacks-up in front of me?'

'Heroin? That will destroy him? Won't it?'

'Like in the leaflets? Not immediately. And not always.'

'I didn't know that.'

'You know, I think I'm more worldly-wise than you, Dave.'

'There must be someone you can trust.'

'Yeah. You.'

The words were like an arrow. It went straight into Dave's heart. He knew he could not extricate himself now. He had to help the kid.

Dave looked down into the car park. A Jensen had just pulled up. 'He's back.' Scott looked afraid for the first time. 'The stairs. Don't want to meet him coming out of the lift.' Dave nodded.

'Hurry!'

Dave looked down again at the Jensen and saw Keen alight. He was shocked to see a familiar figure from his past gracefully slipping out from the passenger side. It was Mrs Czarnecki, the wife of the coroner.

'Dave! Come on!'

Grabbing his sports bag, Dave rushed from the room, slamming the door, pausing for the briefest of moments as Scott replaced the key under the flower pot.

Then they hurtled down the stairs, even as they could see the lift was being summoned from the ground floor.

CHAPTER TWELVE

MRS CZAR LEANED BACK in the Bauhaus chair. She was the only person Fab knew who could sit comfortably and elegantly in them. He'd bought the design classics purely for show. He didn't like women much, but he had to admit she looked a picture of beauty. Her glistening and hypnotic, dark eyes, high cheekbones, and slender, swan-like neck reminded him of the legendary Queen Nefertiti. Or Audrey Hepburn in *Breakfast at Tiffany's*. Maybe it was the elegant black dress she was wearing. All she needed was a long cigarette holder to complete her Hollywood star look. She looked nothing like her adopted parents, the Pells, who were unmistakably Southern England. Just one glance at Mrs Czar and you could see she was from somewhere more exotic.

'I thought Brighton for the summer children's outing,' he suggested.

'Why not?' she agreed.

'Good. What can I get you?'

'Vodka on the rocks.'

As Fabulous, wearing an elegant blue Nehru suit, poured her drink, he continued. 'Our friends from the yacht club can take some of them out for the weekend.'

'How generous of them,' she smiled.

'Provided, of course, your Virgin Soldiers came along ...'

She looked teasingly at him. 'As chaperones, you mean?'

Fabulous laughed. 'Naturally, Julia. They'll feel so much safer with you ladies around.' He passed her her drink.

'*And* Uncle Fab,' she smirked.

'Of course. Because it's a dangerous world out there.'

'And you do have your enemies,' she pointed out. 'Those reporters?'

Fabulous shrugged. 'If I see them dancing in my headlamps, I will run over every one of them.'

'In your Enfield?' she smiled.

'In the Jensen. Because I need to hurt them. Badly. And then reverse over them to finish them off. 'Cos I'm infallible, me. I'm like the pope.'

'Don't you mean "invulnerable", John?' said Mrs Czar smoothly. She was using his first name deliberately, as a reminder that she had known him for decades, long before he became known as Fabulous Keen.

'I mean no one can touch me. I can touch *them*, but they can't touch me. Those are the rules.'

'I'll drink to that,' Mrs Czar said. 'Cheers.' And they chinked glasses. She sipped her drink and grimaced. 'Water!'

'Are you sure?'

'Quite sure. I think your cleaner must be a secret drinker.' Fabulous tasted his own vodka and tonic. 'You're right. But Elsie would never do that. She's been with me for years.' He looked puzzled around the room, but everything looked in order.

'Well, someone's done it,' she said. 'Check the gin.'

He did. 'It's okay.' He checked the others. 'They're all okay.'

'Just the vodka,' she pointed out. 'Your regular tipple.'

'Interesting,' he murmured, trying to figure out what this meant and what was going on.

'Could one of those reporters have got in?' His expression told her the answer.

'You don't still leave a spare under the pot plant? Oh, John.'

'They wouldn't dare. No one's going to print those allegations that girl made. Big wailing crybaby. She was asking for it.'

'Well, it's either Elsie, or someone's been in the apartment,' Mrs Czar shrugged.

'I thought the story was dead,' he ruminated. 'All right, let the pus come to the surface. I don't care,' he added bullishly.

'There's nothing incriminating a reporter could have found?'

'Nothing. I'm far too careful.'

'You're sure, John?'

'Quite sure.'

'Good.'

'Gin and tonic?'

'I guess it'll have to be.'

Fab sat opposite her on the leather sofa. They both sipped their drinks, reflecting on the mysterious intrusion. 'I can't get it out of my mind, Julia. Someone's been here,' said Fab. 'You know what it feels like? Like I've been violated. I don't like being violated.'

'Maybe there's an innocent explanation?'

'Maybe.'

'And you're positive there's nothing a reporter could use? You're absolutely positive?'

'Of course,' said a relaxed Fab. 'Unless…the ledger!' Suddenly, he was on edge.

'What ledger? What are you talking about?'

'The one I use to make sure I'm always in the black.'

'What do you mean?'

An awful thought hit him. 'Oh, fuck!'

He jumped up, put his drink down and ran for the bedroom. Going immediately to the desk, he opened the top right-hand drawer.

The relief he felt when he saw the ledger was still there was vast.

'It's okay,' he called back to Julia. 'It's okay. It's still there.' He exhaled, and started to calm down. Not that a reporter could have really made sense of it. But he should be more careful in future.

And then he saw it: lying on top of *The Enchiridion of Indulgences*.

A liquorice pipe.

CHAPTER THIRTEEN

IT WAS NEARLY two decades since Dave had seen Mrs Czar in that solemn procession, as the Virgin Soldiers, including his mother, escorted the Canon through the streets to the King Edward VIII docks. Even from a distance, as he saw her exiting the Jensen, he could see she was still the elegant and radiant woman he had once admired from afar, as a boy.

He could just imagine her fragrant perfume wafting towards him now. He recalled it from later, when he had made deliveries as an errand boy, and had packages for her husband, the coroner. Her chic Georgian townhouse was filled with her subtle but exquisite scent. Dressed in his fishtail parka, with his desert boots and red socks, ready for when he was old enough to be a true mod and drive a scooter, he would wait in the hallway for Mrs Czar to sign his signature book, his boyhood admiration now giving way to teenage lust.

He would listen intently for the swish of her black nylons rubbing against each other, as she approached him, noting just the very slightest hint of a sag in her stockings at the knees, and imagining how they were held up, as she walked towards him in her tight black pencil skirt, set off nicely by the crispest white blouse, and–

He wondered what she was doing with Keen right now. And whether there was any chance their paths would ever cross in the future?

'Dave?' said Scott. 'Dave! Are you listening? Are you following what I'm saying?'

They were continuing their conversation in a nearby café, a few streets back from the Thames. The place was trying to attract tourists visiting the Tower of London close-by, so it had a knights in armour theme.

'Sure,' said Dave. 'You said you hate all this knights and chivalry crap.'

Scott looked around at the various faux-medieval artefacts and tapestries on the wall. 'It's a pathetic lie for sad bastards. The dragons should have slain them all.'

'I take it the "party-goers" were Knights of St Pancras?'

'Some. Wanting me to be their "squire", their "boy companion". You should see what they wanted me to wear. Perverts. I fucking hate them. Others were toffs. And Fab loaned us out to the canvas shoe brigade, as well.'

'Who?'

'Yachties. We were taken on boat rides as a "special treat". But if you fight back, they say you'll go over the side.'

'So what can you do?'

'I'll show you.' Scott looked cautiously around. 'I'll wait until a lorry goes by.' After several minutes, two lorries thundered by, but the boy still hesitated. 'Sorry. No good. Not in me. Has to be a genuine threat to work. Anyway, you'd be arrested.'

'For what?'

'The howl.'

'The howl?'

'It's the most piercing, deathlike howl you ever heard. On a really weird frequency. I've no control over it. Just came out of me. Freaked out Reliant Scimitar. Made him back off.'

'Sounds like a primal scream. Or shamanic scream.' Dave had read Janov's book on the subject when he was trying to understand his father's mental illness. 'An animal howl. Keeps predators at bay. Didn't know it worked.'

'Once. Can't do it again.'

'So what happened the next time?'

'The next time I bit Vanden Plas's ear. And spat in Mantis's face.'

Scott grinned. 'They didn't like that. Threatened to drug me, so then I had to make the best of it with Cobra. But, you know, there are still other ways kids can put these bastards off ...'

Dave looked at him blankly.

'Poor hygiene. Hey – they fight dirty, so why shouldn't we?'

Dave nodded. 'I've seen how resourceful kids can be.'

'You don't know the half of it,' grinned Scott. He looked meaningfully at Dave who had no idea what he getting at. Scott considered enlightening him, then changed his mind. 'Let's put it this way – I didn't feel the "discomfort" he did.' He smirked as he remembered. 'So they don't choose me anymore.'

'I've got to get going,' said Dave. 'And you should, too. Don't they have a curfew or something?'

Scott shrugged indifferently. 'Anyway, I never really understood what you were doing in Keen's apartment. Apart from trying to blow up his comptometer?'

Dave patted his sports bag. 'Borrowing his Spanish Inquisition robes. Hot date. I hope.'

Scott looked impressed. 'That takes balls. I reckon we could bring this off together.'

Dave got up. 'Yeah, we need to work out a plan. Next time, Scott.'

'It's him or us, Dave. Kill or be killed. There's no other way. So we'll meet up again very soon?'

'Absolutely. Definitely. You bet.' Scott looked coldly up at him.

'What's the matter?' asked Dave, noting the boy's sudden change of expression.

'That's three positives, Dave. I'm starting to doubt you.'

'I ... I thought that rule only applied to negatives?' Dave protested.

Scott looked suspiciously at him. 'Are you for real, Dave, or are you full of shit like everybody else?'

'Well I ...'

'Are you on our side or not?'

'For sure. You got it. One hundred per cent.'

PART II

JUNE TO JULY 1976

'It's a fucking Werewolf!'

CHAPTER FOURTEEN

METROPOLITAN POLICE COLD CASE UNIT NOVEMBER
3RD 2016
Detective Inspector Mary Read
A PROFILE OF MRS JEAN MAUDLING

Jean Ryan was born in Ballana, Ireland, in 1925, emigrating to Britain in 1940. In 1944, she was a singer at The Eight Veils club in Old Compton Street, Soho, London. Between 1942 and 1945, four women were murdered by the 'Blackout Strangler' in Soho. One of the victims was Jenny Clarkson, another singer at The Eight Veils who was Jean's best friend. The identity of the 'Blackout Strangler' has never been discovered.

We have investigated and found no connection between these murders and Jean's subsequent death by strangulation in 1957.

John Keen, later known as the TV celebrity 'Fabulous' Keen, was a doorman at The Eight Veils during this period, but we have investigated and found he had no connection with this case, despite various allegations on conspiracy websites.

At The Eight Veils, Jean met Peter Maudling, a young scientist working for the Ministry of Agriculture, and they married in 1944. In 1945, the couple went out to the British colony of Nigeria. Their daughter Annie was born in Nigeria in the same year. Peter was often away for long periods 'up country' and Jean began a relationship with Ernest Gambo, their houseboy.

When their interracial relationship was discovered, there was a scandal. Women like Jean were described as having 'gone native'. The Maudlings were sent home in disgrace in 1947 and Peter Maudling was forced to resign from the colonial service.

Peter subsequently took up a post as a seed analyst with seed merchants M&R Pell, at the King Edward VIII docks, East London. The family bought a house: 2, Mordle Street, Stoke Basing, close to the docks.

Peter's job was well-paid, and Jean had a sophisticated taste in clothes. She would regularly wear fur coats, muffs and stoles and this was the subject of much gossip in the neighbourhood.

Peter began drinking heavily. His wife's infidelities, expensive tastes, and his loss of status may have contributed to his subsequent mental illness. He used a derelict property at 10, Mordle Street to produce 'moonshine' beer. The couple spent several periods of time apart up to the time of Jean's death.

Their son, David, was born in 1949.

Jean craved respectability and hoped to achieve this by becoming a leading member of her local Catholic church, St Mary's. She joined the Virgin Soldiers, a women's organisation affiliated to the Knights of St Pancras, an order of wealthy businessmen who dedicate themselves to helping poor and disadvantaged children.

John Keen was the Grand Master of the East London Province of the Knights of St Pancras at this time, but, again, this has no relevance to the case.

According to Jean's daughter Annie, her mother had two secret, extra-marital relationships:

Bill Peat, a chemistry teacher and Knight of St Pancras who also sang in St Mary's church choir with Jean.

Ernest Gambo, who emigrated to Britain and took a job as a stevedore in the King Edward VIII docks.

Annie also states that her mother and Canon Williams, the local priest and chaplain of the Knights of St Pancras, were 'very close', but insisted that there was no impropriety in their relationship.

Jean bought a copy of *The Fourpenny One* comic for her son David on Saturday 9th March 1957, from a local newsagent, Stanley Cooper, who had a shop in Commercial Lane, just off Commercial Road. A next-door neighbour, Mr Ross, recalls seeing Jean Maudling entering the newsagent's premises and overheard her attacking Cooper, screaming, 'I'll give you a fourpenny one, you bastard.' He estimates the time as approximately 11.00AM.

This is the last confirmed sighting of Jean before she disappeared.

Cooper was taken to Stoke Basing Hospital on Saturday 9th March at 6.00PM. His facial injuries indicated he had been hit with a blunt trauma instrument, almost certainly the blood-stained knuckleduster found in Jean's shopping basket.

On Tuesday 12th March 1957, Peter Maudling reported his wife missing to the local police.

Jean was known to regularly spend time away from the marital home. So the local police believed she had gone off to begin a new life with 'one of her fancy men'. They did not suspect foul play.

We know that all five men: Peter Maudling; Stanley Cooper; Canon Williams; Ernest Gambo, and Bill Peat, were in contact with Jean around the time of her murder on or shortly after 9th March 1957.

We will next consider each of them as persons of interest in this case.

CHAPTER FIFTEEN

IT WAS January 1957, and young Dave was waiting to go to confession at St Mary's. Canon Williams had a stentorian voice and Dave could hear him telling the penitent in the cubicle to say six 'Our Fathers' as a penance and 'Try to keep your temper under control in future … well, yes … even if you *were* provoked. Tell her I'll visit her in hospital.'

Then the green light flashed for Dave to enter. As he hurried forward, he saw that the penitent leaving the cubicle was Mr Cooper, the newsagent, who scowled menacingly at him. But, for once, Dave was not afraid. He knew he was safe from Mr Cooper in the church. He entered the box, knelt down, and began: 'Bless me, Father, for I have sinned. It's been two weeks since my last confession.'

'And what do you have to confess, my son?' asked the shadowy figure of the Canon, just visible through the communicating grille.

'I've told lies.'

'Yes.'

'I've been cheeky.'

'Yes.'

Outside the confessional, the Canon was friendly towards Dave; but now he sounded cold, remote, and bored. So Dave thought he'd better liven things up a bit by admitting to one of his more interesting crimes.

'I stole money from the black babies missionary box.'

There was silence at the other end. Then the Canon responded:

'Why did you steal from starving black babies? They were relying on that money for their next meal!'

'I needed it, 'Dave explained.

'So did they,' shouted the furious Canon. 'They will starve to death – thanks to you!'

'There wasn't enough in there. And it took a lot of work to get it out,' said the boy defensively. 'You turn the box upside down, rattle it a bit until you see the coins through the slot, and then you use a knife …'

The Canon interrupted him. 'That missionary box is church property, you blasphemous little boy! What did you want the money for?'

'So I could buy my comic.'

'What comic?'

'Please, Father, I wanted a *Fourpenny One*.'

The Canon opened the dividing hatch in the confessional and snarled, 'And here it is,' as he punched Dave in the face.

As a dazed Dave staggered out of the confessional, he saw Mr Cooper kneeling in a nearby pew, saying his penance. Looking heavenwards, the newsagent smiled and silently thanked God.

* * *

As he prepared for his appointment with Joy, Dave wondered why he was thinking about Mr Cooper, the Canon, and that painful childhood memory. He often had unwanted recollections of his past now, and there was always a reason. He concluded it must be the robes he had filched from Fabulous Keen. Canon Williams was, after all, the chaplain of the Knights of St Pancras. And the Canon certainly had a temper. There had been that procession through the streets when the ex-cavalryman priest had exchanged blows with a protestant who accused him of having a harem of nuns. And there were other occasions when he had incurred the Canon's wrath as a kid.

Donning the robes, Dave put the pointed, purple capirote on his head, and, clutching his script proposal for Joy, headed for the *Shandy* office. So why think about the confessional, he wondered? There must be some connection he hadn't quite made yet. Something to do with sins, maybe? Mr Cooper being punished with six 'Our Fathers' for beating up his wife?

And then he saw it. It was obvious, once he had made the connection. Stealing money from the black babies missionary box was an act of blasphemy; it showed a lack of respect for the Church; and now he was wearing the sacred robes of a Grand Master of the Knights of Saint Pancras: surely a supreme act of blasphemy. He realised just how good blasphemy felt. He must do it more often.

His plan was to impress Joy with his robes, just as Greg had impressed her with his Mrs Thatcher witch cloak. To bring out the drama of the epic saga that he was going to propose to her. Joy had loved the Mrs Thatcher witch outfit: she would be terrified by Torquemada.

He burst into her office proclaiming, 'Prepare to be examined for deviation! All Deviants must die!'

Nothing prepared Dave for Joy's reaction. At the sight of Torquemada, she roared with laughter; she absolutely howled, practically falling off her chair, she just couldn't stop.

'Oh, fuck – I'll wet myself! That is brilliant, Dave! That is so good!'

'You knew it was me?' said Torquemada, somewhat crestfallen.

'Who else could it possibly be?' asked Joy.

'That's true,' said Torquemada.

She collapsed with laughter again, the tears streaming down her face. 'Oh, no. No. No!' She had to keep looking away, but when she looked back she just fell apart laughing again. 'It's too much. It's too much.' And banged her fist on her desk.

'I'm glad you like it. I was worried you might be scared,' said Torquemada.

'Scared?' Joy looked baffled. 'Why the fuck would I be scared? Where did you get it?'

'Don't ask.'

'It's so bad, Dave, it's good.' She had another attack of the giggles. 'I like men who make me laugh.'

That sounded encouraging, he thought. He handed over his storyline.

She started to read his proposal as he removed his hood and robes. 'Oh,' she said demurely, looking rather disappointed. 'I thought you were going to examine me for deviation?'

'I can put the mask and stuff back on?' he suggested quickly.

'Missed your chance.'

He waited nervously, wondering what her reaction would be to his story. So far, his track record with Joy was zero, whereas Greg was her star writer. He'd had a huge hit with *Feral Meryl*, the story of a wild girl brought up by the wolves of Berkshire. The sequel, *The Return of Feral Meryl*, had just begun in *Shandy*. As well as his *Slaves of War Orphan School*, inspired by Mrs Thatcher.

It was generally male script writers that Joy worked with, as female journalists tended to sneer at cheap 'bog-paper' comics like *Shandy*, which they thought were beneath them, and wouldn't further their careers. They were more interested in writing for the glamorous glossies such as *Mumsy for Today's Young Mums, Twinset, Get It On!* and *My Gang*. So guys like Greg and Dave had a clear field all to themselves. After all his failures, Dave wondered, could he finally score?

'I don't believe this,' said Joy as she got to the end of the first page. 'I don't fucking believe it.'

'It is based on facts,' explained Dave warily. 'I researched it carefully.'

Joy carried on to the end of the second page. 'No. I just don't believe it.'

Oh, shit, thought Dave. So all his efforts, all that research, all that thought, had been for nothing. Again. Just what did it take for him to break into girls' comics?

'Jesus,' said Joy as she reached the third page. She looked up at him. 'You? You? *You* really wrote … *this?'*

Dave nodded fearfully.

'Bloody hell,' she said.

Judging by her grim expression, he knew it was not going well. He got out a liquorice pipe and chewed it nervously.

She looked up from her reading, saw him with the pipe and took it out of his mouth. 'Don't do that.' She looked at him reprovingly. 'They're bad for you.'

She put it in her guillotine and sliced the bowl off. Then lit a cigarette and continued reading.

'Well?' he asked apprehensively.

'Shush,' she said. She looked up at him suspiciously. '*This*, from the author of *My Dead Little Pony*? And *Tower Block Tessa* whose mother is a bag lady and father sleeps in a burnt-out car and is training to be an Olympic swimmer by swimming in the water tank on the 30th floor?'

'You remember them well.'

As she read through to the end, she shook her head constantly. Finally, she put it down, and sighed exhaling a lungful of smoke. 'I don't know what to say.'

'Put me out of my misery, Joy.'

'It's brilliant, Dave.'

Dave's jaw dropped. 'It is?'

'Yes, it's fucking brilliant.'

He was so used to failure with her, he had no idea how to react to success.

'It's a cracking story, Dave. I didn't think you had it in you. It's one of the most beautiful, heart-rending, deeply emotional serials I've ever read.' She looked warily at him. 'Are you sure you didn't steal it?'

'It's inspired by the film, of course.'

She looked up at him, her beautiful dark eyes close to tears. 'I had no idea you could be so sensitive.'

'I just needed your guidance, Joy.'

The story was called *The Defiant Chums* and was clearly inspired by *The Defiant Ones*: the film about two escaped prisoners, one white and one black, who are chained together and on the run from the authorities.

Dave's version was set in medieval Spain, when the punishment for any Jew or Arab who did not convert to Christianity was death. Torquemada, head of the Spanish Inquisition, had decreed their children should be parted from their parents, enslaved and Christianised 'for the good of their souls.' But the two orphans, whose parents have been executed for their beliefs, refuse. The Jewish girl, Aliza, and the Arab girl, Nasrin, are shackled together and await burning at the stake. They are forced to wear *sanbenitos*: dresses of execution with designs of Hell's flames, demons, dragons and snakes on them.

The two 'deviants' manage to escape and go on the run, pursued by Torquemada. They learn about each other's culture, about Judaism and Islam. Aliza explains her name means 'Joy' and Nasrin says her name means 'Wild Rose'. Torquemada is determined that the 'deviants' will not get away: they must be 'cleansed' of their crimes. But, after many adventures and narrow escapes, where they save each other's lives, the two friends finally set sail for Palestine and a new life together.

'They're lovely, heart-warming characters,' said Joy. 'I particularly like Aliza. She's such a positive, strong young woman.'

'Yes,' mused Dave, stroking his chin. 'I'm trying to think where I got her character from.'

'A story of reconciliation between Arab and Jew: it's never been done. Because all the media want to do is stir up hatred between them.' Joy smiled to herself. 'This'll prove to my dad I'm not wasting my time in comics.'

Her father was the radical journalist, Lawrence of Fitzrovia. He disapproved of her working for Fleetpit Publications. He believed she should be doing something more worthwhile with her life.

'I'm so moved, Dave,' Joy continued. 'It's even better than *Slaves of War Orphan School*. It's so lovely.' Tears rolled down her cheeks. 'It's beautiful. It's making me cry.'

Dave tenderly stroked her hair. Then ran an exploratory hand gently down her back. She said nothing as she clearly waited for his next move. Dave was determined not to miss his chance again. So he put on his Torquemada hood again and caressed her neck with his hand, which, to a casual observer, would have looked like he was sizing Joy up for the gallows. He knew she liked dressing up and role-playing, so he figured this was the perfect time. He remembered Joy saying her friend Sophie recommended saying the Lord's Prayer backwards during sex. As he could barely remember the prayer the right way around, he wasn't going to try that. But he thought some words might be appropriate.

'*Credo in unum Deum, Patrem omnipotentem* ...'

It was all he could remember from his church days and he had no idea what it meant, but he thought it sounded pretty cool.

'Dave, what are you doing?' asked a bewildered Joy.

'Examining you for deviation?' suggested Torquemada.

'Bad timing,' said Joy, pushing him away.

Dave took off his hood and sighed. Somehow, he could never get it right.

She saw the look of disappointment on his face as she appraised him. 'You know, I would fuck you again, Dave, if you lost a bit of weight.'

'I'm on a diet tomorrow, Joy.' Dave despondently picked up his robes, ready to leave. Not that a diet would do him any good, he reflected. Somehow with Joy it would always be the wrong place, the wrong time, the wrong robes.

'Actually,' Joy decided, 'I'll fuck you anyway. Let me lock the door. Draw the blinds.'

She had already taken her top off when he turned back from the window.

CHAPTER SIXTEEN

DAVE AND SCOTT met again on a hot and airless Saturday afternoon at the King Edward VIII docks, now a deserted wasteland, the long line of cranes towering over them, rusting and silent.

They discussed Scott's new plan to dispose of Keen. It was ingenious, and Dave had to admit it seemed foolproof. Older teenagers from both schools were involved. Four from Castle Ramparts and three from Mildencroft. They'd kept the numbers down so there was less chance of the wardens finding out. But it still needed an adult to lure Keen into their trap, and this was where Dave came in.

'Trouble is,' said Scott, 'by the time everything's set up, I've calculated it'll be September. Still, it'll be worth it.'

'And there's a problem,' said Dave. 'I went to take his robes back a couple of days later. Waited till he left and sneaked into the building. Only he'd changed the lock. So he knows someone's been in.'

'I told you! I told you the vodka would alert him!'

'Then I guess he checked to see if anything was missing, so he's bound to see his robes are gone.'

'Doesn't make any difference to the plan,' decided Scott. 'He doesn't know who we are. We can still go ahead.'

'Uh-huh,' said Dave.

'You're not chickening out?' asked Scott.

That wasn't the case at all. Dave was firmly committed to Scott's plan. But something in the back of Dave's mind – doubtless his mother again – was suggesting something much sooner than September, and much worse.

So he tried to block her out of his mind. He stared out across the eerie, windswept, industrial wilderness, the hot air shimmering as it rose from the cracked concrete. 'When I was an errand boy, in '65,' said Dave, 'I remember all those cranes dipping in salute when Churchill's funeral barge went by.'

'They told us about it at school,' said Scott. 'It was powerful. Our teacher had tears in her eyes.'

'Only it wasn't true,' said Dave. 'The dockers hated Churchill. Said he was a warmonger. I heard them arguing about it. Especially 'cos his funeral was on a Saturday, their day off. The bosses made them do it.'

'Everything's a lie,' said Scott. 'Hey – wouldn't round here make a great album cover for *Who's Next?*'

'*Teenage Wasteland?*' said Dave. 'It's certainly where I wasted my teenage years.'

'Was The Who where you got the idea for *The Damned?*' Scott asked. 'Kids given medication that turns them into zombies. Albums melted down in furnaces by the Insinerators? Music banned. Like *Lifehouse*. People living in government-controlled "experience suits" inside "the Grid"?'

'No. But that's what my sister said when I sent her a copy of *Aaagh!*' Dave said. 'She's a big Who fan.'

'And you're not?'

'Emerson, Lake and Palmer.'

Scott looked disapproving. 'Oh, dear.'

Talking about music was working, Dave realised. It was a safe subject to distract him from the heinous thought lurking in the back of his mind. Mistake. It wasn't safe at all. The heinous thought refused to be distracted and now turned itself into a music track and his stomach lurched as it played inside his head.

Then, just to be sure he got the message, he saw his mother in the distance, barely visible across the dock. She was standing by one of the rusting cranes and, despite the distance, he knew it was her. Because she looked stunning in an ermine cape with chinchilla trim.

'D'you see a woman over there, Scott?'

'Where?'

'Just there. By that crane.'

'No.'

She might not be visible to other people, but the track she was playing in his head was real enough. And he knew what she wanted him to do.

Far from being fearful of him getting involved with Keen, she was now actively encouraging him to kill the celebrity.

Whether because he was her murderer or was involved in some way, was not yet clear. She had not chosen to share this information with him.

But it had to be done her way.

The track was "Bang Bang" by Nancy Sinatra.

* * *

Jean had used this method before, so Dave was ready for it and ignored it. Over the next week or so, she upped the ante by playing "The Man Who Shot Liberty Valance", "Shadows of Paris" (from the film the *Shot In The Dark*) and "El Paso" by Marty Robbins. He was ready for her, though, and drowned them all out with Emerson, Lake and Palmer. Her music was no match for *Brain Salad Surgery*. That good old Moog kept them all at bay. That, and the work. He worked like crazy to block her out. He typed up all the episodes of *The Defiant Chums* in record time. And had sex with Joy at every possible opportunity. At this rate he'd turn into a workaholic *and* a sexaholic.

But it was very much on Joy's terms: location, method and erogenous zones. His own preferences were not taken into account. It had begun with the office sexual encounter. He was disappointed to see she had shaved her armpits, and hadn't been able to hide his crestfallen expression in time. Joy's face tightened at his lack of interest in the rest of her. 'Something wrong, Dave?'

'No.'

'You could've fooled me.' She pointed to her breasts. 'Say goodbye to them, Dave, because you won't be seeing them again.' She started to put her top back on.

'No. Wait. Sorry. I was just so stunned by their beauty,' he lied.

'And so you should be.' She looked at him impatiently. 'Well, come on then. Do it or don't do it. You won't get another chance.'

He didn't know how to explain his fur needs to Joy. He had a feeling she wouldn't understand.

She stood there, waiting, hands on hips. 'Do you want it? Yes or no?'

'Yes,' he said.

'Then get your trousers off right now.'

Keeping Joy happy in the bedroom and the workplace did the trick, and kept his mother at bay. Joy found an artist, and his story *The Defiant Chums* appeared in *Shandy* in record time. It needed to.

Joy explained it to Dave as she looked up at her multicoloured popularity chart. 'See? *Return of Feral Meryl* is dive-bombing.'

'Greg not doing well? That's a pity,' said Dave with fake concern.

'Yes. Got to cancel it,' grimaced Joy. 'My fault. I should have realised. Girls like wolves and ponies. They don't like baboons. They find them scary.'

'Ah, yes,' said Dave with grim satisfaction. 'And this time Mandy meets Andrea, a girl who was kidnapped and brought up by baboons in a safari park after a female baboon's offspring was run over by a visitor. So Andrea is now her best friend.'

'It seemed a good idea at the time,' said Joy weakly.

'And once again, Mandy has to hide who her friend really is,' said Dave relishing the details. 'But while other girls put blue eyeshadow on their eyelids, Andrea puts it on her face and draws a red lipstick stripe down her nose, so she looks like a hamadryad baboon. But the other girls aren't actually suspicious until Andrea starts grooming Mandy, removing fluff from her jumper. A classic Greg script – if I may say so – making no fucking sense at all.'

'I thought when Meryl returned from the wilds, it might pick up in the votes,' said Joy. 'She's left the wolves of Berkshire because she just wants to be with Mandy. Mandy felt she had betrayed Meryl. Now she had to choose between the two wild girls: Feral Meryl and Andrea Ape Face.'

Dave quoted from the latest issue of *Shandy*. 'Who will I choose as my best friend? And – where will it all end?'

'Very soon,' said a determined Joy. 'After that episode where Andrea is jumping up and down on the teacher's car and chewing her windscreen wipers.'

'And I believe his *Slaves of War Orphan School* hasn't worked out either?' said Dave, hiding a smirk.

'Classic artist con trick,' said Joy.

'Bummer,' said Dave sympathetically. 'Great sample pages?'

'Yep. Once he'd got the gig and the story was scheduled …'

'… pissed it off,' concluded Dave, shaking his head sorrowfully.

'Thatcher as a witch looks pathetic. She's about as scary as Valerie Singleton. So it's dead in the water.'

'Ding-dong.'

'I've got to break the news to Greg,' said Joy, lighting a cigarette. 'Not looking forward to it.'

'I'll stay and help,' said Dave, smiling in anticipation. 'Ah. And here he is.'

It took a moment for Dave and Joy to absorb the full impact of what Greg was wearing and another moment or two to react to it and respond.

He was wearing black leather lederhosen.

Anticipating their derision, Greg attempted a nonchalant swagger, which was difficult in lederhosen.

'Greg, why are you wearing a school satchel?' Dave asked finally, once he'd recovered from the shock.

'Leni and I are going to the opening night of 'Bavarian Beer Hall', Greg explained. He nervously opened a red and white packet of German Mercedes cigarettes and lit one.

'I'd have thought a meerschaum pipe was more appropriate,' observed Joy.

'Don't start,' said Greg, inhaling deeply. 'I just saw Ron and I got enough crap from him.'

'What did Ron say?' asked Joy. Greg hesitated.

'Come on, Greg,' said Dave. 'You can tell us.'

'Yes,' encouraged Joy. 'You're among friends. We'll understand.'

'He said, "Fucking hell, chum. You look like a fucking Nazi nancy boy. You big leather fag. Shagging Eva Braun. You're a fucking disgrace".'

It was several minutes before Dave and Joy stopped laughing.

'Look, I don't care what any of you think,' said Greg defensively. 'There is *nothing* Leni can do or say that will ever, *ever* embarrass me. So don't waste your time hoping. Okay? All right? Because I have no shame.'

'We noticed,' said Joy.

'We're carrying your shame for you, Greg,' said Dave.

'After she sent me into Boots to buy an enema kit and I got a lecture on "dubious practices", nothing will ever, *ever* embarrass me again,' said Greg rather bitterly.

Then Leni entered. The statuesque Brunhilda was dressed for the event in landhaus-style, with a leather bodice, low cut blouse with puff sleeves and short skirt, looking every inch the Bavarian serving wench.

'Ah! There you are, schnookieputz,' she said. She tugged Greg's cheek affectionately. 'Mein kleiner liebchen. Isn't he sweet?' she asked Joy and Dave.

'No, not really,' said Dave and Joy in unison.

'He reminds me of my daddy when I was a little girl. I was so cute. I had plaits over my head and a little leather jerkin.'

'You were … cute?' said Joy in disbelief, looking up at the giantess.

'Mein schnookie,' said Leni, running her fingers through Greg's hair. 'Now, schnookie. I wanted to ask you. Did you take it into the electrical repair shop?'

'Yes, yes. They said they can fix it. I'll pick it up later,' said Greg hastily. 'Er – you wanted to see me, Joy?'

But Dave was too quick for him. 'Fix what, Greg?'

'Pick up what exactly, Greg?' asked Joy.

'Nothing,' said Greg, barely maintaining his composure.

But a smiling Leni was happy to tell them. 'My vibrator. It's an excellent model. German, of course. Industrial strength. I burnt out the motor.'

'Really? Now, you see, I would find *that* embarrassing, Greg,' said Dave.

'Definitely,' said Joy.

'I don't see why,' shrugged Greg, desperately maintaining his cool. 'It's because it'd been adapted for American use. 110 volt.'

'Mmm,' said Dave skeptically.

'Wrong voltage. So when she plugged it in–'

'Please, spare us the details,' said Joy raising a hand in protest. 'You're making me blush.'

'Me, too,' said Dave.

'So, what did you want to tell me?' said Greg, desperately changing the subject.

'It's not good news. I'm afraid I've got to cancel *Slaves* and *Feral Meryl.*'

Greg looked shocked. 'What? Oh, no. Shit. But they're in mid-story,' he protested.

Joy indicated her chart. 'Sorry. But they're way down in the charts.'

'Dropping like a stone,' Dave added helpfully.

Greg looked at their low position on the graphs and his face went white.

'So they've got to finish, next episode,' said Joy. 'Have Meryl return to the Wolves of Berkshire. Andrea goes back to her safari park. And Mrs Thatcher fucks off on her broomstick.'

'But I need more time to kill them off properly,' protested Greg. 'I want to do it with some style, some finesse.'

'How much style can you have, wearing lederhosen?' Dave asked.

'No time for finesse. The readers don't give a shit. Just get rid of them,' ordered Joy.

'Thank goodness *The Defiant Chums* has started, eh, Greg?' smiled Dave. He nodded to the chart, which showed his story soaring ahead of all the others. 'My story's a huge hit.'

'Congratulations,' said Leni. 'I'm impressed.'

'Thanks, Leni. I appreciate that,' said Dave.

Greg's mouth tightened petulantly. Then he quickly recovered. 'Defiant *chums*? *Chums*?' he sneered contemptuously.

'What's wrong with that?'

'Chums. That's so uncool. So dated. Sounds like Ron.' He hooked his thumbs into his leather braces. 'It's a really shit title,' he added venomously.

'Well, it seems the readers disagree with you, Greg,' said Dave. 'And not for the first time.' He gave a smug smile. 'It would seem I'm now Joy's star writer, so any way I can help you get your mojo back, you only have to ask. I'm so happy to pass on my wisdom. For instance, you might want to focus more on your research.'

'I won't need to, when they've got rid of Ron and I'm your boss,' retorted Greg 'Which is going to be happening very soon. Right, Leni?'

'Ja, Ja, I'm working on it, schnookie,' said Leni.

'Plus,' smirked Greg, 'I'm going to the States, to LA, with Leni, for the American launch of *Megahits* and *Sassy Girl*.'

'It's going to be a big launch,' said Leni, 'and I need my schnookie by my side.'

'Particularly if they don't repair your vibrator,' said Dave.

'Then we're driving to Arizona on vacation,' smiled Greg.

'Las Vegas. Grand Canyon. Hopi Land,' Leni added.

'Holiday of a lifetime,' said Greg triumphantly, 'So I will be moving on from writing for cheap 'bog paper' comics like *Shandy*, *Pinafore*, and *The Spanker*, which I'm surprised you two don't find … embarrassing.'

'That's because we're too busy being embarrassed for you, Greg,' said Dave.

'There's no need. I'm with the glossies now,' said Greg arrogantly.

'And while we're in LA,' smiled Leni, caressing him fondly, 'I can have lots of nookie with my schnookie.'

Dave and Joy looked intently at Greg for any sign of embarrassment at the intimate term of endearment, but, to their disappointment, he maintained his cool. Instead, he looked at them defiantly and silently mouthed something.

'Pardon? Was that, "I have no shame," Greg?' asked Dave.

'It was, *fuck you*, Dave', said Greg.

'You'll be embarrassed eventually, Greg,' Dave warned. 'I'm looking forward to it.'

'What is there to be embarrassed about normal bodily needs and functions?' shrugged a puzzled Leni. 'It's like the other morning I was in the toilet, and I asked Greg to …'

'We have to go. We have to go. We'll be late,' said Greg hurriedly, and hauled Leni out of the office before she could elaborate further.

'Watch you don't get Teutonic todger rot,' said Joy sweetly.

CHAPTER SEVENTEEN

WITH HIS MOTHER AT BAY, Dave was able to continue with his homicidal plans, changing the endings of *The Caning Commando*. It was a compulsion, something he needed to do. He wasn't entirely sure why. He had an appetite for it that still needed satisfying. But his experience with Detective Inspector Ferguson showed him he was somehow protected by Fate. And now Fate had found him the right targets: adults like Mr Cooper, who ill-treated kids and needed to die. He was merely the pathfinder, showing the readers the way. It was remote killing. Like bomber pilots who never see the consequences of their actions. Or politicians. It was the modern way. An order written down on a piece of paper, and people the politician never sees die in a hail of bullets or are blown apart with high explosive bombs. It was safe.

If it was good enough for pilots and politicians, why not for Dave?

The latest episode of *Caning Commando*, featuring Winston Churchill, was one of his favourites. While Greg was away in LA, he sat back in *The Spanker* offices to enjoy it. Especially the homicidal ending.

Rear Window

In the school assembly hall, Victor Grabham, the Caning

Commando, sat on the stage close to his hero Winston Churchill, and his chest swelled with pride. The Prime Minister was inspecting coastal defences and had graciously agreed to visit the nearby Golden Hind Academy in Lower Belting Bottom, and give a talk to his pupils.

The Commando's assistant, Alf Mast, was, of course, too common to join the assembled boys. He was in the boiler room guarding the end of the secret tunnel which enabled the intrepid pair to leave the school on their commando missions without being observed. Grabham hoped he wasn't snoozing on the job, dreaming of 'bumpy men', or he would be due a striping later.

The Prime Minister described his school days to the enthralled boys. " 'Study the pattern on the carpet, Churchill," said my Greek teacher. Then he delivered six of the best in the place provided by nature for the purpose. He gave me a jolly good swishing, as good as a fellow could wish for.'

'And he *was* the best. He once thrashed eleven pupils in eight minutes,' said Winston proudly. But the boys looked unimpressed. That was nothing. Victor Grabham could easily thrash an *entire* class in half that time.

'Yes,' continued the great man. 'Afterwards, my backside looked as though I'd sat on a freshly painted park bench.' The boys howled with laughter.

'And being caned taught me discipline,' said Winston. 'So take your medicine, boys, as bravely as you can. And then you can wallow in the glory that is a boy's right after being caned.'

'And now you will take your medicine, Prime Minister!' snarled a masked, blue cloaked figure bursting out of the secret tunnel and onto the stage. Grabham recognised him immediately. It was the Oberspankerfuhrer! The Blue Man! The leader of the feared Wackem SS, whose canes were attached to the periscope of a U-boat for six months, so they were hardened in brine, and whose arse had been frozen solid on the Russian Front.

The Oberspankerfuhrer brought out a lethal cane as his Wackem SS poured onto the stage and pointed their canes menacingly at Grabham. The Caning Commando had been caught with his trousers down by his greatest enemy. But how was this possible?

Then Alf Mast emerged from the tunnel and Grabham knew the answer. 'I was asleep in my hammock, dreaming of 'bumpy men', sir,' the Cockney lad explained, 'when this gentleman …' He pointed to the Oberspankerfuhrer, '… wanted to know the way into the school.'

'And why did you let him?' asked Grabham.

'Because he said he was a teacher, sir, so, naturally, I showed him our secret tunnel.'

'Naturally,' sighed Grabham. 'A man wearing a mask and blue cloak, the authentic, yet unexplainable attire of German public school teachers, and with a German accent even thicker than you, yet it didn't arouse your suspicions?'

'No, sir. I'm just too thick to know that, sir.'

A leering, giant Nazi stepped forward. 'Time for some horseplay,' grinned the Oberspankerfuhrer.

'No!' cried Grabham, because he knew just what this meant. 'Horsing' was a common and equally unexplainable caning method in public schools.

The Nazi was going to 'horse' Churchill! The giant bent over and the struggling Prime Minister was hoisted onto his back, his feet dangling off the floor.

'No!' cried Grabham. 'Not that. I'll take the striping for him.'

'Don't worry, Victor, your thrashing will come,' sneered the Oberspankerfuhrer. 'Soon you will run the gauntlet of my men, every one of them an expert caner.'

It was a terrible thing for the Caning Commando to watch. But the valiant war-leader uttered not a sound as the Oberspankerfuhrer subjected Winston to a cruel fusillade. Again and again his rod came down on the great man's broad nether cheeks while the 'horse' held him in a rigid grip, so he was powerless to even squirm.

'I have nothing to offer you, Winston, but tears, snot and fear,' laughed the Oberspankerfuhrer, paraphrasing the famous speech as he thrashed him again and again.

The Prime Minister's caning was filmed by a Nazi cameraman. 'We will show the newsreel in Chermany and the people will laugh to see your humiliation,' he jeered.

The audience of boys were as outraged as Grabham, but –

surrounded by the sinister Wackem SS – there was nothing they could do.

The Commando could see the Oberspankerfuhrer was using the infamous 'cavalry cut' on Churchill, a method that was banned in British classrooms. The stroke starts with the cane held over the head and then is brought downward in a circular motion, enabling the *entire* rear end to be flogged. The Blue Man caned with absolute precision, leaving a perfect set of parallel stripes each just one cane-diameter apart, on the great man.

But, under the force of the Oberspankerfuhrer's ferocious blows, the 'horse' holding him staggered forward and Grabham saw his chance. As the 'horse' stepped over a trapdoor in the stage, designed for theatre productions and pantomime, Grabham punched aside his guards and threw the control lever in the wings.

The trapdoor swung open and the 'horse' and the PM plunged into the basement below, quickly followed by the Blue Man. Seizing a Wackem SS's cane, the Caning Commando leapt into the void after them.

Down below, the 'horse' had broken Winston's fall, and he lay unconscious on the ground. Before the Blue Man could strike another blow, the Caning Commando was upon him.

'You blackguard!' he snarled, laying into the Oberspankerfuhrer. 'It's time to Carpet Bum the Hun!'

But the Nazi only laughed as the Caning Commando thrashed him. 'All the rods in Great Britain are wasted on my behind,' he jeered, 'because my arse was frozen solid on the Russian Front. I am invulnerable. You lose, Victor! You lose!'

Meanwhile, up above, Alf Mast led the boys in a revolt against the Wackem SS. 'Bring 'em down with a good hard swish!' he exhorted them. The boys laughed as they grabbed their enemy's canes and thrashed them. 'Well hit, Carruthers!'

'Well caught, Fritz!' 'Up the school!' 'Come on, you dry bobs!' For Alf Mast it was a dream come true: he was fighting alongside the posh boys!

Down below, Grabham's savage flogging cut through the seat of the Blue Man's trousers and the Commando could see *red* cheeks rising and *red* weals tingle and swell.

'No … it is not possible,' cried the Oberspankerfuhrer.

'Not so blue now,' jeered Grabham, 'you're starting to blush!'

In a panic, the Nazi fled down the tunnel, leapt into his Underpanzer – a high-speed armoured car – and roared away. His submarine was waiting just off the coast to take him to safety.

As he approached the coastal cliffs, he turned back and laughed maniacally. 'We will meet again, Caning Commando! Ja! Ja!'

He braked for the cliffs but nothing happened. He looked shocked and tried again. Again, nothing happened.

And he hurtled over the edge to his death.

'Jaaaaaaaaaaaaaa!'

'How?' asked the baffled Caning Commando watching the scene through binoculars.

'That was down to me, sir,' revealed Alf Mast appearing at his side. 'After I showed them into the tunnel, I saw that German Underpanzer outside and I thought I should practice the exercises in my commando sabotage manual, what I've been reading.'

'You've learnt how to read, Mast? I had no idea you were so advanced.'

'Yes, sir. Although I still have trouble with the big words, sir.'

'Like what?'

'Like "the", sir.'

Grabham leafed through the manual. 'Hmm. Yes. It's making sense now. Here on page 47 there are detailed instructions on how to expertly sabotage the brakes of an enemy vehicle without danger of detection. So that's what you did, eh, Mast?'

'No, sir.'

'No?'

'I tried to read it, sir. But it was too difficult, so I just ripped the cables out.'

'Now that's what I would expect from a halfwit. Either way, you are redeemed, my boy,' said the teacher.

'Could you learn me to be a fullwit, sir?

'I'm afraid that's out of the question, Mast. You are that rare bulldog breed – a nitwit. You have the scientific skills that lead one to believe you are aspiring to be a half-wit, but in truth you are little more than a fraction wit. Or something beginning with F.'

'I should like to learn more, sir.'

'Lad, leave learning to the higher apes and humans,' said Grabham. 'You are not to be troubled by logic or advanced thinking. As long as you can remember which end to wipe, you'll be fine.'

Now the Caning Commando had to apologise to Winston Churchill for the terrible indignity he had undergone. 'I am so sorry, Prime Minister. The film of your ordeal has, of course, been destroyed.'

But Winston actually looked cheerful. 'Don't worry, my boy,' he chuckled. 'The thrashing brought back splendid memories for me. It was like looking through a window in time. I could see myself as a schoolboy once again,' he recalled, lighting an enormous two-hander cigar.

'Yes. Happy days,' Winston reflected. 'Bent over the flogging block at Harrow. Teacher using a five-foot-long birch soaked in brine to thrash me "on the bare". Drew blood with the first cut. Blood sprayed up the walls,' he laughed. 'Oh, yes, indeed. Birch twigs embedded in your flesh. Getting your chums to squeeze the twigs out later. Best days of a boy's life, eh?'

'Sounds really *Harrowing*,' said Grabham.

'*Spanks* for the memory, Caning Commando,' said Winston, exchanging terrible comic book puns.

Winston tapped his ample rear. 'Only today I have a bit more padding, eh?'

'It's what makes this country *Great* Britain, sir,' said the Caning Commando proudly. 'That behind every one of its leaders is a red rear.

'Thank you, Prime Minister.'

* * *

Dave had copied the brake sabotage instructions directly from an authentic commando manual from the period, and it showed the readers exactly how it could be done.

He would never know who they were and where they were and why they would do it. They would rarely show up on his radar because letters to *The Spanker*, telling him about their kills, would obviously incriminate them. So their stories would always remain unknown. But he was sure they were out there somewhere, hard at work carrying out his lethal suggestions.

CHAPTER EIGHTEEN

MELISSA BRADLEY HAD WARNED her parents there would be consequences if they sent her to that horrible boarding school. But their smug expressions showed they were thinking, 'What can you possibly do to us, Melissa? We will always win. Because we are older and we are wiser than you, and we have the power.'

But, correction, they were wrong. *She* had the power now. Thanks to *The Spanker*. Thanks to the Caning Commando.

Things got out of control after she spent a miserable time in a psychiatric ward at Christmas. Her parents had said they would let her out for Christmas if she behaved herself, but then the fifteen-year old had started swearing and attacking them again, calling them cruel, evil bastards, so they felt she had, unfortunately, still not learnt her lesson.

They made her stay for another month and had her pumped full of drugs. Her father was a doctor and her mother a matron, so they had used their connections to have her sectioned. The psychiatrist, who was a good friend of theirs, agreed she should be given head-fucking drugs as a cure for taking head-fucking drugs. It was that easy. For what? Being a rebellious teenager. She'd smoked some dope, dropped some acid, fooled around, dressed as a punk, stayed out late, but so what? It wasn't a crime.

According to her parents it was. She hated them. And, anyway, they weren't her real parents; she and her younger brother Craig were adopted.

In the past, she had tried to meet them halfway, to connect. That's why she made them a 'space cake'. She thought it would make them relax, chill out, so everything would be cool between them. They really enjoyed the cake and were so touched their daughter had made them just for them. But when she told them it was a cannabis cake, they insisted on going to hospital to have their stomachs pumped. The cake didn't even make them giggle. They were that straight.

She had pretended to learn her lesson and be a good little zombie in future, so they did finally let her out of the psychiatric ward. But it hadn't really lasted. They were constantly checking up on her, invading her privacy. They were determined to 'bring her to her senses'. For her own good. And she was determined they were going to fail. She was a fighter; they would never break her.

Things came to a head when they got the police to bust a party she attended. Her friends were arrested for smoking and selling dope. now her friends wanted nothing more to do with her. So she'd smashed up her bedroom in protest. They decided to send her away to a private boarding school. It sounded like some kind of middle-class borstal for 'difficult' girls. There were alarms on the windows in case the girls tried to get out at night (or boys tried to get in) and CCTV cameras in every room and in the grounds. The school would teach Melissa to 'obey the rules'.

So what was the point of having a daughter if they sent her away to boarding school? They didn't get it, did they? This wasn't just 'a phase she was going through'. It's who she was. It was over. She wasn't going. They said she was, and they said they had the power. They were used to their patients obeying and looking up to them in awe, and couldn't understand why their own daughter should defy them.

While she was in hospital, Craig had brought her a pile of his *Spanker* comics for her to read and they seemed pretty boring to her. And stupid. Especially *Gas Mask*, which Craig agreed was 'pretty pathetic' but he still liked it "Because of the brilliant artwork'. Craig told her the Caning Commando would cheer her up, and make her laugh and she had to admit it was fairly funny in a stupid sort of way.

But then she noticed *The Caning Commando* story, which gave detailed information on how kids could obtain and prepare a tasteless and odourless poison. And that really had her attention. She did seriously think about trying it on them. But, after the cannabis cake incident, she doubted she would get away with it. Too many questions would be asked: another of the Bradleys' friends in their medical Mafia was a pathologist. There were other homicidal ideas in other episodes of the Commando, but none of them were really suitable for bumping her parents off.

And then, just before she was due to be sent to her posh borstal, she saw the perfect solution in the latest issue of *The Spanker*.

As Doctor Bradley drove down the notoriously steep hill just outside their property, he put his foot on the brakes as usual, and nothing happened. He tried again. Nothing. 'There's no brakes!' he screamed to his wife, who looked aghast at her husband.

The car sped up, and they knew that sharp bend at the bottom of the hill, that accident black spot, was coming up fast, and they had to slow down, but there was nothing they could do. He pressed the brakes six more times without any effect. He lost control of the vehicle and it hurtled off the road, smashed into a tree, rolling over and over, before colliding with the wall of a house, where it exploded into flames.

Neither of them survived.

CHAPTER NINETEEN

'WELCOME HOME, GREG,' grinned Dave. His assistant editor had just come back from his trip to the States with Leni and, by way of celebration, Dave was sending him down a sewer.

It was the latest *Aaagh!* challenge from the readers. A giant sewer pipe ran through the vast, eerie basement of Fleetpit House. It was the River Fleet storm relief pipe. When the water level rose above a certain point in the sewer system, the flow was diverted into this relief tunnel. So, in that parched summer of 1976, it was safe for Greg to descend into the sewers.

Greg had told Dave and Joy very little about his glamorous American trip, other than that *Megahits* and *Sassy Girl* had been successfully launched onto the US market, although there was no job forthcoming on the glossies, after all. Instead, Leni seemed to be using Greg as her personal assistant. But he still had high hopes that she would promote him to managing editor soon, and this was why he was still going out with her and putting up with her eccentric behaviour.

Dave and Joy knew there would be great opportunities for them to take the piss out of him, so they got him drunk in the Hoop and Grapes on his return and encouraged him to tell all.

Wearing a fringed suede jacket and cowboy boots with two-inch heels, he stood at the bar with them, and they noticed he was wincing and holding his back. That seemed like a good opening gambit for their interrogation.

'Are you all right, Greg?' said a concerned Joy. 'You seem to be in some pain?'

'It's my back,' explained Greg. 'Had to carry a suitcase with all her healing crystals and sacred stones in. She never goes anywhere without them.'

'A suitcase full of rocks? That must have weighed a ton. Must have cost her a fortune?' probed Dave.

'Normally. But she told the airline she needed the crystals for her health. You know the way diabetics carry special food everywhere? Well, she carries special rocks everywhere. So they had to make an exception for her.'

'Oh, they'd never buy that!'

'Have you ever tried arguing with Leni?' said Greg bitterly. 'It's just easier to give in. So I did my back in.'

'So then you went to Las Vegas, the Grand Canyon and up into Hopi Land?' prompted Joy.

'Yeah, the Third Mesa,' scowled Greg.

'That must have been exciting!' said Joy.

'It must have been amazing,' agreed Dave.

'We did sweat lodges. Slept under the stars. She's a regular visitor. The Hopis can't stand her, of course, but you know Leni, she's completely oblivious. I probably shouldn't say anything about that,' said Greg, recalling some awkward incident.

'I'll get some more drinks in,' said Dave.

Plied with more alcohol, Greg elaborated. 'So we went and saw a Tribal Elder and she asked him what she could do to help the Hopis. So this old guy looks her straight in the eye and says, "The best thing the white man – *or the white woman* – can do, is to go away and *leave us alone*." "Ja, ja" says Leni. "You are so right." '

'She didn't take the hint?' enquired Joy.

'This is hilarious,' said Greg, now pretty drunk. 'No, I shouldn't really say …'

'Come on, Greg, you know you want to,' encouraged Dave.

'Well …' grinned Greg, 'She thinks she's some kind of Hopi Messiah. She thinks she's the True White Brother.'

'Surely she would be the True White Sister?' said Dave.

'Although she is built like a man,' said Joy.

'Double-D?' said Dave. 'Something wrong with your eyesight, Joy?'

'I meant, she's got to be over six foot tall.'

'The True White Brother can be either gender,' Greg explained. 'According to Hopi prophecy, at the time of Purification, the True White Brother will appear, all powerful, and no one can stand against him. All must listen to him or great evil will befall the world. If he comes out of the East, the destruction will not be so bad. But if he comes out of the West, he will have no mercy.'

'And you and Leni came out from the west, from LA!' said Dave. 'Oh, shit! That's worrying.'

'So that's what she means when she talks about preparing for Purification,' said Joy fearfully. 'This is scary stuff, Greg.'

There was enough ammunition here for Dave and Joy to take the piss out of Greg for weeks.

'But how can they recognise the True White Brother? How do they know it's Leni?' asked Joy.

'Because he will bring with him the Holy Tablets of Stone, and–'

'Ah! That's so that's where the stones come in!' said Dave excitedly.

'That's right, so then she–' started Greg. He stopped as he saw the look on their faces.

'No, please. Carry on,' said Dave. ' Tell us more about the True White Brother. Joy and I both seek spiritual enlightenment.'

'Yes,' agreed Joy. 'I want to know how Leni gets her rocks off.'

'Oh, fuck off, the pair of you,' said Greg.

* * *

The exotic and colourful Third Mesa and Hopi Land seemed a long way away now, as Greg, wearing protective clothing and a helmet, descended into the Fleetpit sewer pipe with a cameraman and a worker from the Water Board. 'Bye, Greg,' waved Dave cheerfully as he watched his sullen assistant disappear into the echoing, eerie depths, and the lid was firmly clamped down on them.

Satisfied that Greg's dreams of fame and fortune were dashed, Dave wandered off into the murky vaults of the building, where half an acre of famous magazines and comics, going back nearly a hundred years, were stored. This was where they both belonged, Dave reflected. Nothing good had ever come out of Fleetpit. It was always associated with darkness, death and failure.

It was believed that the name Fleetpit came from the site having once been a Roman burial pit or a cock fighting pit or a plague pit or a cesspit or a bear pit. Or possibly all of them. As Dave was fond of saying, 'Our comics have brought shame on a plague pit.'

Certainly, there was a Bear Alley close to Fleetpit, as well as a Gunpowder Alley. Dave's personal theory was the name Fleetpit came from the manufacture of gunpowder. He had read that 'gong' farmers – or 'night soil' collectors – from all over London were charged by the King, with or without the consent of the householders. They would then bring their slopping barrels back to the Fleet factory and pour them into giant pits. Vast vats of 'gong' would be stored here. 'Not that different to today,' thought Dave, as he glanced at the endless rows of bound volumes of old publications and artwork wrapped in brown paper.

The gong would then be heated up, processed and converted into gunpowder. Sir John Evelyn had singled the Fleetpits out for criticism as a foul and polluted stain on London in his *Fumifugium: or The Inconvenience of the Aer and Smoak of London dissipated* (1661). He recommended that sweet-smelling trees should be planted around the Fleetpits to purify the air and take care of the foul fumes. Evelyn was actually the merchant of death who owned the Fleetpits and he had written the book so he could get the site cleaned up at the taxpayers' expense.

'*Psst*! Son! Over here,' a voice called to Dave from the darkness. It was Mr Cooper. He'd been going through a sack of young readers' letters he'd stolen from the *But Why?* office when everyone had gone home. Stealing the readers' 35p postal orders to join the *But Why?* Club, which entitled them to a special question mark metal badge, a membership certificate personally signed by "Big Q" and a book of answers. He threw the forms, the readers' letters and the envelopes in the furnace, then counted the postal orders up. Nearly twenty quid. Not a bad haul this time. Depriving kids had reminded him of the good old days when he was a newsagent and regularly humiliated them, especially Dave, his bastard son, and now here he was walking right by; he had to be good for a few quid.

The scar-faced storeman beckoned Dave to join him over in Aisle 13, the Black Museum of Comics. Dave had stayed out of his way ever since he discovered the ex-newsagent was his father, but he couldn't avoid him forever. 'I was wondering if you could spare your old man a tenner?' the browncoat whined.

'Why would I give you anymore money ... dad?'

'I'm skint, son.'

'Your problem, not mine.'

'But I'm going to be out of a job soon.'

'Good.' Dave started to leave. 'Then I won't have to look at your face every day.'

'Don't be like that, son,' the storeman followed him along Aisle 13. 'It's 'cos they're closing Fleetpit down soon.'

'Don't be stupid,' said Dave. 'This place will never close.'

'They're moving to a new building. Across the water. Not just Fleetpit Publications, but the parent company, everything's gonna be published there in future.'

'What?'

'So all this is going to be destroyed.'

'No. It's not possible.'

'It's true,' leered Mr Cooper.

'But ... it's a hundred years' worth of popular publications! *The History of the Second World War. The Great War.* I've even seen *The History of the Crimean War.* Over in that corner.'

'Really beautiful old books? Massive, weigh a ton?'

'They're the ones. With wonderful illustrations, protected by rice paper.'

'Flogged them last month.'

Dave reeled from the news. 'But they can't. They're part of our national heritage.'

'Dave, no one gives a fuck.'

'I don't understand.'

'I do. Changing times. I was a newsagent, remember?'

'Not the bound volumes? Not the back issues of *The Fourpenny One*?'

'Yeah. They're all due to be incinerated.'

'But I'd know.'

'That's probably why you don't know – 'cos you're a … fan.' The storeman spat out the word. 'So you fans, who love all this kind of shit, and complain about us using artwork to block up drains and as dartboards, can't make a fuss. That's why Fleetpit have kept it very quiet. See?'

The thought that the old hotel was finally closing down and its great cultural heritage, good and bad – mainly bad – would be thrown away, shocked Dave. The bowels of Fleetpit were about to be finally emptied and vast piles of the nation's popular culture would end up in flames or on rubbish heaps. It was a huge scandal in the making. But he had too many problems of his own. He daren't make a fuss.

'I can't get involved. Goodbye.'

'But you are involved, son. When Fleetpit House shuts down, you'll be homeless.'

'So I'll need to hold onto my money.' Dave headed for the exit.

Mr Cooper called after him. 'If you pay me, I'll tell you who killed your mother.'

Dave stopped. He turned back. 'That's easy … *dad*. I think you killed her. And, looking at your face. I *know* you did.'

'That's why I couldn't say nothing to the rozzers, Dave. 'Cos I had the motive, and they'd have fitted me up. But it's not true, son. Honest. But I reckon I know who it was.'

'Who?'

'Wedge first.'

Deep down, Dave didn't believe it was Cooper, even though he knew he was capable of it. But Cooper knew more about that time when his mother disappeared than he could ever know. He had to solve her murder. If he didn't, she would just keep driving him crazy until he did. He was holding her at bay for the time being, but not forever. He handed Cooper two five-pound notes.

'Thanks, Dave.' Cooper's hideous face twisted in a smile. He beckoned him to sit down on a pile of bound volumes of *The Fourpenny One*. He sat opposite him on a stack of *Tranny* magazines and

Radiogram Fun comics. 'All right. I'll tell you. It was the nig-nog. The one she met in Nigeria. I reckon he done for her.'

'Ernie? Fuck you.'

'Do you want to know the truth or not?'

'I'm listening.'

'That last year, before she disappeared, he turns up. Gets a job on the docks. Lived in Draughtboard Alley. She was giving herself airs and graces, swanning round in her furs, when all the time she was secretly having it off with a darkie.'

'Ernie was a good man. He taught me to play football. I liked him. He had no reason to kill her.'

'Ah!' said Cooper. 'But when your mum and I were together, she poured out her sorrows to me. And, of course, I'd be all sympathetic-like.'

'Just tell me what you know.'

'Back in Nigeria, Ernie was her houseboy and he was very respectful towards her. 'Cos they daren't touch a white woman, Dave. See? Oh, no. Not out there. What? Wife of the District Officer? They'd cut his knackers off.'

'Wasn't she busy bringing up Annie?'

'The bratling? That's what she called your sister. She wasn't the mothering type. She said a baby don't need its mum once it's off the tit. So she had all that spare time on her hands.'

Dave gritted his teeth, trying hard to ignore Cooper's offensive words. 'What happened?'

'Ernie would come in and read poetry to her, 'cos she liked that, see? But he still kept his distance. Still shows her proper respect. Probably 'cos he was scared. So in the end she had to take her clothes off and say to him, 'I want you to do the same to me as your boss does.''

'Then why would Ernie strangle her?'

'He could fly off the handle, see? Get really angry. I saw them together, a few days before she disappeared. In the park. I'm listening on the other side of the bushes, like, and he'd got the hump because she wouldn't go away with him and start a new life together. That's what he wanted. He said he wanted to take care of you and Annie, too, and he was earning good money on the docks. But she said no. Well, what could he offer her, Dave? Six kids and a council house. That's why I reckon he done it, Dave.'

Cooper leered as he saw the expression on Dave's face. 'He's a nig-nog, Dave. What do you expect?'

Dave picked up a bound volume of *The Fourpenny One* and smashed Cooper hard across the face with it.

'You shouldn't have done that, Dave,' Cooper snarled after him as he walked away. 'I make a bad enemy.'

Cooper had told him important information about Ernie. He didn't believe Ernie had killed Jean, but it had filled in some of the gaps in her past. But he hadn't answered the most puzzling question of all: why would his mother have slept with Cooper?

CHAPTER TWENTY

HE FOUND HIMSELF PONDERING, yet again, on the mystery of his mother's murder. It always seemed to come back to Konrad. The boy who had died. The Canon still seemed to be the main suspect. Peter Maudling had accused him of being responsible, before they took him away and fried his brains.

Konrad had been staying at a weekend holiday home run by the Knights and the Virgin Soldiers and, according to the inquest, had climbed out onto the roof, slipped, and fallen to his death. He was known to be a disturbed child. The Canon and Mrs Czar confirmed this version of events, but Dave's mum was not asked to give evidence. The coroner, Mr Czar, recorded a verdict of death by misadventure.

His whole school turned out for Konrad's funeral. Mother St Vincent, head of the Sisters of Sorrow, said a little soul had gone to Jesus, and there was a splendid Requiem Die-castMass in his honour, officiated over by a sombre Canon. but Dave sensed something was wrong. Especially with the things he knew about the Canon, and how his mother was always warning him never, *ever*, to be alone with him.

But, like the other kids, he saw his time as a pupil at St. Mary's rather like being a prisoner in the German POW camp in *The Wooden Horse*. You didn't get involved in the misfortunes of other prisoners, you had enough misfortunes of your own. You got through your sentence as best you could, keeping your head down, avoiding the attention of the guards, always on the look out for a way to escape.

Konrad had found a way. Not a wooden horse, but a wooden box.

Jean was still keeping up her relentless demands on him not only to solve her murder, but to deal with Fabulous Keen. And he was still ignoring her. They had had these mental battles before. She may have won in the past, but he was ready for her this time.

Even though she had now introduced a date: July 22.

Just two weeks away.

He didn't care if the clock was ticking. It wasn't going to happen.

She sat opposite him in his turret, lit a Park Drive and announced: '22nd July, the Feast of Mary Magdalene. Fabulous Keen will be at the Knights of St Pancras ceremony.'

'So?'

'So it's the perfect opportunity for you to kill him.'

'How?'

'You know how.'

'Enlighten me.'

'You've got the robes. Cooper's gun. And a copy of the Order of Service. Do you want me to draw you a diagram? Because if you do, you've got one of those as well. It gives you the layout of the Lodge Room.'

'It's too risky. No, it's not too risky. It's insane.'

'When has that ever stopped you?'

'Dressing up as a Knight and shooting Keen? How would I get away afterwards?'

'That's a detail I'm sure you can take care of.'

'No. I'm going to wait until September. *That's* the perfect opportunity.'

'It's not right to get kids involved, Dave. It's your responsibility.'

'Why is it my responsibility?'

'Because you're my son. You have to do this. Alone.'

'Make up your mind, mum. First you tell me I should keep away from Keen, now you want me to murder him.'

'No, you decided that. It was your conscience that made that decision.'

'September is fine. So stop nagging me, mum. Don't interfere.'

'Do the right thing, Dave. Don't get kids to do your dirty work. They've been through enough.'

'I know what they've been through. That's why I agreed to help them.'

'You know Keen got me to play Mary Magdalene? He and other knights gathered round me, watching me as I danced. Treated me like a prostitute. It was so humiliating.'

'To be fair, you didn't have to do it, mum. You could have said "no".'

'No one says "no" to Keen.'

'Well, I'm saying "no" to you now. And I don't care if you play "El Paso" at full blast again.'

She regarded him coldly. 'I should have thought you'd want to avenge your mother.'

'Avenge your humiliation? Or your death? You never make it entirely clear.'

'That's because you're meant to work it out. You're the detective.'

'But you're still holding back information.'

'What do you mean?'

'Like: why did you get involved with a creep like Cooper?'

'There's no time to go into that now. You realise I will be in your mind constantly, until you agree?'

'I figured that, mum. But, with work and sex, and Emerson, Lake and Palmer, I'm pretty certain I can keep you at bay. Try as hard as you like; I won't let my guard down.'

'Don't make me up the ante, son. If you suppress your inner voice, it will just come back louder than ever. I will endlessly remind you of what you have to do on the 22nd of July.'

'Do your worst, mum. If necessary, I will take up smoking, drinking and jogging, as well as liquorice, to keep you out of my head. How's that? Give up, because you're never going to win.'

Dave took the album 'Brain Salad Surgery' out of its eerie Giger cover and began to play it. And just for good measure, he decided to read a book at the same time. That would really drown her out. He pulled a book off the shelf at random.

It was *Catch 22*.

CHAPTER TWENTY-ONE

IT WAS a Saturday morning, and Dave was lying next to Joy, reflecting that their relationship was going really well. She was starting to understand his needs as well as her own. She wasn't shaving under her arms, for example. She knew he had a fur fetish and she was trying to relate to it. Anything weird or unusual, Joy was up for. It was missionary position sex that was not for her. So he figured he was on a winning streak.

Joy turned to him. 'Dave,' she said, 'I know it's a fetish, and, of course, I approve of fetishes. The weirder they are, the better.'

'That's what I thought.'

'But–'

'But what, Joy?'

'Do you always have to have sex with my armpit? Armpit sex is getting boring.'

'We could switch to your other armpit, if you like?'

'Not really. I don't really understand it, Dave.'

'It's because your armpit is furry on the inside. It's Eldorado. I'd love to crawl into it. I'd love to live in your armpit, Joy.'

'Okay. But we still need to make progress.'

'Progress?'

She shot him a warning look. 'You need to up your game, Dave.'

'I do?'

'Definitely. If you want our relationship to work. Why don't we find something else in my book?'

'Okay.'

Joy brought out a coffee table book with different positions and opened it at random. 'Let's see...what about this one? Position 22. That looks fun.'

'Position 22? Definitely not. That is completely out of the question.'

'What's wrong with position 22?

'I don't like the number, Joy. It's a bad number.'

'It's not like it's 666.'

'Let's go back to your armpit.'

'But there's so much more to me, Dave. I need to feel the rest of me is valued, too.'

'But it is. And it's not just your body that fascinates me, Joy. It's your mind, too.'

'Really? You're not just saying that?'

'No. There's your thrift. You can go through a charity shop like a plague of locusts.'

'That's a nice thing to say,' smiled Joy. 'Thanks, Dave. Okay, Let's watch something instead. I got a *Twilight Zone* tape from the States.'

'Cool.'

Joy was keen to try out her new Betamax player.

The episode unfolded. It featured a dancer who was hospitalised for exhaustion. A nightmare and a series of creepy events lead her to the hospital morgue, room 22. When she leaves the hospital, she is booked, by coincidence, on Flight 22. She relives her nightmare, doesn't take the flight, and the plane explodes in mid-air.

'I thought "Twenty Two" was a pretty good episode,' said Joy afterwards.

Dave scowled heavenwards. 'Okay, okay. Okay. I get the message. It's a little on the nose, isn't it?'

'What are you talking about?'

'That weird coincidence in the *Twilight Zone*. "Twenty Two".'

'I believe in coincidences. I think they're like omens trying to tell us something,' said Joy.

'You're probably right. I think coincidences are going on all around us, all the time, and we don't take any notice of them usually. And then, for some reason, our subconscious brings them to our attention.'

'Because of a guilty conscience or something?'

'I prefer the "or something". Whatever it is, I don't care.' Dave looked heavenwards again and muttered, 'You're wasting your time. Okay?'

'We should do stories like *Twilight Zone* in comics.'

'Maybe in *Aaagh!*? Give me a proposal. If you wrote a *Twilight Zone*-style series that would really impress your dad.'

'I doubt it,' said Joy sullenly, rolling a spliff.

'Why not?'

'I sent him my favourite episode of *White Death*, which I was really proud of. The one where the natives of Bikini atoll die in the fall-out following a nuclear test.'

'Their children play in the radioactive "snow", with tragic consequences.'

'Then the fucking scientists responsible are attacked and eaten by White Death as they test the water around the islands for radiation.'

'Yeah, that was brilliant, Joy. I like the double meaning of white death.'

'And you know what my dad did? The tosser! He wrote back, "Why are you wasting your talents and education writing for children's comics? Let me introduce you to people on *The Guardian* and *New Statesmen* so you can have a career in real journalism."'

'What a snob,' said Dave.

'No! He's not a snob,' said Joy touchily. 'Don't you insult my dad. Okay? He's just a bit ..."North London".'

'Well, it was a bit harsh,' said Dave.

'I thought so. I'll show him,' she growled. 'I'm going to make it without any help from the great Lawrence of Fitzrovia.'

'Good for you. Good for you.'

''Cos writing for *The Guardian* doesn't change a thing, Dave. It's preaching to the converted. Whereas we're reaching impressionable kids.'

'Scaring the hell out of them with *White Death* makes a lot more sense,' agreed Dave, chewing on his liquorice pipe. 'You realise they'll be having nightmares about great white sharks coming to get them for the rest of their lives?'

'I hope so,' said Joy drawing on her spliff.

He tried to reassure her. 'It's interesting, Joy. You've got a dad issue. I've got a mum issue. So we compliment each other.'

'What do you mean I have a dad issue?' snarled Joy. 'I have no such thing. How dare you? How fucking dare you?'

'Oh. Okay. So we should ignore what our mums and dads want us to do.'

'Well, yours is dead. So that's easy for you.'

'If only,' sighed Dave.

Seeking advice on how he might up his game, Dave thought he would have a boys' night out at The Eight Veils. Greg was away for the weekend. Leni had a pilot's licence, and she had hired a monoplane for the weekend. They were flying over Wiltshire looking for more of the recently discovered 'saucer nests' that were starting to appear in the wheat fields. She wanted Greg to take photos of this strange new phenomena. As the True White Brother, she needed to be there to welcome the aliens. So it was just Dave, Ron and the Major drinking in the Soho club.

'You're worrying unnecessarily, Dave,' said the Major. 'All this modern nonsense about whether you're satisfying women or not. Who cares?'

'You're sure?' said Dave uneasily.

'Absolutely,' said the Major. 'You need a real woman who is just happy you're screwing her. Not some dickless bloke. Isn't that right, Ron?'

'I tried telling him, Major.'

'I'd rather shag a sandbag,' continued the Major. 'Oh, by crikey, yes. Seriously, Dave,' he said, twirling his handlebar moustache. He was still wearing his all-year round, threadbare, camel hair coat with velvet collar, despite the heat, and had his trusty portable typewriter by his side. 'How badly do you want to get laid to put up with that abuse? You could abuse yourself. Take out the middle woman. I'll give you a subscription to *Members Only.*'

'Or there's Naked City down the road,' suggested Ron. 'I've brought my torch, so we can read the prices.'

'I'm not sure. Even a scary lay is better than no lay,' mused Dave.

'We're men of the world, Dave. You should listen to us,' said the Major. 'Ron here is a mine of information on the opposite sex. Right, Ron?'

'That's right, Major.'

'He started that romance comic in the 50's. *Forces Sweetheart.*'

The two of them chanted, 'On land, sea and air, she'd go anywhere!'

'She was the Forces Sweetheart, dreaming of a dashing officer …' said Ron.

'… but sweaty privates were all she had to look forward to!' said the Major.

'She was a military mattress!' they roared together.

'But I'm out of date now,' reflected Ron bitterly, knocking back another drink. 'Over the hill. You think I'm for the chop. Got nothing to offer anymore. Right, Dave?'

Oh no, Ron,' Dave lied smoothly. 'You're like a vintage wine that matures with age.'

'My last success for the trendy teenage market was over ten years ago with *Tranny.*'

'It was very "gear" in its day, Ron,' Dave reassured him. '*It's fast. It's fab. It's 78rpm.*'

Dave went up to the bar to get another round and a packet of cigarettes for Ron. The Major and Ron had introduced him to Paula, the owner, who had run the club since the forties.

'The cigarettes are 22p, love, and with the drinks, that's two pound twenty all together.'

'Of course,' sighed Dave.

'I remember when your mum brought you in as a baby,' said Paula, a heavily made-up, glamorous septuagenarian. 'You would crawl around on the carpet.'

'Ah. So that's why I love the smell of stale beer.'

'You were a funny looking thing,' said Paula appraising him with an expert eye. 'Which is odd, 'cos your parents were both very good looking.'

'Thanks. My self-esteem needed lowering.'

'Your mum did well for herself. I was so pleased for her.'

'She often talked fondly about you, Paula. I actually named a couple of my stories after you.'

'The gentlemen want it, they got to pay for it, that's what I told your mum. "Pearls for my girls. Furs from sirs." And she loved her furs, did your mum.'

'You don't remember which furs?'

'No. Sorry.'

'Chinchilla? Mink? Sable? Marten? Rabbit?'

'It was so long ago now, dearie. Ah. Your poor mum. I was sorry to hear about her disappearing.' Paula looked meaningfully at Dave. 'You do know she was quite a naughty girl before she got religion?'

'And afterwards,' sighed Dave.

'And why not? You didn't know if you were going to die, with the bombs, so what was wrong with a knee trembler in the blackout? Made you feel alive. I was just the same in the first war.'

'Really?'

'Oh, yes. We were very naughty. It was worse than the sixties back then. And drugs? You lot think you discovered them, but we had cocaine, marijuana, and opium, too. Chinese laundries was where you got 'em in my day. Did I ever tell you I danced with Ivor Novello, dear? That kept my home fires burning.'

'Hurry up with those drinks,' called the Major.

'Didn't Fabulous Keen used to work here?' asked Dave as he gathered up the drinks.

She didn't answer, so he persisted. 'Wasn't he your doorman?'

Paula looked grim-faced, the wrinkle lines on her face standing out through her white make-up. 'I don't want to talk about John Keen.'

'Why not?'

'He's dangerous.'

Dave put the drinks down again. 'In what way?'

'Drug-dealing. Pimping. Tried to get my girls on the game.' There was fear in her eyes as she added, 'You don't want to mess with Keen, dearie. He may be a "national treasure" now, but he's the nastiest piece of work I've ever met, and I've met more than my share.'

'He left? Or what happened to him?'

'The Major saw him off,' she said, nodding in the writer's direction. 'Ask him about "Fabulous" Keen.'

'That must have taken some guts.'

'Well, someone had to get rid of him, Dave,' she said. 'Someone had to stand up and be counted.'

CHAPTER TWENTY-TWO

'DAVE – ARE YOU LISTENING TO ME?' snapped Joy. In preparation for the publicity stunt for her shop *Time Machine*, he was now wearing his gorilla suit as King Kong, and she was dressed as Fay Wray, with a blonde wig and a slinky, long white dress her friend Sophie had stolen from Biba before they closed down.

'Do I have to wear this suit?' he complained. 'I'm boiling.'

'I thought you liked it? And it's cooler this evening. It's about 22 degrees.'

'Yeah, of course,' he said. 'What else would it be?' It was July 22nd tomorrow and, despite his mother's best efforts, he figured he was going to make it. Just one day to go, he told himself. He could do it.

'Can you carry Stella Louise and Stella Jeanne down to the car, please?'

'I could put them both in the *Baby Jane* wheelchair and save myself a trip?'

'No, they might get damaged bumping down the steps.'

'True,' said Dave. 'Look what happened to Baby Jane.'

So the gorilla took Stella Louise down the stairs first. She was dressed as Mrs Peel from *The Avengers* in a tight leather outfit. 'I thought about a headscarf, but it doesn't really go with the leather. So I've glued her wig on instead,' fussed Joy.

He carried the mannequin out to Joy's convertible: a white Lotus Elan +2. The registration number was H227WDD, but so what? He just ignored it. It was the perfect car for Mrs Peel, he reflected, as he put her in the back.

'I'm worried about bugs hitting them in the face,' continued Joy, wiping the mannequin's cheek. 'Poor Stella Louise. She already has clingfilm over her wrists because her paint is peeling so badly.'

'So she really is Mrs Peel?' said Dave.

'Very good,' laughed Joy.

Mrs Peel was joined in the back by Stella Jeanne, dressed as Barbarella. Then King Kong and Fay Wray climbed in the front and they left Marble Arch and drove around the West End, handing out leaflets for *Time Machine*.

'You know, Dave, I do worry about what would happen to them if I died.'

'That's on my mind, too,' said the gorilla as Joy swerved erratically through the heavy traffic. He took no notice of the Number 22 bus heading for Oxford Circus.

'I don't know who would be as happy to have them, and keep them together.'

'You think they'd want to stay together?'

'Oh, definitely. Although I never think of them as liking each other all that much.'

Mrs Peel and Barbarella stared vacantly ahead, pointedly ignoring each other. Dave looked appreciatively at Joy. He liked her obsession with shop dummies because it made his fur fetish seem normal. It stopped him thinking about the passing minicab, with 22 22 22 written on the side.

'It's not like I actually think they have thoughts, they're just objects of art to me,' said Joy hastily.

'Of course,' said Dave reassuringly.

'But I was annoyed when Sophie told me she liked Stella Louise, but not Stella Jeanne. It's like if someone tells you they don't like your cat: ouch.'

'Joy, can I turn up the *The Avengers* theme?' It made a difference as he passed out *Time Machine* leaflets to shoppers. Because his mum was, of course, relentlessly playing 'Bang Bang', 'The Man Who Shot Liberty

Valance' and 'El Paso' inside his head. And it took his mind off the *Evening News* billboard: '22 die in Tropical Storm'.

It was the advert in Piccadilly Circus that finally freaked him out. *Confessions of a Driving Instructor* altered before his eyes into *Confessions of Dave Maudling*.

Then, nearby, he saw a billboard proclaiming: *The Message,* and beneath it, *Romeo and Juliet.* This became *The Message* and *Mary Magdalene.*

Of course, he realised, if his mother was his inner voice and/or had possessed him, she could change his entire perception of reality. This was confirmed at the Dominion in Tottenham Court Road, which was showing Lee Marvin and Roger Moore's *Shout at the Devil.* The title turned into *Shoot Fabulous Keen.* And as they drove past a poster for the science fiction movie *Future World,* starring Peter Fonda and Yul Brynner, its slogan was modified to read 'Where the only way to survive is to kill Keen'.

Outside her shop in Neal Street, Joy's assistant was on hand to take publicity shots. But, as Dave stepped out of the car, Jean Maudling increased the pressure once again with 'The Shadows of Paris'. The piercing violin and haunting accordion were played at full volume, filling his skull with deafening sound.

Dave jumped up and down in agony, holding his head. Joy looked on approvingly. 'Very good. Very King Kong.' She turned to her assistant. 'Make sure you get plenty of shots.'

The clincher was the all-black poster for *The Omen.* It showed Gregory Peck and Lee Remick, and a shadowy child transforming into a wolf. The text read:

'You have been warned. If something frightening happens to you today, think about it. It may be The Omen.'

'Okay, okay. I give in. I'll do it!' Dave yelled skywards – as it could hardly be heavenwards, given what he was going to do.

Surprisingly, the poster hadn't been altered to get its message across. But his mother, or whatever was driving him: muse; demons; guilty conscience; fate; or the antichrist, wasn't going to stop until it got its way. Now Dave knew what crazy people meant when they said 'The voices made me do it.' He would have to do it. He roared in agony.

'All right. That's enough,' said Joy reproachfully. 'Don't overdo it.

Don't want to frighten the customers.' Joy turned to her assistant. 'I think we've got enough stills. I'll see that guy now. What's his name? Curtis? And, Dave, perhaps you'd like to sit in on the interview? Tell me what you think of him as a possible manager for the shop.'

She looked around for Dave, but the gorilla was running into her shop.

'Dave?'

'No time. Something I need.' The clock was ticking: he only had a few hours left and there was much work to do.

* * *

In a cramped, artificially lit, dim basement room of the *Time Machine* that acted as her office, the handsome, debonair Curtis was waiting for Joy. Dave had shot in and out of the shop without explaining just what the heck was going on and why he was acting even weirder than usual.

Still bemused by his behaviour, Joy carefully descended the narrow, twisting, ancient staircase, holding tightly to its rope banister. She skirted around the adjoining toilet, with the door half hanging off its hinges, squeezed around boxes of stock, and stepped over the gaps in the cracked paving slabs, before finally reaching the basement and her interviewee.

She could see Curtis was wearing an Antony Price suit. She was an expert when it came to suits. She could identify any suit from just one glance. Curtis reminded her of Bryan Ferry, in particular, his look on the cover of *Another Time, Another Place*.

This surprised her, because she knew Curtis had previously been the manager of that hippy comic shop *The Last Night of the World*. This was run on very relaxed lines: money would be thrown into a cardboard box and customers were told to 'fuck off' if they looked too straight. So she had expected a scruffy, long-haired, dope-smoker in flared jeans.

Curtis had turned the shop from near bankruptcy into a successful business and, looking down at his CV, she noted he did have an accountancy degree, so perhaps this explained his suited and booted look. Normally, she would be hostile to Suits, but she knew a Suit was exactly what she needed to run her business while she was away learning the ins and outs of publishing at Fleetpit.

'My mother's from Scotland,' said Curtis by way of introduction, speaking in his soft, husky, compelling voice.

'You're half human then,' smiled Joy.

'She's from Falkirk.'

'I take that back.'

'She told me all about the Battle of Falkirk,' said Curtis conversationally. 'William Wallace. I've seen the two-handed sword he used for his invasion of England.'

'Aye. It needs to visit England more often ...' said Joy darkly.

'It's a massive weapon,' Curtis pointed out.

'That's Scottish men for you,' said Joy.

'I must get up there for Hogmanay. Enjoy a dram or three.'

'You heard about that, then?'

'Truthfully,' said Curtis, casting his eyes slowly over her curves in her clinging Biba dress, 'My heart's in Scotland, Joy.'

'So what the fuck are you doing in London?'

Curtis flicked back a lock of his jet-black hair. 'I want to change comics, Joy. Lose that blokeyness. Make them appeal more to women. It shouldn't just be about American superheroes. There's so much we can learn from the French: *Metal Hurlant. Valerian.* Moebius. Druillet. Bilal. They're so suave. Sensual. Dangerous ...'

Curtis had done his homework on Joy. He knew she was more into French science fiction *bandes dessinées*, American underground and Warren comics, like *Creepy* and *Eerie*, rather than superhero comics. He was crawling more than Uriah Heep, and she knew it. But few bosses can resist a crawler. Especially when he looked as suave and elegant as her father, Lawrence of Fitzrovia.

However, she was also used to the attention of handsome men, as well as oddities like Dave. 'I have several other applicants to see. I'll let you know, Curtis,' she said primly.

He looked around the poorly ventilated basement, which broke every imaginable fire and safety law. 'It's a great office.'

'You think? No one's ever said that to me before.'

'It's so light and airy. You could probably get another three desks in here. At least.'

'When could you start?'

CHAPTER TWENTY-THREE

THE FABER-KNOX HALL was an ugly, red brick, turn-of-the-century building, adjoining the dismal grey, prison-like church of St Mary's. There was a Parish noticeboard outside the hall, displaying the days for Bingo Eyes Down, Bible Study, Slimmers Night, Virgin Soldiers, Scouts and Cubs, Guides and Brownies.

And, sure enough, there it was: Knights of Saint Pancras. Feast of Mary Magdalene. July 22nd. So Keen would be there.

Dave had done a quick recce the night before. On the other side of the church was his primary school with the Presbytery, and beyond that, the Convent of the Sisters of Sorrow. He had sketched a map of the church and the hall, including the alleyways behind them, ready for him to make his escape afterwards. On his layout of the Faber-Knox Hall he wrote: 'Here Be Knights'.

According to the church noticeboard, there was now a new parish priest at St Mary's. Dave was relieved. He was glad the Canon would not be present at the gathering of the Knights of St Pancras.

Having studied the documents he had taken from Keen's apartment, he knew the front door to the hall would be locked on the night. The knights would enter through the church. There was an anteroom inside the hall, which acted as the regalia dressing room. But he would arrive at the last minute, already wearing his Torquemada mask and robes. He knew the password, the rituals, and all their other traditions, like the trick dagger, filled with fake blood, that they used at initiation ceremonies to intimidate new members.

He'd assemble with the other knights and, when he identified Keen from his voice, draw Cooper's gun, and kill him.

And so it was, on the 22nd of June, the day of the Feast of Mary Magdalene, Dave coolly walked through the silent church and into the dressing room of the adjoining Faber-Knox hall.

The doorkeeper, similarly robed, blocked his path. 'Give the password, stranger.'

'Knights of St Pancras shall rule'.

'Pass, friend.' The doorkeeper stepped aside for Dave to pass through the anteroom and into the knights' den itself.

Inside, the Faber-Knox Hall was a typically featureless hall, serving many community functions: barn dance club; meetings of Alcoholics Anonymous; jumble sales; Irish nights; quiz evenings, and coffee morning fundraisers.

But tonight it was the Lodge Room of the Knights of St Pancras. The stark strip-lights were turned off and only candlelight illuminated the robed knights dutifully standing in a semi-circle within. The dark, eerie room could have been anywhere. It could have been a cave, a crypt, or a dungeon, especially with the eerie music now playing. Its mundane reality, as the place for weekly beetle drives and Christmas dinner for the homeless, was lost in its all-enveloping, menacing blackness.

Dave remembered how Ernie told him he had walked past a man-eating lion because he was wearing a charm of invisibility.

'But you must never turn your head, Davey, or you'll break the spell, and then the lion will eat you!'

Ernie's words gave him courage, and he walked towards his fellow knights with complete confidence to join their sinister circle.

A hooded knight was playing weird processional music on an electronic keyboard. The music seemed familiar. It was a haunting, sad lament. Solemn drums were beating. There was the sinister clicking of castanets. Wailing trumpets. A bell was ringing. And a distant, eerie chorus rose to a crescendo and filled the hall.

Yes, it was definitely familiar. But where had he heard it before?

The knights, who had formed a circle, swayed slowly in time to the music. Naturally, Dave swayed too.

And then he had it. He had heard it before at the cinema. It was Spaghetti Western music.

It was remarkably similar to the amazing finale music from *The Good, the Bad and the Ugly*. That final shoot-out between Tuco, Angel Eyes and Blondie.

He remembered the colour supplement article about the knights. It said Faber-Knox was inspired by *Semana Santa*, the Processions of the Brotherhoods, enacted in Spanish cities during Holy Week.

The penitents, dressed in their sinister, colourful, hooded robes, swayed in time to slow music as they carried heavy floats of Christ and the Virgin Mary in procession through the streets.

The article suggested the composer, Ennio Morricone, may have been influenced by the music of *Semana Santa*, especially as the Spaghetti Westerns were filmed in the same part of Spain.

Whether it was true or not, Dave found himself looking round the circle of knights for the evil eyes of a Lee Van Cleef, visible through the eye-slits of his hood.

Or an Eli Wallach.

Or a Clint Eastwood.

No, *he* was Blondie.

The revolver was right there in his pocket, reassuringly heavy. As soon as Keen identified himself, he was going to draw. But he had to be cool, and wait for the right moment, like Clint Eastwood.

The music swelled to a new peak as four knights, also swaying from side to side, brought forth a bier with the gold skull statue of Mary Magdalene from Keen's apartment, and placed it on a candle-lit altar inside the circle of knights.

Then a fifth figure entered the hall. Dave assumed, as the knights stopped swaying, and turned in deference to him, that it had to be the Grand Master.

The Grand Master addressed his knights as the music now faded into the background. 'My brothers, we are here today to celebrate the Feast of Mary Magdalene. The Whore and the Holy One. She who they call Life and we call Death.'

Dave recognised his voice. It was Keen, all right. He had obviously obtained a new Nazareno robe and capirote. He wouldn't imagine the man who had stolen his costume would be present at the Feast. Only an idiot would do something so stupid. And that's what Dave was banking on.

'Traditionally, brothers,' continued the Grand Master, 'we would have a painted whore play Mary Magdalene. To disport herself and show us her unclean beauty. But tonight needs to be a more … *private* occasion.'

Dave wondered why there was the change of plan, why no floorshow? It didn't matter. He clutched the gun. Keen was still going to die.

'So our knight chaplain will address the Magdalene.'

A brother stepped forward and addressed the gold statue.

'God's sentence hangs over all your sex and his punishment weighs down upon you.' He pointed an accusing finger at the skull inside the statue. 'You are the devil's gateway; you are she who first violated the forbidden tree of knowledge and broke the law of God.'

Dave's stomach lurched as he recognised the Canon's voice.

'Because of you, Our Saviour had to die,' said the Canon sorrowfully. 'Because of you, the Son of God was crucified.'

He turned to the congregation. 'Because of her!'

The knights angrily murmured their agreement: 'Because of her!' 'Because of women!' 'Slut!' 'Whore!'

The Canon turned back to the skull and continued his one-sided conversation with it. 'It was you who coaxed your way around man whom the devil had not the force to attack and made him weak. "Woman … you are the gate to hell." Not my words, but the words of Tertullian, the father of Christianity.'

He spoke to the brothers again. 'But … let us also remember, the words of St Augustine. "If you do away with harlots, the world will be convulsed with lust." So … what are we to do? Hmm? St Augustine had the answer. He said: "Give me chastity, O Lord … but not yet." '

The knights nodded their agreement.

'And forgive ourselves,' said the knight chaplain, 'the disobedience of our bodies that, despite our best intentions, are aroused by temptresses. Of our own members, over which we have such little control.'

Once again, the hooded assembly nodded their heartfelt agreement.

Then the Grand Master stepped forward again and Dave started to draw the gun from his robes …

'Thank you, knight chaplain.'

The Grand Master addressed his knights. 'Brothers, take these words to heart, and bear them with you in all your activities of life.

'And now … there is a most serious matter to be dealt with. There is one amongst us who is an intruder, who has come here tonight to learn our secrets.'

The brothers looked around at each other through their eye slits. Dave, too, looked at the knights on either side of him.

'Such a one will surely incur the curse of God.'

The knights nodded their heads and Dave nodded with them. Then he realised they were all looking in his direction. He felt a slight clench in his bowels as the Spaghetti Western music began again.

He couldn't pull his gun now; he'd lost the element of surprise and the brothers were closing in on him. If he started to draw, they'd seize hold of him.

'His name,' continued the Grand Master, 'will become a byword and a reproach among all honourable men. He deserves the reception that the devil himself received from God: to be cast into eternal torture.'

He pointed in Dave's direction. 'You. Step forward.'

Dave reluctantly stepped out of the circle as the Spaghetti Western music grew louder once more.

Too late, he realised the whole thing was a trap. Keen had anticipated his burglar might have the temerity to masquerade as a knight.

The Grand Master addressed his knights. 'Should he be spared, brothers? Or should he suffer The Penalty? The white ball, brothers? Or … the black ball?'

The Canon went round the circle with a chalice and the knights dropped balls into it.

'What exactly is The Penalty?' asked Dave.

The Grand Master picked up a ceremonial dagger from the altar.

'The ancient penalty of having your throat cut for being a spy, an intruder and revealing the secrets of the Brotherhood.'

The Canon showed Keen the chalice. It was filled with black balls.

'I've been blackballed,' thought Dave.

'So mote it be,' said the Grand Master holding the dagger. It could still be a fake dagger, of course, Dave thought desperately.

'Wait. Let me explain.'

'Be quiet and accept your sentence,' said the Canon.

'At least give me the right of reply,' Dave pleaded.

'When Jesus was hanging on the cross, he had no right of reply. Neither do you,' said the Canon.

'It's a fake, right? You stab it in me and joke blood comes out. Right?' The Grand Master advanced on him with the dagger.

'It's just for show right? To scare me?' said Dave. 'Then you'll let me go home? Well, let me tell you, it's worked. I'm scared. Okay?'

'Take his mask off,' ordered the Grand Master.

'Why?' asked Dave.

'So I can slit your throat.'

'You – you don't really mean that,' said Dave as two knights closed in on him.

The Grand Master raised the dagger. 'You must pay for your blasphemy.'

Then he backed away in alarm as he saw Dave was pointing a gun in his face and was about to squeeze the trigger.

'No!' yelled the Canon, hurling himself on Dave. They rolled together on the ground, the ex-cavalryman smashing his fist into Dave's masked face. He began tearing at the mask to rip it off.

'You've stuck two fingers up at the Church and I'm going to break them,' he snarled. 'Followed by every bone in your body.'

Then the gun went off, and the Canon staggered back, shot through the heart. His shocked eyes were visible briefly through the slits of his hood before he keeled over. The music had stopped. There was silence in the room. A knight checked the Canon's pulse and slowly looked up at the others. 'He's dead. The Canon's dead.'

Keen wrenched the gun out of Dave's hand and two of the knights grasped hold of him.

'Who sent you? Who wanted me dead?' asked Keen pointing the gun at Dave.

'No one. It was just me,' he admitted weakly.

Keen angrily ripped his capirote off and stared coldly into Dave's eyes. 'I am your judge, jury and executioner, and you are dead.'

He turned to the others. 'Get his hood off. I want to see his face.'

'Let's see who this idiot savant is,' said a knight.

As they started to yank Dave's hood off, Keen stepped closer, and warned him, '*Get Carter* has nothing on me, son, and what I'm going to do to you.'

Then he stepped back in alarm as he gazed into the slavering, twisted, bloody fangs and bristle-haired face of a werewolf.

Shopping for a suitable mask in *Time Machine*, Dave had been torn between the Timberwolf, the Yeti and the Wolfman. They were all Don Post classics – rubber whole-head latex masks, but he settled for the furriest: the Bloody Werewolf. He had needed the fur to give him the courage to go through with his assassination mission.

'It's a fucking werewolf!' exclaimed a shocked Keen. The two horrified knights involuntarily let go of him.

Dave emitted a spontaneous and hideous howl, which he had absolutely no control over, and came from somewhere very deep within him. His primal scream reverberated all around the Faber-Knox Hall.

It shocked and confused the predators, and by the time they'd realised what was going on, Dave was out through the back window of the building, dropping down into the alleyway, and legging it, ripping off his robe and discarding it as he ran. But he took off his Don Post classic and held onto it as he ran. Knowing he had got away with it, and they had no idea who he was, lightened his steps. To them, he was a man with no name. Knowing the Canon was dead, and he'd shot him, didn't make him feel guilty or bad. On the contrary, it lifted his spirits. Because he knew just what the Canon was: a predator.

There were no trumpets, castanets, insistent drums, or wailing chorus; no triumphant Spaghetti Western music playing, as he headed off into the sunset. And yet there was. Inside his head. Courtesy of his mother.

PART III

AUGUST TO OCTOBER 1976

*'I should have shot the Sheriff. I shot the Deputy.
Sorry about that.'*

CHAPTER TWENTY-FOUR

METROPOLITAN POLICE COLD CASE UNIT NOVEMBER
3RD 2016
Detective Inspector Mary Read
PERSONS OF INTEREST

CANON WILLIAMS

Canon Charles Williams resigned as parish priest of St Mary's two months after the death of Mrs Maudling, and spent some years in the missions, establishing a Boys Town for homeless orphans in Burma.

He returned to the UK in 1966, and became parish priest of St Mary's once again. In September 1968, there was an incident when Peter Maudling was detained under the Mental Health Act and the Canon tried to comfort him. Mr Maudling attacked the Canon, and had to be restrained. Hospital records show Peter persistently claimed the Canon was responsible for his wife's death: police officers were called to the hospital and he made a written statement over several pages.

I have seen this statement. It is rambling, incoherent and largely incomprehensible. Most of it consists of meaningless scrawls and doodles. The few recognisable words, written in block capitals, are 'BASTARD', 'CANON', 'MURDERER' and 'I LOVE YOU JEAN'.

In view of Mr Maudling's serious mental illness, the police took no further action. A course of electric shock treatment and medication were effective in helping him make a good recovery. On his release from hospital, he did not repeat his allegations to the police and told them he 'did not want to talk about it anymore'.

The Canon left St Mary's in November 1968 and became parish priest of a further three churches in East London. He died from a heart attack on July 22nd 1976, at the Faber-Knox Hall adjoining St Mary's church. He had remained the chaplain of the Knights of St Pancras and it was during one of their meetings that he became unwell and died.

STANLEY COOPER

Stanley Cooper, the newsagent, had a history of violence and was well known to Stoke Basing police. His wife Doreen disappeared in February 1963. According to his next-door neighbour, Mr Ross, there were rumours Cooper had murdered her. Cooper sold his newsagents shop in 1973, and took a job as a storeman at Fleetpit Publications in Farringdon Street, coincidentally the same company that David Maudling, Jean's son, worked for. Cooper left the company in 1976, at the time Fleetpit were about to move to new premises in Southwark, and, despite exhaustive enquiries, his subsequent whereabouts are unknown.

ERNEST GAMBO

Ernest Gambo found work as a stevedore at the King Edward VIII docks in 1956, apparently so he could continue his relationship with Jean Maudling. Annie Maudling has told us her mother confided to her, shortly before she died, that Gambo asked her to divorce her husband. He wanted to marry her and look after her and her two children. She told him this was impossible and he became angry and stormed off. Following Jean's disappearance, Gambo left the docks in July 1957, and returned to Nigeria. We have been unable to trace his subsequent whereabouts. We have been unable to confirm a report that he died in Nigeria during the civil war in 1969.

PETER MAUDLING

Mrs Maudling's husband died of liver failure on November 6th 1971, two years after his release from St Ninian's Psychiatric Hospital. According to his daughter Annie, he was besotted with his wife, tolerated her infidelities, and would never harm her. It could be significant that he regularly used the upper floor of 10 Mordle Street to produce his 'moonshine' alcohol. It is possible that he could have been aware of activity in the basement when a 'secret room' was created, behind which Jean Maudling was buried. Or he may have been involved himself in some way.

BILL PEAT

In addition to singing in the choir at St Mary's with Jean, Bill Peat was also a chemistry teacher at St Joseph's and later taught Dave Maudling, Jean's son. He retired from teaching in 1983. Now 91, he lives in sheltered accommodation and currently writes popular chemistry textbooks for A level and university students. His solicitor informs us he is suffering from dementia and is too unwell to be interviewed. His client regrets he is unable to be of any assistance to us in our enquiries.

CONCLUSION

We want to help the family and provide answers to Jean Maudling's children, Annie and David (if his current whereabouts can be located) about what happened to their mother.

But, in the absence of new information, we are unable to draw any conclusions as to what occurred and the identity of the murderer, particularly as many of the possible suspects and witnesses are now dead.

Allegations about the involvement of TV celebrity John 'Fabulous' Keen that have appeared on the internet are outside the scope of this enquiry, which is now closed.

CHAPTER TWENTY-FIVE

DAVE FINISHED work in time to sneak up to his turret home and watch the regional news. It had extended coverage of the funeral of Canon Williams who, the reporter announced, had died of a heart attack. She described his distinguished career. He had gone to public school, then joined the army; the Royal Horse Artillery, where he acquired a reputation as a fine horseman. This was followed by the priesthood, the English College in Rome, and parish priest of St Mary's. His many achievements included setting up a Boys Town in the Far East. Dave wondered idly why he hadn't set up a Girls Town, but, of course, he knew the reason why.

There was nothing about his reputation for violence. Dave recalled that business about the hosts. In the Sundays following his First Holy Communion, he'd kept the hosts on his tongue and taken them home and hidden them in his Warfix foreign legion *Fort Africa*. Inspired by the illustration on the box, which showed foreign legionnaires enthusiastically, but bloodlessly, bayoneting Bedouins, he'd enjoyed many great games with the legionnaires protecting the hosts. Canon Williams had to be called and *Fort Africa* was exorcised. The Canon had to eat all the stale hosts and wasn't very happy about it. While his mother was out of the room making some tea, he'd belted the boy round the face and called him a 'blasphemous little shit'.

Dave could see why such an upper-class character, with a sense of entitlement that went back hundreds of years, would feel he had a *droit de seigneur* on vulnerable kids like Konrad. And why his mother would form a 'friendship' with him. After all, she had been trained by Paula to attract gentlemen. She had aspired to enter his elite world, but, to the Canon, she would have always been Mary Magdalene.

Dave was glad he was dead.

The Canon's coffin was escorted by the Knights of St Pancras, who wore their usual funereal top hats, black suits and cloaks, and carried silver canes. He recognised Mr Peat amongst the knights and Mr Czar, the coroner. He must have been essential for the death certificate, passing the Canon's murder off as 'natural causes'.

The knights had many members in the police and medical professions and would have called in favours to avoid an enquiry that would have exposed their secret ceremonies and activities to public scrutiny. There was no sign of Fabulous Keen, though.

But he did see his old headmistress, Mother St Vincent, 'Vinegar Bottle', now more hateful, ancient and vinegary than ever, following the funeral cortège. She was pushed in a wheelchair by Mrs Czar, as lovely as ever in her Virgin Soldier robes. He tried to banish his lecherous thoughts about her, but his mind wouldn't permit that. Mrs Czar reminded him of Mrs Robinson in *The Graduate*. He would have loved to play the part of Benjamin, who was seduced by Mrs Robinson.

* * *

'To the Canon,' said Fabulous Keen. He was resplendent in a turquoise Nehru suit with silver stripes.

'To the Canon,' said the other three, chinking their glasses.

'I like to think,' said Fabulous, 'he's paid his dues and he's up there in Heaven, riding across the sky.'

'With servants waiting on him in the clouds, and his silver service with him,' said Mr Peat sarcastically.

'Don't fucking mock, Bill,' sneered Keen. 'You're not an Angry Young Man anymore. You're not Jack fucking Kerouac.' Peat blanched under Keen's withering look.

Keen turned his attention to the film on his eyeball TV, and shook his head.

'See that? You see that? That is disgraceful. They should be ashamed of themselves.'

Mr Peat winced. Mr Czar chuckled. And Detective Inspector George Wallace grinned.

'My Godfathers,' said Fab, shaking his head, and continuing to avidly watch the tape. 'You were definitely right to confiscate this, Inspector.'

'I'm going to miss the Canon,' said Peat, trying not to look at the images on the TV, and wriggling uncomfortably in the Bauhaus chair.

'Yes, we all will,' agreed Keen. 'He took one for the team.'

'He took one for you, Fab,' said the Inspector.

Keen nodded. 'I'd be dead if it weren't for him. You know, I've been giving it some thought, and I still think our mystery man is a pro.'

'I have to admit, the werewolf mask was a master stroke,' admitted Mr Czar. Despite being a second generation White Russian who had settled in Britain, he still spoke with a thick Russian accent.

'Gate-crashing one of our ceremonies to make his hit,' said the Inspector, 'he must have balls of steel.'

'He's got more front than Brighton and Margate,' agreed Keen. 'Anything from the prints on the shooter?' The Inspector shook his head.

'I want you to find out his name, where he lives, what he does, and why he wants to kill me,' said Keen. 'And then I'm going to nail this bastard.'

He was distracted by the TV again. 'Now *that* should definitely not be allowed. Bloody hell. Can you freeze frame it?' The Inspector operated the Betamax.

'Thanks. I still haven't got the hang of this bloody machine. That's the one. Look at that. Amputees. Oh, that is disgusting.'

'Supposing it is a professional,' said Mr Czar, 'you realise he will try again?'

'And I'll be ready this time.'

'Then they'll send another, and another, until the job is done. They won't stop until you're dead. You know that's how it works.'

Mr Peat sighed. He was now sitting, rather more comfortably, on the Pop Art, yellow hand. 'I still say you're blowing this out of all proportion, Fab. I just don't think this man is part of an organisation, or is a professional hitman. He sounded genuinely scared to me.'

'So what does our chemistry teacher believe?' asked Keen.

'Well …' said Mr Peat cautiously, 'It's like I said at the time, I think he's an idiot savant. I mean, who else would leave a liquorice pipe in your desk?'

'Maybe a boy?' suggested Mr Czar. 'From one of the homes?'

'Have to be a big lad,' said the Inspector.

'Some of them are,' nodded Mr Czar. He leaned forward. 'What if he was at one of your parties, and has some…grudge against you? Saw your robes in the wardrobe, and read about our Brotherhood.'

'Why should any kid have a grudge against me?' asked Keen indignantly. 'My parties are a great opportunity for them to network, meet important people, make something of themselves.'

'They get strange ideas sometimes. And, whoever it is, he has inside knowledge.'

'I talked to the wardens,' said Keen. 'They checked their records. Who was allowed out that evening. They say it's impossible.'

'Kids wouldn't have the balls to pull a stroke like this,' agreed the Inspector.

'So we should be looking for a lone nutter,' Mr Peat insisted. Keen, Mr Czar and the Inspector looked at him with derision.

'Sure. Like Lee Harvey Oswald and Sirhan bloody Sirhan,' said Keen.

CHAPTER TWENTY-SIX

'BLOODY HELL,' said Scott. 'You took a chance coming here.'

'Had to see you,' said Dave. 'Explain what went wrong.'

'They didn't ask to see any ID?'

'No. Just told them I was your Uncle Ken. Bloke at reception—'

'McClaren. Housemaster. Real bastard.'

'That's the one. Said "You don't look like a drug-dealer. On you go, mate." Got me to sign the visitor's book and I was in.'

'You're cool, Dave,' said Scott admiringly. 'I can see how you shot the Sheriff.'

'No. I *should* have shot the Sheriff. I shot the Deputy. Sorry about that,' said Dave.

'You *actually* went to one of his Ku Klux Klan meetings, and were going to off him?'

'Until the Canon got in the way. But that's okay. He's another rotten apple.'

'I don't think he ever came to any of the parties. I don't remember him.'

'He wouldn't need to. He had other ways of getting to kids.'

They were sitting in Scott's room, which he shared with three other teenagers. It smelt of night breath, testosterone, and b.o. The wallpaper had practically disappeared under the rock posters. There were four bunk beds. Chest expanders, weights, nunchakus and piles of L.P.'s were stacked in a corner. Bookshelves dominated the room, with counter-culture volumes like *The Sacred Mushroom and the Cross*, T Lobsang Rampa's *The Third Eye*, and *The Origin of Consciousness in the Breakdown of the Bicameral Mind*. The latter was one psychology book that, surprisingly, Dave didn't have, and he figured it must have just been published. There were popular culture novels: *The Rats,* the entire *Gor* series, *Pan Book of Horror Stories*, endless *Perry Rhodans, Mandingo,* and *How to be Topp.* As well as neat piles of *Aaagh!* and *The Spanker.* A giant poster of Farrah was pinned to the ceiling, who smiled winsomely down on them.

'We knew something had happened, even before your call.'

'What do you mean?'

'Keen turned up here with two bodyguards, heavy dudes. Went into the warden's office and was asking a lot of questions. Then they were checking where we all were that night. Next thing we know: all the parties are cancelled.'

'They're not taking any chances,' noted Dave.

'So it's great. We're off the hook.'

'Off the meat hook?'

'Thanks to you. No more parties. Yes!' Scott punched the air. 'Although they're watching where we go now,' he added as an afterthought. 'We can't just come and go as we like.'

'I figured if you weren't allowed out, I should come to you,' said Dave.

'They must be desperate to find the killer.'

'And here I am all the time, hiding in plain sight,' grinned Dave. He realised just how much he liked taking chances. In fact, he was addicted to it. He'd crossed the line. Gone through the pain barrier. And he wanted more. Being normal was boring – not that he ever *was* normal – but he needed that adrenalin rush he felt when he'd been about to shoot Fabulous Keen, and gunned down the Canon instead.

'So where are the others?' he asked.

'Downstairs, playing table tennis.'

'D'you want to bring them up, so I can say hello?'

'Better not. Don't want it to look like we're having a meeting up here, just in case they're watching us.'

'Okay. About the plan. Now my way didn't work out, we've got to go for yours.'

Scott was taken aback. 'But we're safe right now, Dave. You don't have to worry about us.'

'For the time being. But for how long? I've checked the route, the location, gone over the cover story. It's all perfect. One hundred per cent. Say the word and I'm ready to rock and roll.'

'I don't know. I think we need to cool it for a while. Until Keen's relaxed and got rid of his bodyguards, anyway.'

'If you say so.' Dave was impatient for action.

Scott feared Dave's newfound bravado might be covering his fear, and in a sense he was right. Being manic was Dave's way of keeping his former cowardice at bay.

Scott looked thoughtfully at him. 'Look, are you sure you want to do this, Dave? I'll understand – and I know the others will, too – if you want to drop out. You've done enough for us.'

'Not only is it still on, Scott, but I'm looking forward to it.' Dave picked up the nunchakus and spun them to emphasise his words.

Scott ducked. 'That's great, Dave. That's great. We knew we could rely on you.'

'So when?' asked Dave, still quite manic as he twirled the nunchakus. 'When do we do it?'

The boy looked soberly at Dave.

'Come on, Scott. When do we launch Operation Grim Reaper?'

'When it's party time.'

CHAPTER TWENTY-SEVEN

IT WAS WHEN he was 20 and working for Angus, Angus and Angus of Aberdeen, for their senior citizen's magazines: *Kith and Kin, Health and Wealth,* and *Housebound.* Visitors would come into the office and step over the ancient, threadbare, worn-out carpet in the reception area. After an elderly author tripped on it and went flying, Dave had suggested it was time for a new carpet. But approval for such an important item required the permission of the directors. So it had gone all the way up to Mr Angus Senior himself.

After two weeks, Mr Angus Senior's response was sent all the way back down to the editor of *Kith and Kin.* There was to be no new carpet, but, instead, he decreed that the carpet should be turned round so the worn area would now be under the staff desks and filing cabinets. The furniture was duly removed from the office, and the carpet turned around, only to discover the concealed area was equally worn out from a similar move twenty years earlier.

Dave was telling his favourite Angus, Angus and Angus story to Joy in the pub. It usually got a few laughs, but, instead, she looked at him blankly.

'So what's the punchline, Dave?' she asked.

'That *is* the punchline of the story, Joy.'

'I don't get it. It's very sensible of them.'

'Ah. Right. Okay.'

'Anyway, that's not why we're here, is it, Dave?'

'No.'

'Dave, are you really serious about me?' asked Joy, lighting yet another cigarette. She had said they needed to have a serious talk about their relationship, so they'd gone to the pub round the corner from her flat in Marble Arch.

He leaned forward and looked tenderly into her eyes. 'Oh, Joy, you know how I feel about you.'

'I know how you feel about my armpit, Dave.'

'It's always on my mind, Joy.'

'Really?'

'Yes. Every time I see the word 'Fleetpit', I think of your armpit.'

His eyes still locked on hers, sending her romantic thoughts, he breathed out deeply with his nostrils. This caused the cigarette ash in the ashtray to fly up all over Joy's white top. He tried to rectify the situation by wiping the ash away, but he only served to rub it in, and made things worse. Joy watched silently as Dave rubbed her chest.

When he had finished, she asked coldly: 'I suppose you'd like me to grow a moustache, too?'

'Oh, Joy, would you?' he said excitedly, 'Is it possible? It would make me the happiest of men.'

She angrily stubbed her cigarette out and lit another as he smiled at the thought: 'My girlfriend growing a moustache especially for me. How about that? You know, I remember seeing the bearded lady in a fairground sideshow. So sexy. She was Ukrainian. I know, because I went and asked for her autograph. They rate bearded ladies in the Ukraine. They recognise the similarity to the vagina, you see?'

'I could buy a false beard if you wanted?' suggested Joy tightly. 'Then it might look even more like a vagina.'

'You've got a point there,' he agreed.

'Only it wouldn't *be* a vagina, would it, Dave?'

'But if you're considering buying a false beard ...'

'Yes?'

'I should tell you, I have one already. I was just waiting for this opportunity to mention it.'

'You have a beard you'd like me to wear?'

'I bought it on the off-chance that you'd be up for it?'

'While we're having sex?'

'It was a difficult decision. Joy. I was torn between The Lumberjack and The Abraham Lincoln. But in the end I went for The Viking. It's big and red and bushy. You'll love it. I can't wait to show you.'

Joy got up. 'Okay, that's it.'

'We're going back to your place?'

'Briefly.'

Half an hour later, Dave, clutching the few possessions he had left there, hurriedly left Joy's apartment and stumbled down the stairs.

'And I hope you trip and break your fucking neck!' Joy called down after him.

* * *

'Nice free holiday, was it, Greg?' sneered Dave.

'Two weeks on a Greek island, all expenses paid. Just one of the perks of going out with Leni,' grinned Greg. 'And now Guthrie's back,' he said, leaning back in his chair and clicking his pen, 'they'll definitely get rid of Ron. And maybe the board will forget about my fashion *faux pas* and see me as a responsible Suit?'

'They'll never forget,' said Dave.

Especially, he thought, as Greg was currently wearing white shorts that were far too short for him, and went right up to his crotch. Just so he could show off his sun-tanned legs, and a bit more besides. His hair was also all wavy, like a perm, strongly suggesting he'd spent a lot of time swimming in the sea. His candy-striped top completed the beach-bum look. Bum was the operative word. Guthrie had spent nearly a year in a Greek prison under the country's oppressive anti-gay laws. Leni and Greg had been dispatched to get him out.

'We were working all the time, you know,' said Greg. 'I was there because of my local knowledge of Greek culture. Proved invaluable in freeing Guthrie.'

'Greg, you spent six months on an army base when your dad was stationed in Cyprus.'

'But it still gave me an understanding of the people, their way of life.'

'You were eight years old.'

'Those are the perks of being Leni's right hand man,' said Greg smugly. 'Have some *baklava*,' he handed over a small square of the sticky sweet. 'Might cheer you up, help you get over Joy.'

'Oh, I'll get her back,' said Dave confidently.

'Fat chance,' jeered Greg. 'I'd throw myself on my sword, if I were you. Or onto the centrefold of *Members Only*.'

'I just need to smooth things over with her.'

Greg grinned. 'That would take a steamroller. The woman's got a corrugated soul.'

Wiping that grin off your face would cheer me up, Greg, thought Dave. It would help my pain go away, if I was enjoying your pain.

'Well, if anyone could break Guthrie out of a Greek prison it was Leni,' Dave admitted.

'That's why they sent her,' nodded Greg.

'Guthrie coming out of the closet on a Greek beach with Dmitri was maybe not such a good idea.'

'Yeah, I thought that whole anti-gay thing with the Greek Colonels was over, now they got rid of them. But it seems not. Some local police chief decided to make an example of him.'

'I'm surprised they didn't arrest you, as well, in your flimsy white shorts. If they saw you in your lederhosen, you'd be in jail quicker than you can say, "Ooh! Betty!" '

'We thought he was banged up for life. But two weeks negotiating with the locals, and a *lot* of retsina and drachmas – on Fleetpit's account of course – and it was sorted.'

Dave scowled jealously in response.

'I'm afraid it took that long, Dave,' sighed Greg sadly. 'It was tough. Leni and I, we just never stopped.' He added: 'On our mission of mercy.'

'You're lucky it wasn't a Turkish prison,' glowered Dave. 'Just been reading *Midnight Express*.'

Greg shrugged. 'Guthrie didn't look too bad. And he brought Dmitri back with him. He's put him in charge of photocopying.'

'That's nice. We really need someone in charge of photocopying.'

'So Guthrie's taken back his old job as managing editor of the girls and romantic comics. Which means Ron is even more irrelevant.'

'Yeah,' agreed Dave. 'He's definitely on the way out.'

'Such a waste,' sighed Greg. 'D-Day veteran, and he's never written about his experiences. All that great material going to waste: people being blown up, machine-gunned in the water, limbs being torn off, dying horribly.'

'He needs to let go of his pain,' sighed Dave.

Dave decided Leni was the answer. He'd make a move on her. That would make the pain of losing Joy go away. He'd lost her because of his stupid obsession with fur. And, if Greg was to be believed, it was for good. If only he could get fur out of his head. He'd read the psychology books; he knew the reason for his fetish, so why wouldn't it just fucking go away? Was he going to be cursed with fur lust for the rest of his life?

'He did once admit he machine-gunned a field of cattle in the war,' said Greg.

'But that's not as interesting as machine-gunning Germans, is it?'

Dave reflected that he'd probably have to crouch down under Leni's desk, wedged in behind her modesty panel, to keep her happy, but if that made the pain go away, so be it.

And there was a bonus: all the pain he'd give Greg by being Leni's new schnookie.

* * *

'Let's see what the pendulum says,' said Leni.

She and Dave watched it sway to and fro. In some unfathomable way, she received her answer. 'It says "yes".' She turned to Dave. 'So you want it? You've got it. We have nookie tonight at your place? Ja?'

'Maybe better at your place, Leni. My flat's a bit crowded.'

'Okay. My place. You will be my stallion for the night.'

'Strictly speaking, Leni, I should be your *uhlan*, your cavalryman. That's if I'm riding you, of course.'

'I know what I mean.'

'I'll have my lance at the ready.'

'But no sherbet breaks, Dave. I expect rigid liquorice.'

'I'll do my best. What about Greg?'

'He won't be there. And if he does turn up, it won't matter. It's our blindfold evening.'

'Okay. See you this evening.' He turned to leave her office.

'Wait,' the publisher commanded. 'Aren't you forgetting something?'

'What?'

She pointed to the space under her desk, concealed from public view by her modesty panel.

* * *

That evening, Dave duly turned up at Leni's New Age-style apartment. There was an altar to Sathya Sai Baba, surrounded by Arthurian pre-Raphaelite prints, as well as air-brushed paintings of angels and dolphins, with framed photos of Osho, Ouspensky, Madam Blavatsky and, surprisingly, Roger Daltrey.

Leni sprayed Dave's hair with sea water.

'It is holy sea water, specially blessed, that I took from the Pacific and carried up to the Hopis on the Third Mesa.'

' "Specially blessed?" Oh. Really? By whom?'

'Be me, of course. I am the True White Brother.'

'So we're having some kind of … spiritual sex?' asked Dave warily.

'No. It's because I want to make your hair all curly like Roger Daltrey.' She pointed to a photo of Daltrey as the Pinball Wizard.

'Do you mind if I pretend you're him when we're fucking? I really have the hots for him. I loved *Tommy*. Great spiritual truths are revealed in that film, Dave.'

'With Oliver Reed?'

'The universe sends many unusual messengers in the end times as we prepare for purification.'

'Fair enough.' Greg's curly hair was suddenly explained. 'So is that how it works with you and Greg?'

'Ja. He pretends to be Roger Daltrey, also. It is very satisfying.'

'But Greg is better looking than Roger Daltrey.'

'This is true,' agreed Leni. 'Daltrey is a bit ugly, but he is much sexier. Success is so sexy. That's what matters. And Greg is a failure. A loser. You know he will never be managing editor?'

'I didn't, but that's good to know.'

The knowledge delighted Dave. However, there was a possible drawback. 'So what about me? Does that mean I'm a loser, too?'

'No. No, not at all, schnookie,' she reassured him. 'You do look like Daltrey. Well. A little bit.'

'Ah. Well, at least I don't remind you of someone unhealthy, like your dad.'

'No. You look more like my uncle. Now. Let me see your flipper fingers.'

Dave was so busy meeting Leni's meticulous criteria, including saying "My G-G-G-G-Generation, baby," at the appropriate moment, that he had no time to focus on his own fur fetish.

Afterwards, she said approvingly that she was pleased he didn't try having armpit sex with her, especially as she had luxuriant foliage there, herself.

He decided against telling her that he hadn't made a move on her armpits because it would have felt like he was being unfaithful to Joy.

She explained the reason she grew her armpit hair was because it helped her lymphatic drains.

He didn't know what that meant and decided it was better not to ask.

She made some green snot to eat, which she called 'spirulina' and said was a super-food, and would get all the toxins out of his system. He couldn't face it, and opted for a liquorice pipe instead. As she wolfed down his spirulina as well as her own, she chatted happily away.

'Greg and I would sometimes watch you and Joy having armpit sex from over in the *Hot Pants* office.'

'What?'

'Ja. It looks out across the courtyard towards the *Shandy* office, so we had an excellent view. You must have forgotten to pull down the blind?'

'Oh, shit. How embarrassing.'

'No. It was very interesting. Although I should have dismissed you both for having sex in the office, of course.'

'That was nice of you. Thanks.'

'Greg wanted me to.'

'Greg wanted you to sack us?'

'But I explained to him that you were not having penetrative sex, so, strictly speaking, it was not a sackable offence.'

'So what did Greg say?'

'He said we should consult the pendulum. But it confirmed I should not sack you.'

'That's a relief.'

'So Greg suggested tossing a coin to be sure the pendulum was right. If it was heads I would sack you. But it was tails. Even when Greg made it best of three.'

Dave realised that having a fling with Leni wasn't making the pain go away. It was actually making it worse. Especially hearing about Greg.

And he realised that Joy, even without a moustache, was the woman for him.

* * *

He was still thinking about Joy the next day as he entered the photocopying room and joined the queue. He tried getting Dmitri to do his photocopying, but the handsome young Greek just gave him a contemptuous look and said, 'I don't photocopy. I am in charge of photocopy.'

'You just sit there and do nothing all day?'

'That is job of supervisor.'

'Do you even load the photocopier?'

'No.

So he just sat around, 'supervising', looking at magazines like *Him International*. He had film-star good looks and was nineteen, according to Greg. Dave could understand how Guthrie had risked everything for Dmitri. He would risk anything for Joy, now he had lost her. Aware of Dave's eyes on him, Dmitri pouted and gave him an arrogant look that said: 'Don't even think it. I'm well out of your league.'

But at least I'm closer to your age group, thought Dave. Not that it would do him any good. It was like Leni had said: it was success that mattered, not age. Success that everyone found sexy.

And, if Leni was right, Greg and he were seen as losers. Even though they had produced the smash-hit *Aaagh!* which must count for something. It was, at least, their first step on the road to fame and fortune. And to pulling the female equivalent of Dmitri. Some gorgeous girl who would help Dave forget Joy. Although Dave suspected Greg, with his love for his dead, car-crazy friend Bernie, would secretly be happier with someone like Dmitri.

Dmitri continued pouting, presumably thinking Dave hadn't got the message. Don't pout at me, Dmitri, thought Dave. I understand the need for you to have an imaginary job. I've read *Hollywood Babylon*. Gay Hollywood stars need their gardeners, handy men, stable boys, and pool boys as a cover for their secret relationships. In Britain, we have our 'photocopy supervisors.'

Finally, Dave was at the front of the queue and it was his turn at the photocopier. He raised the lid and saw there was still a piece of paper inside. He looked round to see who had left it behind, and alert them, but they had gone.

He turned the paper over and saw a message written on it in an angry scrawl in block capitals: 'MAUDLING, I KNOW WHAT YOU DID AND YOU'RE GOING TO PAY, YOU MURDERING BASTARD!

CHAPTER TWENTY-EIGHT

COULD IT MEAN SOMETHING ELSE? Could it be a joke? A mistake? No, not really. The message was crystal clear.

Could Keen have written the note? Dave wondered, his head in a spin. No, it couldn't be. Fab would have been instantly recognisable in Fleetpit House, in his Nehru suits. Could he have sent an assistant? But how could they have set him up to find that note in the photocopier? Whoever it was must have been following him. But that didn't make sense. Keen couldn't possibly know *he* shot the Canon. He was too careful. He'd worn the werewolf mask.

There was only one explanation. One of his past Caning Commando crimes had caught up with him. Someone had figured it out: just like Detective Inspector 'Fiddy' Ferguson.

But it's not meant to be like this, lamented Dave to himself. They're meant to be the perfect, hero-free crimes. Killing by remote control, with no comebacks. That's the whole beauty of them.

In a state of shock, he was barely aware of Ron entering *The Spanker* office to tell him that Quentin Cowley would be interviewing him tomorrow for *Newshound*. Cowley wanted to question him about *Aaagh!* Ron assured him it would not to be a problem. *Aaagh!* was a big-seller so he had the board's full support.

'Just keep batting his criticisms back with bland, safe replies. Like "Well, that's your point of view, Quentin." And "I'm sorry you feel that way." Or, if he goes on about violence in comics, remind him of all the war films they show on Sunday afternoons. Remember, Dave, *Newshound* is live, so they can't edit stuff out like they usually do. So you can make them look pretty stupid.'

'Okay, Ron,' said Dave, in a daze.

Ron looked surprised and pleased that Dave agreed to the interview without any of his usual resistance. He headed for the door. 'Good man. The telly blames everything on comics. Soccer hooliganism: comics' fault. Illiteracy in kids: comics' fault. Devalue the pound – comics' fault.' He turned back at the door. '*And* they fucking stole our readers, too. Worse thing that ever happened to comics was fucking television.'

'Okay, Ron,' said Dave, still in a daze.

'So ... you're going on *Newshound*, eh?' said Greg, not yet sure if this was good or bad for him, or for Dave.

'Okay, Ron,' said Dave.

'It's Greg. Hello? Hello?' Greg clicked his fingers in front of Dave's face. 'Is anyone at home?'

'Sorry. I was far away,' said Dave. 'What were you saying?'

'*Newshound*. Quentin Cowley. The man with the tank tops? I nearly appeared on it myself, you know? Did I ever tell you the story? But thank fuck I managed to get away.'

Dave decided to ignore the threat in the photocopier and it might just go away. Maybe it was just a lone nutter, who wouldn't really do him any harm? Yes, forget about it. That was the best thing to do. Concentrate on the here and now. Greg wants to tell some fucking boring story about *Newshound*. Listen to it. Block everything else out.

'You nearly appeared on *Newshound*? With Quentin Cowley – the guy who wears those awful tank tops? That sounds really intriguing, Greg. Do tell.'

'Are you sure you want to hear it? You always say "intriguing" when you mean something is actually shit.'

'I meant to say, it sounds fascinating, Greg.'

'Okay. But it is a story about one of my great conquests and I know, well, you haven't been getting any lately.'

'You are correct, Greg. I'm seeing less action than a convent mattress and my vital fluids are all intact, whereas you're like an uncapped oil well. But that's why I love to hear stories of your sexual exploits, so I can live vicariously through them.'

'Okay,' said Greg uncertainly. 'Well,' he continued, shaking his curly locks, 'It was three years ago …'

He doesn't know that I shagged Leni, thought Dave. I'll keep that to myself until I can find the right time to reveal it and humiliate the smug bastard.

'She was gorgeous. Looked like Susan George. Seventeen years old. Annabel. The Commanding Officer's daughter. I met her at the Officer's Mess Summer Ball.'

'You were at a Summer Ball?'

'As a waiter. My dad got me the job.'

'Ah.'

'She fancied me more than all those Hooray Henries. But she was strictly off limits. If the CO had found out, he'd have gone spare; dad would have lost his job. Maybe even our house. Who knows? That's what made it so exciting. Forbidden fruit.'

'Uh-huh.'

'I was screwing her all that summer. It was amazing. She just couldn't get enough. She used to like …'

'Can we just get to the *Newshound* bit?'

'Woolworths got burnt down.'

'I remember. It was on the news. Police thought it was a bomb.'

'They thought it was the IRA. Only it wasn't. But they didn't know that then. So *Newshound*, Quentin Cowley, came to interview Annabel's dad. Get the army angle. In his house. Problem was, I was upstairs with Annabel and she was meant to be at college.'

'Shit.'

'So the CO comes up the stairs to see if she's ill, and I shin down the drainpipe.'

'That must have been tricky.'

'Not really. I'm used to that sort of thing. Only guess who's waiting at the bottom? Howard the *Newshound* dog!'

'The bloodhound with the big soulful eyes who follows Quentin everywhere?'

'That's the one. So I'm about to make my getaway and Howard

starts making that strange baying they make. "Roooooo!" He must've thought I was a burglar.'

'Howard attacked you?'

'No. They're watchdogs. But he wouldn't stop howling. Calling for help. So I had to shut him up, didn't I?'

'Oh, no, you didn't, Greg?'

'Well, I had to, Dave.'

'You actually kicked Howard, the legendary *Newshound* dog, loved by millions of kids, and with his very own fan club?'

Greg squirmed. 'Just once. Okay, once or twice. Had to stop him following me. Then I legged it before Cowley came round with his camera crew to find out what was going on.'

'So you didn't pay the wages of sin, Greg.'

'No way,' smirked Greg. 'Got away with it. Had my wicked way, and was on my way.'

'But do we all pay for our sins in the end?' speculated Dave.

* * *

'All right,' said Ron. 'Now don't hang up. Okay? Now before you go out on the ledge, I want you to keep your phone off the hook. And close to the window. Okay? 'Cos I want to hear your scream when you jump.'

The line went dead. Ron winked at Dave as he replaced the receiver. 'Another cross line with Cross Line. Works every time.'

'Good to know you're still offering the comfort of the Lord to troubled souls, Ron,' said Dave.

Quentin Cowley, who was just setting up with the *Newshound* crew, came over to them. 'That's not it, is it? It couldn't be? It's not ... The Desk?' said Quentin excitedly.

Ron said nothing, just puffed away on his cigarette as he removed his racing papers. The legendary glass-topped desk had once belonged to the creator of *Homework:* the Reverend Julius Cambridge. But to Ron, the desk, with its school shield and Latin motto: *Deo patriae litteris* – 'For God, country and learning' – was not a proud memento, but a scalp, the spoils of victory when Fleetpit took over *Homework.*

Quentin lovingly stroked the desk. 'The famous *Homework* desk. I can feel the history. *Homework* made me who I am today. I based my life on *Dan Darwin*, commander of the spaceship *Beagle,* with his mission to understand the evolution of life on alien planets.'

'I do a lot of homework here meself,' said Ron. 'Always studying form. Perusing tables.'

'*Tales from the Blackboard* ...' continued Quentin, lost in his own memories. '*The Boyhood of Bertrand Russell* ... *So you think you could be a ... Magistrate? ... Lives of the Great Headmasters* ...' He smiled at the two of them. 'A young boy is a knowledge sponge. He can't soak up enough.'

'I agree,' said Dave. 'I received a subscription to *Homework* as a punishment. I was shitting logarithms for a week. If it had been today, I'd report my parents to Social Services. It's a crime against trees. What did they do to deserve this abuse?' Whenever Dave was nervous, he got manic and aggressive, and he was particularly nervous now there was mysterious maniac threatening to kill him, plus a hostile interviewer like Quentin Cowley.

'You might as well have called it, *Homework*, incorporating *Detention*,' continued Dave. 'That's about as much pleasure as it gave me.'

Quentin had never met anyone quite like Dave before, so he just ignored him. He turned to Ron. 'You must feel so honoured to sit behind it?'

'Actually, Quentin,' Dave intervened, 'Ron was the man who closed down *Homework* when Fleetpit took it over.'

Quentin looked aghast at Ron, who sat back in his chair, whisky glass in hand, fag hanging from his lower lip.

'It was the first thing he did.'

Ron nodded, 'Merged it with *Scarper* and *Blimey*. We kept *Toffee Nose* and chucked the rest of the magazine away.'

Toffee Nose – a know-it-all kid spouting boring facts – had finally ended up in *The Spanker* after it merged with *The Fourpenny One*. Dave would sometimes recite Toffee Nose's facts to send himself to sleep at night.

Quentin looked horrified. 'Doesn't this desk mean anything to you?

'I'm in comics, son,' replied Ron. 'Not the second-hand furniture business.' And casually flicked his cigarette ash onto the desk.

'I loved the smell of *Homework*,' Quentin reminisced. 'My parents would never let me read comics. They thought they were rough and crude, like the dreadful *Fourpenny One.*'

They had chosen Ron's office for the interview with Dave. Dave was looking rather sharp in an Aquascutum suit, thanks to the insistence of his female fashion police: his mother and Joy. By contrast, the TV crew were wearing paisley shirts with long collars, dungarees and platform shoes. Quentin himself wore one of his famous tank tops. He also had a badge with Howard depicted on it, the symbol of *Newshound*. His beloved dog sat quietly snoozing at his feet.

Dave was mic'd up and took his place on the other side of the desk to Quentin. Quentin carefully removed from a plastic folder the number one issue of *Homework* and placed the large, glossy, juvenile educational to one side, next to the latest issue of *Aaagh!*

Dave leant forward. 'By the way, Quentin, if I may so …?'

'Yes?'

'I'd like to compliment you on that particularly fine tank top you're wearing.' Dave nodded his sarcastic approval at the garment.

'Thanks, Dave,' said Quentin, mystified but flattered.

'Nearest he'll get to a tank,' muttered Ron. 'Good luck, chum.' He sat down out of camera range and was joined by Greg who had just slipped in in time and was keen to hopefully enjoy Dave making a prat of himself on live television.

The cameraman gave a signal. 'On in ten.' Quentin turned to the camera and his speech pattern suddenly changed. He spoke slowly, enunciating every word, in a patronising manner as if his youthful audience were deaf and was lip-reading him, or were complete imbeciles.

'Good afternoon, Newshounds. Today, I have with me Dave Maudling, editor of this children's comic.'

He held up the copy of *Aaagh!* The cover showed a kid from *The Damned* shooting the hated Insinerators who had made rock music illegal. The Insinerators were meant to be wearing black uniforms, but 'Deep Throat' had coloured them blue so they looked like cops. Which was unfortunate.

'*Aaagh!*, a comic that made headlines with its shocking images of a great white shark eating the President of the United States. A comic that caused questions to be asked in the Houses of Parliament about a scene where Her Majesty the Queen is depicted thrown over the shoulder of a shotgun-wielding lorry driver called Street, and carried through the sewers beneath Buckingham Palace. Then she's thrown in the boot of his car with the words, "Calm down, your Maj, don't get your knickers in a twist." '

Dave interrupted: 'He had to put "Her Maj" – Her Majesty – in the boot so he could get her past the army checkpoints. Street's a freedom fighter. Against a military take-over in Britain, which is a real possibility today. Maybe the Houses of Parliament should think about that.'

Quentin ignored him. 'It's also a comic that features a corrupt policeman taking bribes from villains.'

He turned to Dave. 'Dave, what do you say to the accusation that your comic is violent, disrespectful to religion, the monarchy and authority, and is actually encouraging children to commit crimes?'

'I would say that's not true. In *Bent*, we make it clear an A10 police officer is pursuing the corrupt cop.'

'But you're setting a bad example, Dave, so children will stop trusting figures of authority.'

'I think that's a good thing, Quentin. There are a lot of questionable adults out there.'

'And *Carjacks?* Where you actually show children how to steal cars?'

'Harmless fantasy. Like Cowboys and Indians.'

'But children can't run out and actually kill Indians, can they? And you have a war story: *Panzerfaust.* You do know the war has been over for over thirty years?'

'Tell that to my dear old Nan who had her false teeth blown to Hounslow by a doodlebug,' said Dave.

Quentin sniffed. 'If I can draw your attention to a recent line from *Panzerfaust.* Faust says, "God won't help us, so I call on the Devil!" This sounds like black magic to me.'

'It loses something in your delivery. Perhaps if a man was saying it.'

'Then there's *Micky's Mutants*, about the hideous survivors of a nuclear war.'

'What's wrong with that? It's hilarious.'

'So you find nuclear war amusing?'

'We've grown up with the threat of the Bomb. You've got to laugh at it, haven't you?'

'Have you? And *Deathball?* Killing as a sport?'

'After *White Death,* it's our most popular story.' Under so much pressure, Dave was unaware that he had taken a liquorice pipe out of his pocket and put it in his mouth.

Quentin held up the cover of the latest *Aaagh!* 'And *The Damned,* which shows a boy actually gunning down policemen!'

'Colouring error. Those cops are meant to be fascists.'

'I see. A "colouring error"… cops depicted as fascists,' sneered Quentin.

He held up the number one issue of *Homework.* The free gift was still attached to the front: a plastic protractor. There were cover lines on the magazine. 'Make your own school report. How to revise over Christmas.'

'Let's compare it with a periodical that reinforced moral values. This is the number one issue of *Homework* that I swapped with a young viewer for a *Newshound* reporter's clipboard.'

Quentin leafed through its glossy pages. 'A magazine every responsible parent recommended. It was rich in mentally nourishing ideas.' He carefully enunciated every word. 'A paper university.'

'I remember it well.' said Dave. "Treasure Island in Latin begins inside."'

At Quentin's feet, Howard stirred. His beloved master droning on usually sent him to sleep. But now something was nagging him. A scent from long ago. He looked suspiciously around the room and made eye contact with Greg.

Quentin picked up the copy of *Aaagh!* again. 'It compares with this appalling, illiterate, juvenile delinquent comic that has been pumping out its vile content, like raw sewage, onto the children of Britain.'

'A simple "I don't like it" would suffice,' said Dave.

Quentin flicked through the comic and stopped at an image of a furious Black Hammer attacking racist thugs on the terraces. 'A comic that actually *encourages* soccer hooliganism,' he announced.

That was it. Criticising the Black Hammer. His hero. Dave bit through his pipe.

Quentin held the comic up for the cameras. 'On behalf of all responsible parents, I feel a duty to do this to your disgraceful publication.' With pursed lips, he precisely tore *Aaagh!* in half.

'I see,' said Dave.

He picked up the copy of *Homework*. 'On behalf of the bored kids of Britain, I'd like to do this.'

To Quentin's horror, he violently ripped it in half. 'Goodbye "Boyhood of Patrick Moore". Goodbye "Cecil Rhodes, Africa's Saviour." Goodbye "Cutaway of a stapler".'

The ash from Ron's cigarette curled over and fell to the ground. Greg looked on, open-mouthed, at what Dave was doing. While Howard continued staring intently at Greg, the hound's body now tense, and his tail high and stiff.

Dave quoted imaginary scenes from *Homework* as he continued to rip it into smaller pieces. 'Goodbye "Your Royal Betters"... "How the Bible was brought to hotel – a drawer-by-drawer guide"... "Africa: lining your pockets made easy. How to strip-mine a country. What every boy should know." '

'You ignorant oaf!' snarled a livid Quentin and took a savage swing at Dave. But Dave was ready for him, and gave the presenter a resounding fourpenny one, instead.

At the same time, Howard leapt on Greg and sank his teeth deep into his ankle. Screaming with pain, Greg tried to shake the bloodhound off, but there was only one way to make him stop: by booting him off.

He sent Britain's most loved dog yelping and flying across the office. On live TV.

CHAPTER TWENTY-NINE

NOT EVEN THE old Fleet prison down the road or a Greek jail could compare with The Hole.

The *Laarf!* 'Specials'.

They were both given life sentences.

This time, there was no comforting music from *The Great Escape* in his head to comfort him and reassure there would – somehow – be a way out. There was no way out.

Heading for 'Mirth Row', Dave and Greg heard a distant baleful laugh from the *Laarf!* office. They looked at each other and shuddered. It came from editor Tom Morecambe, and sounded like a soul in torment, the wail of a banshee, or the high-pitched scream of a vampire in a Hammer movie, and confirmed 'Abandon hope all ye who enter here.'

It reminded them of their previous stretch on the Devil's Island of comics. They had worked on *Andy's Anorak, Billy Blower, William the Conkerer* and *Dirty Barry.* The latter was possibly the worst. Every week, Dirty Barry was splashed by cars, dogs cocked their legs on him, and he was dive-bombed by pigeons. Or he passed a cess-pit lorry driver who accidentally pressed a lever marked 'Blow' instead of 'Suck' on his tanker, so he was covered in sewage.

Onlookers were always concerned for the boy, until they recognised

Barry through the filth; then they didn't care. It always ended with the same punchline:

'It's all right! It's only Dirty Barry!'

It had taken the combined efforts of Ron, Leni and Joy to stop Dave and Greg being fired. Joy had threatened she would resign. Leni had pointed out that Quentin and Howard had struck the first blows.

But it was Ron who explained to the directors that Dave and Greg could cause more problems if they were on the outside. With their new-found notoriety, they could give exclusives to the tabloids and reveal the secrets of Fleetpit. Secrets such as the legendary hundred-year old archives that were being quietly destroyed as a cost-cutting measure before the move over the water to Southwark. Dave was one of the despised 'aficionados' who felt strongly about the nation's cultural heritage ending up in an incinerator. Ron pointed out it was best to keep potential enemies close.

Aaagh! was banned with immediate effect. But its huge popularity meant it would return in a suitably castrated form. And who better to castrate it than Pete Sullivan, who had just finished a stint as caretaker editor of the children's educational magazine, *'But Why?'* He had almost destroyed *'But Why?'* with his feature on edible mushrooms that children could forage and safely eat. The list of edible fungi included the Death Cap, which was 95% fatal and had no cure. The entire print run had to be sent back from the newsagents to be destroyed.

Yes, thought Dave bitterly, Sullivan would 'take care' of *Aaagh!* and *The Spanker*.

Originally an assistant editor on *Casino for the Man about Town*, Sullivan's time on the soft-porn magazine meant that he saw sexual references everywhere. As he took over *Aaagh!* and *The Spanker* from Dave, he had looked alarmed at the liquorice pipe projecting from his mouth.

'What is it, Pete?' Dave asked curiously. 'What is it about a liquorice pipe that you find offensive? What are you seeing that I'm not seeing? A saxophone? A black man's cock? A dildo? Here. Take a closer look.'

Sullivan looked repelled at the black object and backed away. 'I'd rather you didn't wave that in my face, Dave.'

And so Dave and Greg headed for The Hole, and their life sentence on the infamous *'Specials'*.

The *Laarf! Puzzle Special* was especially mind numbing: spotting the difference with Andy's Anorak. Joining the dots with Billy Blower. And Dirty Barry had fallen into a sewer.

Again.

'Help him find his way out of the sewer maze'.

Greg looked up grimly from editing the *Gambling Madd* fruit machine puzzle game.

Gambling Madd was one of *Laarf*'s most popular characters. Kids loved him. Every week Gambling Madd was bunking off school to play cards or hang out in fruit machine arcades. That was when he wasn't being thrown out of betting shops, bingo halls, casinos, and dog racing stadiums. Often his gambling efforts would pay off and result in him ending up with a huge pile of cash and going out for a slap-up feed.

'So it's okay to have a cartoon strip about a kid who's a compulsive gambler, but it's not okay to have a story about lorry driver fighting for freedom.'

'Can't have working-class heroes, Greg. Look at all the great heroes of fiction: Sherlock Holmes, James Bond, the Scarlet Pimpernel, Richard Hannay. White, rich, upper class. It's deliberate. It's social conditioning.'

'Same with comics,' agreed Greg. 'Dan Darwin. Batman. Caning Commando.'

'They want readers to know their place. Like Alf Mast.'

'Stupid sidekicks.'

'With no future. Like us, Greg. Except they may get a better job as a fruit machine tester.'

Still in a despondent mood, Dave later met up with Scott at a café near Farringdon Station. They'd agreed to stay in touch. The boy was in an upbeat mood because there were still no parties and they were being let out again. Life in Castle Ramparts was actually becoming bearable.

'And if the parties do start again, well, then we deal with Keen.'

'Something to look forward to,' said Dave morosely.

'You must be gutted about *Aaagh!* being banned?' Scott enquired.

'No. I don't care,' shrugged Dave indifferently. 'It's just a comic.'

He then proceeded to talk for thirty minutes about how little he cared about his comic being banned.

'Plus,' he said, in between bites of his sandwich. 'I've lost my girlfriend, my job, and I can't even kill the right fucking knight.'

'The Canon was still a scumbag.'

'I haven't finished yet. I'm doing time in The Hole. And I've discovered who my real dad is. He turns out to be a complete shit who is trying to get money out of me. As opposed to my other dad, who drank himself to death.'

'Some of us at Castle Ramparts went through bad shit,' sympathised Scott. 'But we're going to win this time. You're with a winner.'

'And I'm a loser,' said Dave. 'You really shouldn't hang around with someone like me.'

'Everyone can win, Dave.'

'Not true. They want us to know our place.'

'You mean like Alf Mast? Sleeping in the boiler room?' laughed Scott.

'I should have known my place when I left school. I was an errand boy riding a trade-bike around the docks. And now I'm where I really belong, in The Hole.'

'It sounds like a nightmare.'

'On the contrary, The Hole has much to commend it. I'm actually better off in my slough of despond. Comfier. One day you'll understand, Scott, that life is a plate of shit and every day we eat another mouthful.'

'I don't believe that.'

Dave sighed. 'Anyone who breaks the rules, who dares to challenge them, always ends up in the shit. Like Dirty Barry.'

'You were still right to stand up to Cowley, Dave. He swapped his reporter's clipboard for some kid's valuable number one issue of *Homework*. He's a creep.'

'That's what they're all really like under their cardigans and their tank tops.'

'And you showed us that in *Aaagh!* And showed us we can beat them.'

Dave imitated Quentin and his patronising, careful pronunciation, talking to kids as if they were complete idiots. 'A p-a-p-e-r u-n-i-v-e-r-s-i-t-y.'

'That's why he hated you. 'Cos you showed him up.'

'Don't know about that,' said Dave, starting to enjoy the praise.

'I do. I've seen him at Keen's show-biz parties, with all the other TV stars, snorting coke. He's a fucking hypocrite. Only he's not into kids; he sticks to hookers, who Fab also provides, of course.'

'So I was right not to trust a man who wears a tank top?'

'When I saw him, he was wearing lingerie and was on a dog-leash.'

'Well, he is a newshound.'

'You have no idea of the effect *Aaagh!* had on everyone, Dave. It was massive.'

'Really?' Dave was definitely brightening up now.

'That Saturday *Aaagh!* was banned, there were kids running down the street yelling *'Aaagh's* been banned! *Aaagh's* been banned!'

The world was definitely a sunnier place, even if Dave couldn't actually see the sun as the café windows were fogged up from all the cigarette smoke.

'Aaagh! made a difference, Dave,' said Scott. 'Just remember that.'

CHAPTER THIRTY

DAVE WAS STILL BASKING in the warmth of Scott's words when he returned to The Hole. Not even working on the belated *Laarf! Olympic Special* and Tom Morecambe's hideous laugh, echoing through the long empty, miserable corridors of Mirth Row, could depress him, he decided.

And then he discovered Ron's secret.

All those months he'd been locked in his office, "drowning his sorrows", he had actually been secretly preparing a new comic, which was launched just two weeks after *Aaagh!* was banned.

War Picture Weekly was a huge hit with the readers because, uniquely, it showed combat as it really was, with the barest minimum of censorship. It was written and drawn by servicemen who had experienced World War Two. Not portrayed with the idiocy of the Caning Commando or the equally questionable 'War is Hell but it's still pretty cool' style of baby-boomers like Greg.

The lead story, *Ron's War*, was a fictional version of Ron's wartime exploits beginning with the teenage soldier's role in the D-Day landings on Sword Beach. Normally, comics would have covered the D-Day landing in just a single episode. Instead, Ron outdid the legendary war movie *The Longest Day* by taking an entire 12-episode serial over the first day of the landings alone. He brought out a humanity in the characters, which, aside from *Aaagh!*, had been lacking in comics. The death of Ron's best friend, Ginger, in the first wave of young soldiers hitting the beaches was particularly moving and had many readers in tears.

It was drawn by ex-serviceman Joe Callaghan who, for the first time in a lifetime of working for Fleetpit, had something worthwhile to draw, and put his heart and soul into it. There was a passion and conviction in his characterisation; a truth to the mesmerising detail in his graphic images of the fighting, which not even *The Longest Day* could compete with. Readers preferred it to the film. They would remember Joe's incredible pages all their lives.

They finally had their working-class hero: Ron.

Other stories, like *The Red Devil*, about a World War Two airborne soldier, and *Borstal Boys*, kids growing up in the Blitz, were also written and drawn in a similar hard-hitting vein. The latter revealed darker aspects of the war not generally known. Soldiers throwing away their rifles on returning from Dunkirk. Looting. The King and Queen booed by starving East Enders. The tube stations that were originally locked so people couldn't shelter there during air raids. A priest, Father John Groser, breaking into a food depot when the authorities refused to feed his homeless neighbours. A kid sent to borstal for stealing a few lumps of coal to keep his family warm. The comic was refreshingly free of officer heroes. The war veterans, a writer and artist creative 'League of Gentlemen', had finally told it like it really was, and their audience responded accordingly.

It had taken the challenge of working under a German publisher, to kickstart Ron back into life. To throw caution to the wind and reanimate him and veteran artists and writers desperate to have genuine challenges. *War Picture Weekly* was a sensation.

The only one of Ron's 'rat pack' who was missing seemed to be the Major. This was surprising, as the Major had been a Japanese prisoner of war and had written the shockingly racist, banned 'Bumzai!' episode of *The Caning Commando*, where the teacher fights a cane-wielding Samurai and was awarded a 'purple arse' medal by the Americans for 'giving the Japanese a taste of their own divine wind'.

Ron's success only made Dave slide deeper into his slough of despond. He and Greg had both expected to rule the roost at Fleetpit and they had both thought Ron was washed-up.

They saw him as they returned to The Hole one lunchtime. He gave no sign of his victory, but there was just the slightest curl to his lip and he walked that bit taller, that bit prouder.

And his look said, 'I've cut you two hotshots down to size.'

Dave and Greg's days as the whizz kids, the golden boys of Fleetpit, were over. There would be no escape from The Hole. They were the ones who were washed up. They were lifers.

'Hey,' said Greg, looking up from game-testing the *Laarf!* Olympic game. 'Maybe Ron would be interested in my French resistance story? It's about a British kid, Billy Chief.'

'Billy Chief, eh? That's an unusual surname, Greg. And you say he's a British kid in a French resistance story?

'You see, you must always have a British hero,' said Greg.

'For reader identification. So we have to lead the Russians, the Americans, or the French in the war. 'Cos they're not really cool.'

'Apart from Germans. They're cool?'

'Germans are always cool, Dave. So Billy leads a Paris street gang of French apaches who fight the Nazis using their savage kickboxing skills.'

'Naturally Billy Chief is so much better at the French martial art than the apaches?'

'Oh, naturally. He's British. That's why he leads them. I've got a great title for it.'

'I have an uneasy feeling I know where this is going. Don't, Greg. Please. Spare me.'

'You guessed the title?'

'I'm afraid I have, Greg. But, don't tell me. I'm already about to phone Cross Line.'

'I'm going to call it … *Chief of the Indians.*'

'Yes. Yes, that's what I feared, Greg.'

'What do you think?'

'I think you need to return to your game-testing.'

Dave had devised an Olympic board game for the centre pages of the *Special*.

So he could inflict his pain on the readers once more. And on Greg, which was a significant bonus.

He insisted Greg, as his assistant, game-tested it. This involved doing squat thrusts, press-ups, and running on the spot every time the player was caught by 'The Trainer'. 'Oh, shit, this is agony,' said Greg after doing 10 press-ups. 'Got to take a fag break.'

Dave enjoyed his discomfort. That'll teach him to try and get me sacked, he thought.

'Anyway,' said Greg, inhaling deeply. 'Once the dust's settled, Leni thinks I could still be made managing editor. Or she might make me editor of *LBD*. And then I'm out of this hell-hole.' He grinned. 'It's all yours, mate.'

'I doubt it,' said Dave. 'She's been promising you that for months now. She's just using you, mate.'

Greg shook his head. 'I don't think so. I mean a lot to Leni. We have a very special relationship.'

'That's good to know,' said Dave. 'So you think it could be serious?'

'Oh, yeah.' Greg said cockily. 'We'll probably get engaged.'

'Fantastic,' Dave leered. 'Am I right in thinking she's really into Roger Daltrey?'

'Yes,' said Greg defensively. 'How did you know?'

'And what's that song of his she likes? Let me see. Oh, yes. "My Generation".'

'What?' Greg went white. 'What did you say?'

'My G-G-G-G-G-G-G-G-G...'

'Shut up!' said Greg.

'G-G-G-G-G-G-G-G-G-G-G-G...'

'*Shut up!*'

'G-G-G-G-G-G-Generation, *baby.*'

Dave drank in his pain. It tasted sweet. Under stress, Greg had graduated from pen-clicking to spinning his pen in the air and expertly catching it. He spun it endless times now.

Then he retaliated. 'You know Joy is dating the manager of her shop?'

'Nice try, Greg. But you got that wrong,' said Dave confidently. 'She said he was a creep.'

'That's true. But she also said he had an excellent business brain, and that's what really matters to her. Profits at *Time Machine* have doubled since he took over.'

'But she liked me because I make her laugh.'

'Not enough I'm afraid, Dave. She also told me he reminded her of her dad: Lawrence of Fitzrovia.'

'Whereas you, Dave…' Greg raised an arm and scratched under his arm, making grunting, gorilla noises.

Dave went white and Greg drank in his pain. It tasted sweet. Dave returned to the *Special*. All the *Laarf!* characters, Andy's Anorak, Billy Blower, Gambling Madd and Dirty Barry, took part in the *Olympics Special* and it was the most unfunny yet.

Dave gloomily wondered just how much worse his day could get.

The phone rang and Dave answered it. It was the switchboard. 'The Major for you, Dave.'

'Hi, Major. How's it going?' asked Dave.

'This isn't the Major,' hissed the menacing voice at the other end.

'Who is this?'

'The man who left the message in the photocopier. I know you did it, Maudling. You and the Major.'

'You know what?'

'The Caning Commando? Your murderous ideas for killing adults. Congratulations. They paid off. Someone very close to me died, thanks to you two.'

'I don't know what you're talking about.'

'I've got something in the boot of my car for you, Maudling. Death is waiting and watching for you. D'you hear me, you fuck pig? You are both fucking dead.'

Then the line went dead. The operator came back on. 'Were you cut off, Dave?'

'Yeah. Do you know who that was?'

'I thought it was the Major?'

'No.'

'Oh. Well, it was an internal call.'

Whoever the mystery caller was, he was inside the building.

CHAPTER THIRTY-ONE

'SO DID I tell you how I danced with Ivor Novello? At the Victory Ball in 1919?'

'You may have done, Paula,' said Dave, looking nervously at the entrance to the club.

'All the flappers were in their fancy dress: Britannia, The United States, Cleopatra, Peace, The Sun and the Stars. And I was there with my mistress, you see?'

'Uh-huh,' said Dave.

'Calm down, dearie,' smiled the elderly boss of The Eight Veils. 'The Major said he was on his way. There's nothing to worry about.'

'There's everything to worry about, Paula.' Dave had called the Major directly afterwards. He needed to meet up with him. Warn him his life was in danger. By some nutcase who had discovered what he was up to in *The Caning Commando*. No, what he, Dave, had been up to.

'Joy dust, they called it,' continued Paula. 'They'd all go into the powder room and snort powder, all right, and drop their empty pill boxes in a bin. So I collected the dust from the boxes and decided to have a sniff myself. I said to the other servants, "If it's good enough for our mistresses, it's good enough for me." '

Where was he, thought Dave. He should be here by now. The killer couldn't have struck already, could he? Maybe he's not really a killer?

Maybe he was just making idle threats? Maybe there's something harmless in the boot of his car? Oh, sure.

'So I put on the butterfly gown. Gorgeous it was. Huge floaty, silvery wings on the back.' Paula smiled, still beautiful in her seventies. 'Maybe the joy dust helped a bit, but I've always been mad, you see? Always taken risks.'

'Well you shouldn't,' said Dave, turning his attention to her. 'It just leads to huge fuck-ups. It leads to disaster.'

'It led to me being held in Ivor Novello's arms. Everyone was watching us as we glided round the ballroom. Me, a humble servant girl, the butterfly belle of the ball.'

'Sounds straight out of a girls' comic,' said Dave cynically. Paula looked far away. 'I've remembered that moment all my life. He was so handsome. Course, I didn't know he was one of them. The handsome ones always are.'

'And you got away with it?' asked Dave curiously.

'No,' laughed Paula. 'My mistress was furious. Sacked me and warned me I'd never find work in service again.'

'There, you see?' said Dave triumphantly. 'That's what happens when you take risks. I bet you were blacklisted in all the servant halls. Mr Hudson and Mrs Bridges wouldn't have given you the time of day.'

'Who fucking cares?' laughed Paula. 'I've done all right since.' She leaned forward over the bar. 'You've got to take chances, Dave, you've got to dare, otherwise you never win. I think it was one of my army regulars who said that.'

'And that just proves my point, Paula. If you dare, you *don't* win, you just end up in the shit.'

Who knew just what awful fate the killer had in mind for the Major and himself?

'That's not what I taught your mum, Dave. I said to her, "Reach for the stars, Jean. You've only got one life and you've got to live it to the full."'

'I wish I could believe that,' said Dave.

'Pearls for my girls. Furs from sirs.'

'Same again, Paula.'

'Mind you,' grinned the elegant old lady, pulling a pint. 'Your mother didn't need much teaching. She was a natural.'

'What's the matter with me, Paula?' said Dave. 'Why can't I play by the rules? Why can't I be a boring, play-it-safe wage slave and just do what I'm told, like all the other boring wage slaves?'

Paula looked him straight in the eyes. 'Because you're Jean Ryan's son.'

The Major hurried into the drinking club. 'All right, everyone,' he announced. 'Stand by your beds.'

'Major!' said a relieved Dave.

'I think I'm being followed,' the Major panted, looking fearfully back down the stairs.

Shit, thought Dave. It's started! It's started! The killer is about to burst into the club, clutching his shotgun, like Street, when he kicks open the door of the officers' mess and snarls, 'Here's your dessert, Hooray Henries!'

'Yes, definitely being followed,' said the Major, hanging up his camel hair coat. 'Thought I'd shaken him off, but I fear he's still on my tail.'

'Oh my God!' said Dave. 'Maybe there's a back way out of here? Yes, down the fire escape. Quick! Run, Major! Run!'

'Why, dear boy?'

'I'll try and slow him down,' said Dave, desperately looking around him.

'Why would you do that, dear boy?'

'Because this is my doing, Major. It's all my fault. I am so sorry.'

'Why is it your fault?'

'It's my fault this man is after you! Now just go!'

'A taxi driver's after me. Jumped out in Dean Street. Thought I'd lost him in the crowds. Could you do the necessary? Damnably short of the readies.'

After Dave had paid off the cab driver and bought the Major a double, he coldly reminded him: 'I thought you said you earned more money than the British Prime Minister?'

'Easy come, easy go, dear boy,' he boomed. 'Wives. Horses. Poker. Hotels. Flat broke now.' He held up his portable typewriter. 'Just my trusty typewriter left. In fact, talking of hotels, they just threw me out. Misunderstanding about the bill. Couldn't stay at your place tonight?'

Dave thought of his turret up in Fleetpit House. 'Actually, Major, I don't really have much of a place.'

'Not to worry. Railway waiting room tonight. Know them all. St Pancras, I think. One of the ladies of the night will take pity on me.' He took some black cardboard out of his shoes that covered the holes in them. 'I'll make you two more, Major,' smiled Paula.

'Major, I have to warn you,' said Dave, 'there is some guy out there who's making death threats.'

'Death threats?'

'Against you and me. I think you could be in danger.'

'What did he say?'

'It was an anonymous phone call. He said, "You and the Major. You're both fucking dead." I think it's 'cos he hates *The Caning Commando*,' Dave lied.

'Is that all?' The Major laughed. 'Nothing to worry about. Just forget it, dear boy.'

'He also said he had something in the boot of his car he was going to use on us.'

'That's what they always say. Probably a shotgun.'

'That's what I thought.'

'Hot air, dear boy. Hot air. I used to get those threats from Keen after I had him thrown out of here.'

'Yes. Paula said you dealt with him.'

'Ill-treating the girls. Beating them. Wasn't going to stand for it. Saw too many beatings on the railway. Japanese guards. Bullies. Oh, by crikey yes. Wasn't going to stand for it again. Oh, by crikey no. Caught up with him playing snooker.'

'What did you do?'

'Improvised, dear boy. Always improvise. Learnt that in Burma. Think fast.' The Major made a fist. 'Billiard ball punch with the fist. Broke two of my fingers. Worth it. Solid uppercut. Broke his jaw.'

'Wow!'

'After he was wired up, started making threats. Shotgun. All the rest. Not for long. Called the lads. Ron. Murray. Nobby. Dusty. Ex-soldier-chums. Just like *The League of Gentlemen*. Jack Hawkins. Under my command. We saw Keen off. Slunk away. Like the rat he was, oh, by crikey yes.'

'I saw Ron's comic. Was that them?'

'Absolutely. We all stayed in touch. Dusty wrote *Borstal Boys*. He wasn't in the services until the end. Too young. Sent to borstal for stealing coal off the railways.'

'It looks like a good story.'

'I was surprised Ron allowed him to go that far.' The Major looked at Dave and wagged a reproving finger. 'Probably your bad example on *Aaagh!*, dear boy. You're a bad influence on young Ron.' He chuckled. 'Loved the punch you gave Quentin, by the way.'

'Thanks, Major. I was surprised you weren't in the comic with your POW experiences.'

'Ron wanted me to do another *Bridge Over the River Kwai*. I tried, but it wasn't in me' said the Major thoughtfully. 'Thought it would be easy, knowing how I feel about them. And that hasn't changed. No, sir. You remember I wrote the 'Bumzai' *Caning Commando* story?'

'Vividly,' said Dave.

'Corporal punishment was a daily occurrence. Why I dreamed up *The Caning Commando*. My way of trying to cope with the beatings. I'd make up those stupid stories. The more stupid they were, the better. 'Bumpy men'. 'Carpet bumming the Hun.' So I could laugh at death. Whatever they did to me, it didn't matter quite so much; in my head I was somewhere else. That's how I survived. Thanks to the Caning Commando.'

'Maybe Ronald Searle did the same with St Trinian's?' suggested Dave.

'Maybe,' the Major brooded. 'But afterwards, just before they sent us back to Blighty, we saw our old jailers in Changi. We were invited to watch their executions. They thought we'd like it. Payback.'

The Major looked haunted as he remembered. 'Only we didn't like it at all.'

'Why not?'

'Caused a bit of a scandal at the time,' the Major reminisced. 'Each Japanese guard had just a half-hour trial, and was sentenced to death. Of course they were guilty. Oh, by crikey, yes. Especially the Big Fella. He could crank an engine with just one turn. But he'd prefer to make us do it. Then he'd beat us when we failed. Finally, he'd do it, effortlessly. Like King Arthur pulling Excalibur from the stone. He could knock

down a coconut tree with his hands and feet. Imagine what he did to us
…Yes, I'm afraid so.'

Dave winced.

'So there we are, thin as rakes, covered in green and purple dabs
from ring worm, entering the prison courtyard. And there's the Big
Fella, immaculate in his uniform. He recognises us, of course. Clicks his
heels and bows to us.'

'Like he's finally showing you respect?'

'Maybe. Who knows? Then he runs at the wall. Dashes his
brains out.'

'*What?*'

'Two more of his chums do the same. Our chaps didn't know what
to do at first. Couldn't shoot them. They were sentenced to be hung. So
they herded them back inside at the point of the bayonet. But carefully,
so they couldn't impale themselves and commit hara-kiri.' The Major
breathed out heavily.

'Bloody hell,' said Dave.

'For some reason, I can't get that image of the Big Fella out of my
mind. His head down, running full speed at that wall and then the
sickening thud, and …' he tailed off. 'I can still hear it. Even now.' He
knocked back a double whisky.

'I can't hate them as much as I should. And I really want to hate
them, Dave. I don't understand it. That's why I can't write about any of
it. I need to keep it shallow. Like *The Caning Commando*. Let's change
the subject, shall we, dear boy?'

'About the death threat, Major?'

'Like I said, Dave. Relax. I'll be fine. And so will you. It's just a lone
nutter. Don't encourage him. That's what he wants. Ignore him.' The
Major waved a dismissive hand. 'There's absolutely nothing to worry
about. Same again, eh? Your round?'

CHAPTER THIRTY-TWO

KEEN WAS finally getting around to watching *Tomorrow's Britain*, his last show in the current series. He'd set the timer on the Betamax and he thought he'd got it right this time, but, somehow, he'd still got it wrong; it included the show before his own: *Newshound*. He was just going to just fast forward through it and go straight to *Tomorrow's Britain*. But then he remembered someone telling him that this edition of *Newshound* was quite funny. Quentin Cowley gets into a punch-up with one of his interviewees. Keen never liked Quentin very much, even though they'd done a few lines of coke together. So it would be amusing to see him being humiliated.

He settled down on his sofa and watched as Quentin laid into some idiot, the editor of a stupid comic, because it was too violent. Quite right, too. Kids needed protecting from that kind of filth. It should be banned. He still found *Newshound* tedious, though, because of the way Quentin insisted on talking, like his audience was brain dead or something.

Quentin was saying, 'But you're setting a bad example, Dave, so children will stop trusting figures of authority.'

Fab found himself nodding in agreement. Quentin was absolutely right. Children needed to trust people in authority.

Then he mentioned some Satanic war story. A Nazi calling on Satan to help him? Disgraceful. That should definitely not be allowed.

And frightening kids with a story about nuclear war. Just who was this editor? This irresponsible idiot?

Then the irresponsible idiot put a liquorice pipe in his mouth as he answered more of Quentin's questions.

A liquorice pipe.

Fab freeze-framed it. And gave a delighted double thumbs-up to himself. That beatnik Peat was right, after all.

CHAPTER THIRTY-THREE

GREG WAS GOING stir crazy in The Hole. He had graduated from spinning a pen in the air and catching it, to spinning a scalpel in the air and catching it by the handle.

'Will you stop doing that, Greg?' said Joy.

Greg was feeling particularly despondent after the lacklustre reactions to the game in the *Laarf! Olympic Special* that had just been rushed out.

'We only got one reader's letter. And he wrote in to say he didn't understand it. Despite the clearly written, simple fucking rules.' He looked bitterly at Dave. 'All those squat thrusts, all those press-ups I did. For nothing.'

Dave looked sympathetic. 'Not for nothing. I enjoyed them, Greg.'

'What's the matter with them, man? Are they stupid?' asked Greg. He threw the scalpel into the air again.

'I fear so,' sighed Dave. 'At least *Spanker* readers read the comic the right way up.'

'Greg!' warned Joy.

'It's all right, Joy,' he said, catching it. 'It's just like Russian roulette. Only you don't die. You go to A&E. And I've become really good at it. 'Cos there ain't nothing else to do here except help Dirty Barry through the sewer maze.'

'Stop it! Right now.'

'Why? *Aaagh's* been nuked. Seven million kids hate me for kicking the *Newshound* dog. They'd be so happy if I bled to death. Why shouldn't I play scalpel roulette?'

'Because it's fucking mad?'

'How else do I pass the time, Joy? Throwing paper aeroplanes out of the window? We're not high enough.' He spun the scalpel high in the air. The menacing silver blade spun over and over.

He caught it expertly by the handle. 'Maybe I should throw myself out the window instead?' He threw the weapon into the air again. 'Or set myself "accidentally" alight with cow gum? Hey – that's a lot more fun than the *Laarf! Puzzle Special.*'

'I think he's been getting high on the fixative,' Dave explained to Joy. 'He's been calling me "man" all afternoon.'

Once again, Greg caught the scalpel. 'Nearly,' he grinned.

'I won't tell you again,' warned Joy.

'I think you should do as Joy advises and go back to your pen-clicking, Greg,' Dave advised. 'As we both know, she's made better men than us cry.' Greg finally stopped.

'I think I know how to get your sentence quashed, guys,' she said.

'The guvnor's heard our appeal for clemency?" asked Dave, brightening up.

'No. Not exactly. But I think the board might if you started a new science fiction comic.'

'Science fiction? Oh, no. That will never work,' said Dave.

'Dave's right,' agreed Greg. 'Kids think science fiction is stupid. They want reality. Like *War Picture Weekly.*'

'You do know *The Bionic Woman* is number one on TV?' Joy pointed out.

'On TV maybe,' said Dave. 'But there hasn't been a good sf comic strip since *Dan Darwin.* It was the only decent thing in *Homework.*'

'Yeah, that was brilliant,' said Greg. 'Fantastic artwork. You really shouldn't have torn it up, Dave.'

'But I have seven million *Dan Darwin* fans hating me,' smirked Dave. 'So that takes some of the heat off you, Greg.'

'Will you two clowns just shut up and listen?' snapped Joy. 'I'm trying to get you out of The Hole.'

'Sorry, Joy. But for a moment there, it seemed like you were offering us hope.'

'There is hope. This guy in competitions sent a memo to Leni to say there's going to be a science fiction boom. There's a new film coming out next year: *Star Wars*. I said I'd look into it for her.'

'I remember meeting someone from the film at your *Time Machine* launch party,' Dave recalled. 'I wasn't impressed.'

'That's because you enjoy pissing on everyone's parade, Dave.'

'True,' agreed Dave.

'Some of the images are fantastic. Reminded me of this amazing French comic book, *Valerian*, I've got in the shop.'

'I'm not sure I like the idea of writing escapist fantasy,' pondered Dave. 'What's the point? There should be a point to it.'

'Who cares what the point is?' said Greg desperately. 'Just as long as we get out of The Hole.'

'Science fiction does have meaning,' said Joy. '*Dan Darwin* explored the principles of evolution through life on alien worlds. That's why it was such a great story.'

'But even if Greg and I get it right, Joy,' said Dave, 'Fleetpit is cursed. That's why everything we do here fails.'

'Oh, come on.'

'Seriously. There were pagan abominations carried out on this very site. Rituals we dare not speak of.' He looked meaningfully at her. 'Just to say, the goats left over were very bandy.'

'Well, Ron overcame the curse,' Joy said impatiently.

'Thus far. You know this was convenient for hangings from Newgate and martyr-burning when Tyburn was busy? Fleetpit is the pits.'

'But we're moving soon. To a brand new tower over the water. It's a new start.' This was something Dave didn't want reminding of. It meant losing his turret home. It meant no longer living rent-free in central London. And being able to spend his spare money on furs.

Dave shook his head. 'It was easier getting Guthrie out of a Greek prison, than getting us out of The Hole. We're lifers, Joy.'

'Before you finally turn down the opportunity of a lifetime, Dave,' Joy replied, 'Can I just point out that one of the heroes in *Star Wars* is covered in fur.'

'Tempting. But no.'

From the other end of Mirth Row they could hear the distant, buzz-saw wail of Tom Morecambe's laugh.

'You know it's the *Laarf! Christmas Special* next?' warned Greg. 'Endless shit stories about Dirty Barry falling down sooty chimneys with Santa. Billy Blower blowing up party balloons. Gambling Madd trying to double his Christmas money on the horses.'

'I'm your man, Joy,' said Dave.' When can I start?'

'Whoa, whoa. Back up. I've still got to get Leni on our side and convince her that a science fiction comic is a good idea.'

'It's a brilliant idea,' said Dave. 'What's the problem?'

'No real problem,' said Joy carefully. 'But I think it would help our case if we could work on it together?'

'The three of us?' said Dave.

'Like on *Aaagh!*

Dave realised if he worked closely with Joy again, he might find a way back into her arms. Or her armpits. Especially the left one.

'I think we'd make a good team,' agreed Dave.

'I get it. So you can promote *Time Machine*?' grinned Greg.

'There's got to be something in it for me, too,' said Joy. 'And I do happen to love science fiction.'

'Everybody's exploiting everybody else these days,' said Greg bitterly. 'Why not? Why the hell not?'

'So the Three Musketeers are back in action again?' asked Joy.

'All for one and one for all,' said Dave.

CHAPTER THIRTY-FOUR

'SHOULD WE GET LENI?'

'I don't think so. She's still OD'ing on rescue remedy after he dropped that picture of Roger Daltrey on her head. Accidentally, of course.'

'So what's he doing? Self-harming again?' said Joy as she and Dave entered Mirth Row.

'Much worse. I'm afraid he's completely lost it, Joy. He's in a bad way.'

'Oh, shit.'

'Yeah,' said Dave. 'The poor guy.'

Dave didn't actually care about Greg. In fact, he was enjoying Greg's suffering. But he had noted how Joy had shown compassion to Ron when she thought he was losing the plot. This was something women seemed to do. So he thought it was important to sound like a caring human being,

'Poor guy,' Dave repeated for emphasis. 'I'm really worried about him. I'm afraid Leni seems to have finally broken him.'

'Was it the turd diary they kept?' Joy asked.

'Measuring their turds with a ruler after their volcanic ash colonics? I'm not sure. Whatever that stuff Leni gave him, it was certainly volcanic.'

Joy nodded. 'He showed me that photo-book of jobbies she gave him as a birthday present. She's definitely mad.'

A hideous wail echoed down the corridor. 'That's Tom's worse yet,' noted Joy, recoiling involuntarily. 'It sounds more like an animal in pain than a laugh.'

'That's not Tom Morecambe, I'm afraid,' said Dave. 'It's actually Greg.'

'Greg?' Joy stared at him in disbelief.

Dave nodded sorrowfully. 'He's doing the Mongolian throat singing Leni recommended. She says it will clear his chakras and then he'll be all right again.' Dave sighed, full of concern for his friend. 'Only I don't think he'll ever be all right again.'

There was another wail from the *Specials* office.

'It sounds like the lethal gargle of a rampant sheep mehhing with a twanging elastic band stuck in its throat, don't you think?' noted Dave.

'Or a scary space echo from *2001,*' said Joy.

Inside, Greg was on all fours. 'Greg? Are you okay? What happened? What's the matter?'

By way of reply, Greg made a deep, grunting, menacing, straining throat noise.

'He's resonating, Joy. He just has to hit the right frequency.'

'He sounds like the soundtrack for *Texas Chainsaw Massacre*. Like he's about to murder someone. Or unleash a massive jobby. Greg, just what is this bloody woman doing to you?'

'You should try it, Joy,' said Greg. 'You'd like it. Leni says it's like taking drugs but with no side effects. It's like peyote or ayahuasca. Did you know it can actually reverse time? I can feel my mind literally going backwards.'

'Come on. Let's get you up.'

Greg grimaced. 'That's the problem, Joy. You see the thing is, I can't actually get up. I've done my back in.'

'What? How?'

It turned out that Greg and Leni had spent the weekend in Glastonbury. At the Lemuria Guest House and Healing Retreat run by Nefertiti and Akhenaten near Glastonbury Tor, built over a healing vortex. Nefertiti was giving birth to baby Jesus and guests had come from all over the world, paying for rooms in the B&B, to witness the Second Coming.

The birth was all the more miraculous as Nefertiti was in her late fifties; however the new Messiah was born on the inner plane, and was therefore invisible on the outer plane.

In preparation for the Nativity, Nefertiti had wanted the house cleaned from top to bottom. 'And it was absolutely filthy,' said Greg. 'So it took me forever.'

'You?' said Joy. 'Didn't Nefertiti have a cleaner?'

'Yes, she did. Unfortunately the cleaner resigned. She was afraid she might vacuum up baby Jesus by mistake. That's why I had to do it without a vacuum cleaner. On my hands and knees.'

'But why you?'

'I think it may have been because Nefertiti and The True White Brother are rivals? Leni consulted the pendulum and it said it was a great chance to clean my aura at the same time. It said her own aura was okay.'

'I bet it did,' growled Joy.

'And I'd already messed up my back from carrying her suitcase of rocks.'

'This is insane,' sighed Joy. 'You've got to finish with her, Greg.'

'I think we should do this gradually,' warned Dave. 'Like deprogramming someone who's been in a cult.'

Greg had started throat singing again; he sounded like a didgeridoo in pain.

'Stop, Greg. Right now. D'you hear?' Greg stopped. 'Now, you've got to split up with her. Understand? Tell her it's over. I'm serious. She's a fucking menace. She's ruining your life.'

'Er – I should give this some thought first, Joy,' said Dave.

'What's there to think about?' said Joy angrily. 'Your friend's health – his mental wellbeing – is at stake!'

'I know and that is very much on my mind, Joy,' said a concerned Dave. 'However …'

'However? What's to "however"?'

'However, if Greg dumps Leni now, it will probably mean we won't get out of The Hole and she won't let us do the science fiction comic.'

Joy paused to consider. 'Hmm.'

Dave added gently, 'I really think we should take his deprogramming slowly, Joy. Let's not be in a rush. He is very vulnerable.'

'Okay, carry on, Greg. If you can just hit that right note, you should clear your chakras.'

CHAPTER THIRTY-FIVE

KEEN SMILED AT THE INSPECTOR. His cool hairstyle and lurid Nehru suit contrasted with the Inspector's conservative high street suit and his short back and sides haircut. 'So you tracked him down, Inspector?'

'I tracked him down, John. Got the full S.P.'

Fabulous sat forward. 'I have so much harm I want to cause that young man, so much pain, I almost don't know where to start.'

'But we need to take our time, and take extra care,' warned the grim-faced Inspector.

'I know. I realise that.'

'After all, he is Jean Ryan's son.'

The Inspector and Keen were meeting at the cavernous City Golf Club by St Bride's Church, just off Fleet Street. Keen enjoyed mixing with the journalists who frequented it, so he could tell them about all the wonderful work he did for charity. The walls were decorated with old golf clubs, but it was really just a drinking den when the Fleet Street pubs were closed in the afternoon.

Keen got the Inspector past the authoritarian, uniformed doorman, and remarked how that used to be his job many years ago at The Eight Veils and just how far up in the world he had come since. 'From Sinner to Saint, that's me,' he said. The Inspector smiled noncommittally, knowing Keen was still both, as he was himself.

Keen was excited by the news coming over the ticker-tape machine chugging away in a corner. NASA had just publicly unveiled the space shuttle *Enterprise* in California and Keen wondered about visiting it for *Tomorrow's Britain.*

Keen brought his mind back to the present. 'So what else did you find out, Inspector?'

The burly policeman lowered his voice. 'I visited the premises at Mordle Street. Told the owner I'd had a report of drugs being used on the premises. He was happy to show me around and prove his innocence. Basement room's still bricked up. Hasn't been touched.'

'So Dave Maudling doesn't know how his mother died or that she's buried down the road from where his family used to live.'

'It would seem so,' said the Inspector carefully.

'But he knows she's dead,' speculated Keen. 'And he obviously knows I ordered her death. And maybe knows the Canon was involved.'

'Maybe he remembered some conversation he overheard as a kid?' suggested the Inspector.

Keen leaned forward. 'You'd better alert the other party concerned. Just in case he pays them a visit, too.'

'I've already done so, John.'

Keen sighed and sipped his vodka and tonic. 'I don't know why Jean just didn't forget it. All right, it was unfortunate that Konrad got all upset and jumped off the roof, but he's in Heaven now.'

'You need to be a lot tougher if you're going to survive in this world,' agreed the Inspector, drinking his beer.

'They're not stoic, like our generation,' agreed Keen. 'Things we didn't like, we just put up with. We didn't make a song and dance about everything.'

'This is it.'

'In fact, a lot of youngsters were pleased when the Canon took an interest in them.'

'Exactly. It was an honour for them.'

'I remember it was a beautiful funeral,' recalled Keen. 'Little Konrad's white coffin. And him dressed in white inside. White for innocence. Not like Mother's funeral.' His face clouded over. 'She wore the brown robe of a sinner.'

'I never understood how you put up with her, John,' said the Inspector.

'I had to, she was my mother,' reflected Keen.

'It was a merciful release.'

'I thought Jean would understand about Konrad. She'd never caused us any problems before.'

'You can never trust them, John.'

'But I thought she was different. I thought she understood the official stuff was a smokescreen. That's for the sheep, the bottom feeders, the outer circle. We are what it's really all about.'

'She played Mary Magdalene, John. She understood.'

'She was reading, thinking too much, questioning. Foolish.' Fabulous sighed.

'So.' He shrugged. 'Now I have to deal with her loser son, too.'

'What have you got in mind?'

Keen thought about it for a while. Finally, he decided.

'The usual.'

CHAPTER THIRTY-SIX

THEY WERE OUT OF THE HOLE. They were free. Back on *The Spanker*, and starting work on their new science fiction comic. Greg had stopped scalpel spinning. He'd stopped taking volcanic ash. He was wearing his usual 'man in black' clothes. He was almost normal again. Apart from his filterless German cigarettes: 'Roth Handle' – *Red Hand*. Rough, smelly and dirty.

Non-smoker Dave recoiled from the smoke. 'The fumes in here are even fouler than when you were on the volcanic ash.'

'They're the cigarettes Germans soldiers used to smoke. Leni wants me to be like her dad now.'

Dave raised an eyebrow.

'Don't ask.'

They were playing 'Splatoom!' as they talked. A target was drawn on the wall next to the door and they were taking it in turns to hurl a ball of plasticine at it.

'The skill comes from how much you mould the plasticine in your hand so it sticks to the wall,' said Dave, scoring a bullseye. 'A strong right hand is important.'

'No problem in your case,' said Greg, removing the plasticine from the wall.

'So,' said Dave, ignoring Greg's jibe. 'Our science fiction comic. We'll do stories with robots. Aliens. Dinosaurs. Time Travel.'

'Spaceships. Mutants. Futurecops. Deathgames,' added Greg.

'Still not sure how popular science fiction will be, but it's a small price to pay for us getting out of The Hole.'

'Correction, Dave. It's a big price to pay. For me.' said Greg bitterly, throwing the ball. 'I'm the one who's sleeping with a mad woman.'

'Oh, she's just mildly eccentric,' Dave reassured him.

'She has a Messiah complex.'

'That's not actually a clinical term or a diagnosable disorder. So it's okay.'

'It's not okay, Dave. She thinks she can save the world.'

'So does Superman.'

'Leni is real. I need to get rid of her,' said Greg desperately. 'I need some sanity back in my life.'

'You two will be great together. You'll see.'

'That's good to know. Thanks,' smiled Greg. ''Cos Leni said I'll be in charge of this new comic.'

'What? You? She must be fucking mad.'

'Apparently not, according to you.'

'But I thought I'd be the editor.'

'It was part of the deal. Mate.'

'I see,' said Dave bitterly, taking his turn with the plasticine.

'So ... your *Sunset Boulevard* routine finally paid off?'

'You wouldn't know what a casting couch is,' jeered Greg.

'I know what a casting *desk* is,' said Dave. 'How long did you have to spend crouched underneath it to persuade her?'

'Too long.' Greg shuddered at the memory as he aimed at the target.

'Your tongue must be worn out,' said Dave unsympathetically. 'No wonder you're so quiet these days.'

'I earned my reward. I'm the editor. Not you. Got it?'

'I hope you're going to put a bit more research into your stories, then,' said Dave, viciously hurling the plasticine at the wall with all his might.

'What's to research?' said Greg, collecting the ball. 'It's science fiction. We just make it up.'

He hurled it equally savagely at the wall.

Dave removed it and squeezed it back into a ball. 'Like your *Moby*

Jaw, about a whale swimming up the Thames and crawling on his flippers to attack people in Piccadilly Circus.'

He flung it at Greg who ducked. 'I felt that lacked a certain realism.'

'So what new literary masterpieces are you dreaming up, Dave?' Greg sneered, throwing the ball back at him. 'Another disability classic? What is it this time? A story about a braille mountain climber? Hmm? *Rachel Feels the Rocks?* Where will it all fucking end?'

Dave closed in menacingly on Greg. 'You know I'm getting a little bored with your snide comments and passive aggression.'

'Okay,' said Greg. 'Let's have some real aggression.'

Dave jumped on Greg and they rolled around on the floor, trying to shove plasticine in each other's mouths. 'You ponce around with your equivalent of an LBD,' snarled Dave.

Greg moulded the plasticine to the contours of Dave's face.

'It's how I get laid, Dave. It's how I get to be the editor. Watch and learn, you freak.'

'You only use women as surrogates because you really wanted to fuck Bernie,' jeered Dave, shoving him away. 'When you're fucking them, you're actually thinking of him.'

'Better than wanting to fuck fur coats.'

'Better than being the publisher's gigolo,' said Dave standing up.

'At least I know what to do with her,' Greg retorted. 'What did you do? End up sticking it her ear?' He hurled another lump of plasticine at him.

The missile caught a glum-faced Ron in the face as he entered. He sniffed the air and his eyes flickered wildly from side to side. His lips bared and his hands reached for an invisible Sten gun as he recognised the familiar smell of the enemy.

It was 1944, and he was a nineteen-year old soldier again. Yelling 'Down! Get down!' he hit the ground.

Dave and Greg looked at Ron writhing on the floor, facing invisible enemies, and didn't know what to say. There was a long, uncomfortable silence for several seconds as he lay there, fearfully cursing, 'Fuck-shit-fuck-shit-fuck-shit.'

Then Ron recognised his surroundings. He got up. Adjusted his clothes, dusted himself off and, with a contemptuous curl of his lip at the two of them, walked out of their office.

There was a stunned silence after he had gone. Greg lit another Roth Handle. Finally Dave spoke: 'Leni's dad was probably smoking them on the Atlantic Wall.'

Greg looked at his cigarette. 'That'll be it.' There was a further long silence.

'Are you okay?' Dave asked.

'Not really,' muttered Greg. 'That was bad.'

'That was bad,' agreed Dave.

'You know what?' Greg said, slowly shaking his head. 'I don't think I can do this anymore. There's only so much green snot I can eat. I'm going to end it with her.'

Dave nodded, with genuine empathy for a change. 'I think you have to, Greg. I'm sorry.'

'It'll cost me the editorship, but what the fuck.' Greg stubbed his cigarette out in the ashtray.

Dave went after Ron. He caught up with him as he approached his office.

'Ron! Ron, are you okay?' The managing editor ignored Dave and kept on walking with his usual proud military bearing.

'Ron ... what is it? What did you want? What did you come in for?' Ron didn't reply.

Outside Ron's office, his secretary was sobbing, 'Oh God. That's terrible.'

Joy and Bridget Paris were trying to console her, and seemed close to tears themselves. Deep Throat and Tom Morecambe were close-by, having a hushed conversation with Dmitri and Guthrie.

'What's wrong?' asked Dave, taking in the disturbing scene. 'What's happened?'

An ashen-faced Ron turned to Dave.

'Ron ...?' Dave asked again.

'The Major's dead.'

'How?'

'In Soho. He was stabbed to death.'

CHAPTER THIRTY-SEVEN

AFTER THE FUNERAL, the reception was held at The Eight Veils. As well as the Fleetpit crowd, there were groups of ex-wives and girlfriends and debtors, many of whom knew the Major by different names and ranks, as well as his real name: Private John Taylor of the Army Catering Corps. Some still seemed to think he was a Battle of Britain fighter pilot.

Paula was crying, still stunned by his death. 'I haven't had such a shock since I was a teenager. Woke up next to a dead Chinaman in a Chinese laundry. He'd overdone the pipe of dreams.'

Dave resisted bringing out his own pipe of comfort. He was in a state of shock that someone he cared about was dead, thanks to what he had done.

Leni was standing next to him, crying her heart out, which was surprising as she had never actually met the Major.

Then Dave realised it was because she still hadn't got over her breakup with Greg.

'I've lost my schnookie,' she lamented. 'He dumped me. He dumped me.'

Dave backed away from her emotional outpourings and headed towards Greg, who was keeping well out of her way.

So the weeping, six-footer, dressed in a smart black power suit, turned to Joy for comfort. 'Because I'm so tall, men don't understand

I'm also soft, vulnerable and easily hurt, just like other women,' she sobbed.

Joy gave her a silent 'Like I give a fuck?' look, lit another cigarette and started to sidle away from her.

But Leni pursued her. 'It's easy for you, Joy. Because you're petite, you can get sympathy from men any time you want. They think you're sweet and cute.'

'Let them think what they fucking want,' Joy growled.

'But it's so hard for me, when I've lost my schnookieputz,' complained Leni and she collapsed into tears again.

'Leni, can I remind you, we're here to remember the Major,' said Joy coldly.

'I know. I know. I just can't help myself,' said Leni.

'I don't work on *Mumsy*. I'm not Marjorie Rayner. I can't help you.'

'Ja. Ja,' said Leni. 'I will talk to Marjorie. She will help me get over Greg.'

'Right now, I want to get over the Major's death,' said Joy pointedly.

'Ja. Ja. Group hug. Group hug, everybody.'

The Fleetpit contingent had no choice but to comply with their publisher: Roger Baker, the Caning Commando artist; Joy; Bridget; Deep Throat; Dmitri; Guthrie; Dave; Ron and others. Everyone but Greg, who was hiding in the gents. Ron scowled contemptuously at his tearful enemy, which gave way to an expression of horror as she drew the circle ever closer until his face was crushed into her double-D bosom.

Dave couldn't understand his feelings. He didn't feel self-hatred or guilt at being responsible for the Major's death. Instead, he felt self-hatred and guilt that he didn't feel self-hatred and guilt. What was wrong with him? Was he a sociopath? Probably, he concluded. Then he decided he couldn't be, because he was actually feeling something, only he couldn't put a label on his feelings, except he knew they were painful.

To get away from those feelings, he focused on the details of the murder. The Major had been stabbed with a misericorde, a medieval dagger used to penetrate the gaps in suits of armour and give wounded knights the *coup de grace*. The police knew this because the blade had remained lodged in the Major's body as he fought back. So at least Dave now knew what the killer had in the boot of his car.

As always, the Major had improvised when it came to weapons, and smashed his killer in the face with his portable typewriter before, he fell dying to the ground. His broken machine lay beside him, the keys scattered across the pavement, as the killer made his getaway.

There was speculation that he was someone from the Major's colourful past: a debtor or an angry husband. There were numerous suspects, but Dave knew the truth. It had to be the anonymous caller who worked somewhere in Fleetpit House on any one of its endless publications.

The Major's last *Caning Commando* story had been found in his typewriter case, ready for the artist to break down into pictures and illustrate, and it was now being respectfully passed around for the mourners to read. As Ron handed the story to Dave, its title sent a shockwave of feelings through him.

The Caning Commando. The character the Major had created to save his life, but which, ultimately, had led to his death.

Because of Dave.

Were his feelings his wake-up call? Warning him that it was over? That he should now reject his criminal ways and start a new life? The pain he felt was so intense, it seemed like the only way to make it stop.

To hand himself in. Confess what he'd been doing. And accept the consequences. Take his punishment.

But the demons that drove him didn't see it that way. And they told him a different, far better solution.

Not to feel anything at all. Like comic book heroes.

Like the Caning Commando himself.

Dave remembered how readers never want the heroes they love to change. The most popular remain endlessly in stasis, never ageing, never evolving, never marrying and having families. They face murder and mayhem on a daily basis, and are rarely troubled by it.

At the loss of someone close to them, they feel pain briefly and then it passes. There would be a token scene of mourning, a few cool words and a gritted-teeth glare before they stoically head off into the symbolic darkness.

They had learnt how to bury their feelings.

Dave had spent his life reading and writing such heroes. They had been his role models. They were the only role models he had, apart from Mr Cooper and Ernie Gambo.

If it was good enough for his heroes, it was good enough for him. Their way was the way he would get through this.

Gritting his teeth, he started to read the story.

It was told at the usual frenetic pace, reflecting the speed with which the Major would have written it. Usually around fifteen minutes. Like the other mourners, despite the sadness of the occasion, Dave found himself smiling at the title of the Major's last story:

The Bum Note

It began when Alf Mast was kidnapped by the enemy and taken to Berlin. The kidnapping puzzled Victor Grabham: why would the Germans go to the trouble of kidnapping an idiot like Corporal Punishment who was afflicted with wet rot of the feet and dry rot of the brain? There was one possible explanation. They wanted to discover the secrets of the Caning Commando.

But Grabham knew Alf would never break under interrogation. He could endure extreme torture due to having a goldfish-like memory. And, although he had the ignorance of an entire busload of dullards, his plucky young companion also had the courage of a legless whippet.

Eleven other British schoolboys – intelligent ones – had also been mysteriously kidnapped, and a ticket to the Berlin Opera House had been found at the scene of one of the crimes. Grabham was parachuted into Berlin to find out the truth.

At the Opera House, he discovered yet another of his greatest enemies was responsible: Arsene Assbender, 'The Phantom of the Opera', a mad German composer, his face hideously scarred after the Caning Commando had once thrown hot tea over him.

German soldiers emerged from the wings and turned their guns on the black-robed teacher.

'Drop your cane, Grabham,' sneered Assbender, and the Commando realised he had been led into a deadly trap.

The Phantom gloatingly revealed to Grabham that he had discovered the manuscript of Mozart's legendary missing masterpiece: *The Magic Cane*. And he intended to perform it as the composer originally intended, with Alf Mast as the star!

Grabham was flabbergasted. Mast, the star of an opera?!

It was unthinkable. Why Mast, with his thick Cockney accent, could barely speak the King's English, never mind sing in German!

But now the curtain was going up on the opening night of *The Magic Cane* in front of opera lover Reichsfuhrer Hermann Goering himself. As the orchestra played the overture, Grabham snarled at Assbender: 'I fail to comprehend why you chose Mast, Assbender? I have heard lungfish with greater vocal range, and seen bison with more grace.'

By way of explanation, with a flourish, the mad maestro revealed a row of bent-over British schoolboys whom he was about to thrash. At the end of the line-up was Alf Mast! Under heavy guard, the boys were unable to move. The soldiers also trained their guns on the Caning Commando, so he, too, could do nothing.

Assbender flicked back his flowing mane. 'Every boy has been specially chosen, Grabham. When caned, each one will produce a different note, just as Mozart intended.

'But … there was still *one note* missing to make my singspiel complete. Then I discovered Alf Mast has the perfect falsetto note I was looking for. He will hit the highest note of all.'

Grabham remembered the high note Alf once hit when he caned him for having saucy pictures of 'bumpy men'.

'I fear you're right, Assbender. Unlike his trousers, his voice has never dropped.'

The cheery Cockney agreed. 'My voice never broke, despite you breaking several canes on me, sir.' He was delighted to be thrashed alongside the public school boys. Under normal circumstances, he would have been regarded as much too common to be caned with the toffs.

Waving two canes, the Phantom strode up and down the line of his victims, inflicting a series of blows, which producing a range of high-pitched screams.

From his private box, a sneering Goering smiled his appreciation.

'I am delighted you came to hear my "organ", Caning Commando,' jeered the Phantom.

Then it was Alf Mast's turn. The Phantom raised his canes over Mast's rear.

'And now! Enjoy the star performance of *The Magic Cane*.'

'You swine, Assbender!' snarled Grabham, seething with impotent fury that he could not go to the aid of his companion.

With a gloating, manic laugh, Assbender thrashed the brave young Cockney.

As the blows landed on him, Alf let loose an earth-shattering high C of such lung power that the Opera House chandelier exploded.

The windows smashed.

And even Goering's monocle cracked.

It was the chance Grabham had been waiting for. Taking advantage of the chaos, the sinister, black-robed teacher seized his cane, leapt for the chandelier chain, and swung through the air on it, sending his guards flying. He used it to hurtle across the Opera House to Goering's private box and jumped down inside.

There, he belayed the Reichsmarshal's bounteous buttocks, then threw the screaming Nazi out onto the stage.

Finally, he leapt back down into the orchestra pit to confront the Phantom, as the 'caning chorus', led by Alf Mast, was finishing off their guards.

'Your time has come, Assbender!' the Commando roared as he swung his cane. 'It's time to Carpet Bum the Hun!'

Wielding two canes, the mad organist had the advantage of him at first and delivered a series of lethal blows to the Commando's rear. But the wily teacher could take it: he bit on a bullet, a time-honoured method of surviving a flogging.

Then, spitting out the bullet, it was his turn. 'Know, Assbender, that canes are school swords which the Almighty has committed to the hands of teachers that they may chastise the wicked with them. And you are in for such a chastisement!'

Again and again he struck. 'High and hard, low and mean!' Soon his old enemy was reduced to a blubbering heap.

'Mercy! Mercy!' Assbender begged.

'No chance,' said the teacher. 'My bowels of compassion never move.'

A light aircraft landed outside the opera house. The Commando and the boys just managed to squeeze inside. The aircraft was barely able to take off with so many passengers.

But, finally, it was aloft, narrowly avoiding the roof of the Berlin Opera House. It came under heavy fire from anti-aircraft guns as the pilot desperately tried to gain height.

The Phantom and Goering ordered the gunners to concentrate their fire on the plane. They could not permit the Caning Commando to escape. Not after they had been humiliated by such a first-rate flogging.

A wing strut was broken off by the flak. Then the wing started to tear itself free from the fuselage. It looked like the aircraft would crash.

The Phantom and Goering exchanged triumphant looks.

'Finally it is all over for the Caning Commando,' exulted Goering.

But Grabham courageously climbed out of the plane, as it continued to lurch up into the night sky, with flak bursting all around it.

He desperately clung onto the fuselage as he used his cane to replace the broken strut and stabilise the wing.

And then they flew back towards Blighty and safety, landing in the grounds of the Golden Hind Academy,

'Thank you for rescuing me, sir,' said Alf Mast as they entered the school. 'I was thrilled to be with the posh boys today.'

'And so you should be, Mast. However, that temporary lowering of the boundary between the human and animal kingdoms should not give you any ideas. You must remember your place, boy.'

'I think I remember it, sir,' said Alf uncertainly. 'Is it my tree-ape nest, sir?'

'Indeed it is. Make sure you put fresh straw in it.' The Caning

Commando gave him a cold smile. 'Or there will be music in the music room and I will be beating time with my stick.'

* * *

'The Bum Note' was possibly the most ludicrous and unlikely *Caning Commando* story the Major had ever written – although there were other serious contenders – and it was the perfect tribute to his comic-writing genius.

Ron addressed the mourners. 'The Major didn't deserve what happened to him.'

'You're right,' said Dave sadly. 'He didn't deserve it at all.'

'I hope they find the evil bastard who killed the Major.' The others nodded their agreement.

'They should never have done away with capital punishment,' said Ron.

'And I hope they find him soon,' said Dave. 'Very soon.' The others looked surprised by his vehemence. 'I mean, he could strike again, couldn't he?'

Ron raised his glass. 'To the Major. An officer and a gentleman.'

The mourners raises their glasses in response. 'To the Major. An officer and a gentleman.'

Dave, too, raised his glass to the man he had betrayed and silently asked for his forgiveness. His plan to use the Major as his scapegoat had worked only too well.

'Goodnight, John-Boy.'

As the evening wore on, the legendary tales about the Major grew ever bawdier. Ron told Dave and Greg how, when he and the Major were in Spain looking for artists, they had tried out the slimming belts in a gym.

'We'd had a couple of gallons of that fucking piss-poor Spanish beer and we dropped our strides and tried the weight-loss machines with the vibrating belts. It was all right.

'Then the Major, he says, "I've got an idea, dear boy". So then he turns round and puts the belt around his wedding tackle. And it went like the fucking clappers. "What's it like?" I asked him. "It's shining my privates up splendidly, Ron," he says. "Oh, by crikey yes. They're absolutely sparkling."

'Unfortunately, just as the Major was about to whitewash the wall, in comes the fucking local jefe of police, right in his line of fire. Fucking hell, chum. The Old Bill's uniform ended up looking like a plasterer's overalls.'

The story seemed about as likely to Dave and Greg as the Major's *Caning Commando* stories. But then Dave had to remind himself that truth is generally stranger than fiction, and the Major was a larger than life character.

In effect, it was no less likely than a killer stabbing a comics writer to death, and pursuing a comics editor next.

Meanwhile, Leni was telling Joy about her great idea for the new sf comic.

'We bring back Dan Darwin from *Homework*. We'll get huge publicity for the comic.'

'I don't know, Leni,' said Joy diplomatically. 'Dan Darwin's a famous strip, but it's really a bit old school, don't you think?'

'That's okay,' Leni shrugged. 'Dave and Greg can update it.'

'I don't know if it's really their thing.'

'I can help them. I have lots of ideas. My ex-husband works for NASA.'

'Really?'

'Ja,' Leni chuckled. 'He used to call me his Space Cadet.'

'He knew you were out of touch with reality?'

'No.' Leni looked puzzled. 'Because when NASA get the go-ahead for the civilian space program, I will be high on the list.'

Joy took in this surprising news.

'That's why I married him,' Leni explained. 'And also because he has a big penis. I've done all the basic training. Flying. Deep-sea diving. Going up in the vomit comet.'

'So how could you help with Dan Darwin?'

'Because I know all about the E.T.'s. I want to bring them in from space, you see? I've talked to "the boys" and they tell me they want to come in from the cold.'

' "The boys"?'

'I channel them every night.'

'D'you think … y'know … when you're out there in space,' said Joy very casually, 'you might actually want to stay there, Leni? It could be the best way for you to help "the boys"?'

The statuesque blonde considered this. 'Ja. This is what my ex said. This is why I'm so high on the NASA list. And because I managed to get into Vandenberg Air Force Base. I got to meet the Commander of the Space Shuttle launch program. He thought it was an excellent idea for me to be sent into space.'

'I can see where he's coming from.'

'I really need to talk to Steven Spielberg, too. He's making a film about the E.T.'s.'

'I heard. *Close Encounters?*'

'Ja. He hasn't been returning my calls. Next time I'm in LA, I find him.' Entering a guarded Hollywood film set would be no problem for a woman who could get into Greek prisons, Vandenberg Air Force Base, or meet Tribal Elders on the Third Mesa. Leni's great talent was she was oblivious to rejection. The words 'fuck off' were meaningless to her. They just didn't register on her radar. Joy felt rather sorry for Steven Spielberg.

Joy returned to the subject of Dan Darwin. 'There's also the original creator to consider. How he'd feel about Dan coming back with a new look and a new creative team.'

Leni looked puzzled. 'What's it got to do with him? He doesn't have any say in it. Fleetpit owns Dan Darwin now.'

'But you're going to pay the artist for using his creation, I hope?' asked an apprehensive Joy.

Leni laughed. 'Why?'

'Because it's the *right* thing to do,' said Joy, knocking back her drink.

'We're going to pay him zilch, honey,' said Leni, 'because that's our legal right.'

'You may have a legal right, but do you have a moral right?'

'What's morality got to do with it?' snapped an irritated Leni. The Queen of New Agers didn't like being challenged. The women's raised voices caused a curious Greg and Dave to look over.

'It's theft,' Joy glowered.

'It's *publishing*,' sneered Leni.

'Doesn't matter if it's legal theft, it's still theft,' seethed Joy.

'He should have thought of that before he signed away all his rights,' said Leni.

'He's an artist, not a fucking Suit,' said Joy.

'Tough shit,' Leni snarled 'I own the character. I can do what I like with him. He's my property! So keep your hands off him!'

'Girls, girls,' said a smiling Greg, sauntering over and happy to be the peacemaker. He opened his arms expansively. 'There's need to fight. There's enough of me to go around.'

'Fuck off, Greg!' said Leni and Joy together.

CHAPTER THIRTY-EIGHT

IT WAS JUST three weeks to go before Fleetpit Publications moved from Farringdon Street to join its parent media group in their new headquarters in Southwark. Joy drove Dave and Greg down past Blackfriars Bridge and parked opposite the tower that could be seen clearly across the Thames, now the final scaffolding had been cleared away. The 44-storey, black glass building, 123 metres tall, dominated the London skyline.

'The Bard of Avon tower,' said an impressed Greg.

'How ironic,' drawled Dave, 'that a tower named after William Shakespeare, one of the world's greatest writers, will be producing some of the most lowbrow publications the world has ever known.'

'But we're going to change that, aren't we, Dave?' said Joy.

'Are we?' said Dave uncertainly.

'With *Space Warp*.'

Dave had thought up and had the title approved for his new sf comic. Following her break-up with Greg, Leni had decided Dave should be the editor.

'Featuring the new *Dan Darwin*,' Greg added.

'I still say it's a mistake bringing him back,' said Joy.

'Too late, Joy,' said Dave. 'She's calling that press conference right now to announce the space hero's return.'

'Right outside the Bard,' smiled Joy. 'Perfect.'

They spread out in a line, looking across the river towards South London and the Bard.

'The press will love it,' said Greg. 'It's going to be huge publicity for *Space Warp*.' Joy checked her watch.

'Is it time?' asked a worried Greg.

'Not yet.'

Dave checked his watch. 'Three minutes to eleven.'

They waited in silence as the minutes slowly ticked away. Dave looked blankly ahead, feeling nothing, thinking nothing.

A tense Greg looked anxiously across the river. Joy nervously paced up and down.

Then she went back to the car and looked at her watch again.

'Okay. It's time.'

She switched on the cassette player. 'Thus Spake Zarathustra' from the movie *2001: A Space Odyssey*, boomed out at full blast.

And, at the Eleventh Hour, the sun rose in the heavens and the towering black slab of the Bard gleamed with a mysterious and unearthly light.

It truly resembled the Black Monolith.

'It's a Stargate,' said Dave looking up at it in awe.

'A portal to other times and galaxies,' said Greg equally moved.

'Warping time and space,' said Dave.

'A doorway to other realities,' murmured Joy.

'The perfect command centre for *Space Warp*,' said Dave.

'Let the Space Odyssey begin,' said Greg.

'You realise,' said Joy in a hushed whisper, looking up at the mysterious edifice, 'this could be the most powerful, most meaningful moment in the history of British comics.'

The insistent drums of Zarathustra beat ever louder and the music rose towards an emotional, triumphant crescendo.

'It's inspiring us,' said Greg, speaking in equally hushed tones, absorbing the energy of the dark obelisk. 'To create a comic that's never been done before. A comic that could change its readers lives.'

'At the Eleventh Hour,' said Joy reverentially. 'British comics were rescued from oblivion.'

'With the birth of a new and very different science fiction comic … *Space Warp*,' said Greg.

'And it's in the hands of monkeys,' said Dave, thinking of the movie.

'Yes,' agreed Greg. 'You should have brought along your gorilla suit.'

As the music approached its dramatic, lyrical, soul-soaring finale, a banner was unfurled from the top of the Monolith and ran down the side of the edifice. It read:

TIME MACHINE: Comics. SF. Movie Props. Toys. Collectables. Cinema. Horror. Fantasy. London's ultimate sci-fi shop

'Right on time,' smiled Joy. 'It'll be seen all over London.'

'Leni's going to love you,' grinned Dave.

Joy's banner caught in the wind and flipped over, revealing a caption emblazoned across the other side, which read:

REPENT MALE CHAUVINISTS
YOUR WORLD IS COMING TO AN END

'From my Women's Liberation days,' Joy explained. Dave and Greg looked at her disapprovingly.

'Well, I didn't want the banner to go to waste.'

As it flapped in the wind, she glowered across the water at her unseen staff, who she'd told to enter the Bard and carry out the stunt from the top floor.

'Fucking idiots. I told them to weigh it down. Properly.'

'The slogan is very you, Joy,' said Dave.

'We had some great slogans in those days,' Joy recalled with relish. 'Don't cook dinner. Starve a rat today ... Housewives are unpaid slaves. End human sacrifice. Don't get married.'

'I imagine you were one of those "yelling harpies" who threw stink bombs at the Miss World contest?' suggested Dave.

'Oh, yes,' grinned Joy. 'I was there with my rattle and flour bombs.'

'So that was you?' said an outraged Greg. 'Bernie and I were enjoying lusting after Miss Africa South and Miss Sweden.'

'That was when I decided to stop being a nice person,' Joy explained.

'And you've stayed true to yourself,' said Dave. Joy looked over at the Black Monolith.

'I loved *2001,*' she said. 'Especially the ending.'

Thus Spake Zarathustra had come to its powerful, emotional and epic conclusion.

And all was silence now.

She looked anxiously over at them both. 'We'll get it right this time, won't we, boys?'

CHAPTER THIRTY-NINE

DAVE'S PHONE RANG. It was the anonymous caller. 'The Major got his, Maudling. I'm coming for you next, you fuck pig,' he whispered down the phone.

'F-F-F-Fuck!' said Dave.

'You'll never know where or when, but I'm watching you, fuck pig, waiting for the right moment. I am going to hurt you so bad, you will beg for death. Then I'm going to pour Greek fire all over you.'

'What's that?' asked Dave.

'It's a burning liquid, like napalm,' the caller whispered. 'It bursts into flames on contact with your body. It will stick to your face. You will …'

The caller spoke so softly, Dave had to ask: 'Sorry. It's a bad line. Could you repeat that please?'

'It's a burning liquid …' the caller began.

'I got that. No, just the last bit.'

'I said, it will stick to your face and you will die in agony, you fuck pig.'

'Well, bring it on, you fuck pig. Okay?' Dave snarled down the phone. 'I'll be waiting. And I'm going to make you fucking pay, you bastard. Got it? So fuck you. Fuck you. Fuck you.' He shouted for good measure. 'Fuck you!'

In response, the line had gone dead.

Dave realised he wanted to make the anonymous caller pay for killing the Major so badly, it had taken care of his fear.

He became aware that Greg was sitting opposite, staring wide-eyed at him.

'What was all that about?' asked a concerned Greg

'Oh, just an artist.'

'Just an artist?'

'You know what they're like when we reject their work.'

'Oh, yeah. Artists,' said a dismissive Greg, returning to his editing. 'What? Is he sending you a turd in the post? It's not another dead rat?'

'Dead fish,' said Dave. "I told him his pages hit me like a wet cod. So he's sending me one.'

'Couldn't handle a little constructive criticism, eh?' Greg nodded sympathetically. 'It wasn't Leggett?'

'Leggett?'

'The artist that agent kept locked in her attic so he'd finish his work on time?'

'I don't see how it could be Leggett,' said Dave, looking meaningfully at Greg.

'Oh, yeah.' Greg shuddered as he remembered. 'A bad business.'

'A bad business,' agreed Dave.

'A very bad business.'

'I had no idea, at first, that he was writing secret messages on his artwork.' Dave reflected. 'Saying, "Help me. My agent's holding me against my will." '

'She always saw his messages and whitened them out.'

'When I saw "SOS" on the side of a desk he'd drawn, I became suspicious. Then, when I studied the page closely, I could just see in tiny letters a plea for help she'd missed.'

Greg nodded. 'Not that it did him any good. Because then we whitened his messages out, too.'

'Just until he'd finished drawing his story for us.'

'Well, we had to. We had to get our priorities right. And by then ... well ... it was, sadly, too late.'

'And it did give you a great idea for a story, Greg.'

'*Flora's in the Attic.* A young girl, a talented artist, who is being worked to death by her cruel art agent and never allowed out of the attic.'

'Drawing from dawn to midnight and wondering, "Where will it all end?"'

'Some people thought it was in really bad taste, especially as the agent did actually run a florist's, below.'

'But, you know, I had some sympathy with her: listening to artists' excuses why they're late with their work, day in day out, year in year out, I guess the poor woman just couldn't take anymore *mañana* bullshit. Something inside her ... snapped.'

'I guess something inside Leggett snapped, too. When she opened that attic door and he was waiting for her ...'

Greg winced as he remembered.

'I don't feel that bad about it,' mused Dave. 'He's an artist. What did she expect?'

'They should really be given a mental health assessment before we hire them,' agreed Greg.

'Even so, pity the real-life version of *Flora's in the Attic* ended so badly. No happy ending there, eh?'

'There you go, Dave. Real life always ends badly.'

* * *

A few days later Dave entered *The Spanker* offices after a meeting with Leni. He was in a surprisingly upbeat mood.

'Any luck?' asked Greg hopefully.

'Sorry. The pendulum says it's got to be me. She's really excited about it.'

'Are you sure that's why she was excited? Did you check behind her modesty board?'

'Nobody there. Nope, she's genuinely excited at me going on *Tomorrow's Britain.*'

'I'd have happily done it, you know?'

'I told her that, Greg. But she said "The monster who kicked the *Newshound* dog? I don't think so." '

The *Tomorrow's Britain* star, Fabulous Keen, had rung the publisher asking to do an interview with the editor of *Space Warp*, the man who was bringing back *Dan Darwin*, so it really had to be Dave.

Dave was apprehensive at first, but then he reminded himself that Keen had absolutely no idea who he was. They had only come face to face when Dave was wearing his Spanish Inquisition hood. Of course they had met once before, when Dave was a fifteen-year old errand boy, but that wouldn't connect him with the murderous events at the Feast of Mary Magdalene.

And the interview was to take place at TV Centre, so there was really nothing to worry about. Even if Keen somehow knew it was him, what could he possibly do in a studio, in front of the cameras?

Dave rather enjoyed the thought of flirting with danger.

'You know, now that Leni's out of my life, I've been doing a lot of thinking,' said Greg as Dave got ready to leave.

'Uh-huh,' said Dave.

Greg held up a book. 'I've been reading *The Book of est*. It tears you down and then puts you back together. It's made me realise just how I'm wasting my life here.'

Dave picked it up. 'Luke Rhinehart. Wrote *The Diceman*, where the hero makes important life decisions on the roll of a die.'

'That's him,' said Greg. 'And I've decided the sensible thing for me to do is to hand in my notice and go freelance.'

'I think you're doing absolutely the right thing, Greg,' said Dave. 'It's a very brave decision. To hell with security.'

'Exactly,' said Greg, clicking his pen. 'Who needs a regular income, a pension and paid holidays?' He shrugged his shoulders. 'Fuck it!'

'Fuck it!' agreed Dave. He flicked through the book. 'Yes, this is definitely the way to empowerment and enlightenment.' And the dole queue for you, Greg, he thought to himself. With Greg out of the way, it would bring Joy and him closer again. They could do *Space Warp* together. Long intimate evenings discussing stories, making her laugh. The Two Musketeers.

All for one and one for two.

CHAPTER FORTY

DAVE REFLECTED on his threatening the Major's killer and facing up to Fabulous Keen on the long journey on the Central Line to the studios at White City. He'd always assumed his courage came from his mother or his demons. Then the thought hit him: perhaps it actually came from himself? Was that possible? Because here he was, on the Underground, unconcerned and barely aware of his fellow passengers, any one of whom might be about to thrust a misericorde between his ribs.

It made him think of his boyhood encounter with Mother 'Vinegar Bottle' St Vincent, the Sister of Sorrow who made Mother Theresa look like Audrey Hepburn. He had been talking to his school friends about Konrad, his mother's relationship with the Canon, and the priest's other forms of communion with his young parishioners. He had been overheard by Vinegar Bottle, who made him go and pray in church and ask God for forgiveness for his terrible lies. But that didn't work. The next day he still related, with mischievous glee, the Canon's extra-clerical activities. Something had to be done about young David.

The way Dave originally remembered it was as a compressed memory, stripped of any detail. The nun was squeezing him by the throat and warning him never to speak about what he had seen or heard, or she would personally send him to Hell. It clearly worked, because he had no idea what he had seen or heard.

But now, so many years later, the door to his memories had been opened and he recalled it all vividly as the tube train trundled through to the West End.

He was being escorted down an immaculate blue corridor inside the nunnery. While the other boys were in the playground after school dinner, he was being taken to the Holy of Holies and he felt a strong sense of exultation. He was going to the batcave. His school chums would be so jealous. He was being singled out for being so bad.

The swishing of the nun's robes; their fusty old lady smell; the rattle of her heavy rosary beads against her outsize, lethal crucifix: it all reinforced the little boy's hostility towards her.

And his pride. Because it was unheard of for a primary school kid to enter the nunnery. This was serious business. Nun and boy went through a central hall and, as he took in his surroundings, he was disappointed to find there were no overhead beams, even though he had insisted to his playground pals that at night, the nuns slept hanging upside down from them, like bats.

Then the excited boy was ushered into Mother St Vincent's office. The batcave itself. The Holy of Holies. It was a stark, sparse room furnished only with a desk, filing cabinet, a crucifix, and paintings of the Sacred Heart of Jesus and the founder of the Sisters of Sorrow. The walls were painted with a pastel 'holy' green. There was a stained-glass Gothic window and, unbelievably, it showed a depiction of the martyr St Sebastian, being shot to death by arrows.

Looking back as an adult, this seemed most unlikely. Why would there be an image of an almost nude man, impaled by arrows, in a convent? For a moment, it made Dave doubt the rest of his memories as fanciful delusions, but nevertheless that was his clear recollection with the sunlight streaming through the saint's muscular, naked torso as he was used for target practice.

It was an apparently pain-free death and its hidden significance was lost on the liquorice detective. But it suggested the joy and the sweetness of pain and suffering and of being pierced, yet pure. The wider esoteric implications of this were not generally aired, known or discussed in the outer circle of the religion. The secret meaning and the importance of St Sebastian, who had been a gay icon for centuries, Dave was totally unaware of.

The headmistress was joined by two other nuns, and the three Sisters of Sorrow stared solemnly down at the small boy.

Mother St Vincent knew she had no choice now but to make an example of this defiant child. His parents were not simply working-class folk who could be intimidated into silence by her presence alone. David's father had a good job at Pell's and the firm was an important benefactor of the church. The mother was no better than she should be, with her film-star looks and her fancy furs; however she was also a member of the Virgin Soldiers and the nun sensed there was a defiance about her, too, that she had somehow passed onto her son.

In fact, there had been rumours about Mrs Maudling and the Canon, born out by the boy's rude talk and that disgraceful drawing he was showing his pals, which she'd torn up. So she had wondered whether the poor man had succumbed to the temptress; just as she knew he had succumbed to that wicked little boy, Konrad, who had led him astray.

She had been forced to ask the Canon about Mrs Maudling, but he assured her that they were just friends and 'nothing happened below the belt'.

Mother St Vincent's bat sisters were also present to intimidate the hell out of David and ensure he never spoke of the Canon's behaviour. Yet, already, she could see from the impertinent expression on his face, his horrid eyes gleaming with delight, that this little monster was somehow enlivened by the thought of three nuns dealing with him. The very opposite effect of what she had intended. He was meant to be awed by being ushered into the Holy of Holies and yet, perversely, he was enjoying every moment of it. As far as David was concerned, the more nuns the better. Ten nuns would have been good.

This made the headmistress afraid, and somehow the child knew it; he sensed her fear. He couldn't articulate it in his mind, couldn't vocalise it with words, but the animal in him felt it intuitively and it gave him that slight smirk of triumph that also brought out the inner animal in Mother Saint Vincent. She was a small, Napoleonic woman, so she couldn't tower over him, in fact, they were almost head to head, her features convulsed with rage behind her silver spectacles.

And yet she was afraid, as she seized him by the throat and squeezed. Afraid of just what she might have to do silence this child who was endlessly talking about Konrad and the Canon and things that must *never* be spoken about. Because she had to protect the Church. Nothing must ever damage its reputation. That need and that fear drove her to violence, so, in that moment, she definitely wanted to kill him.

The boy knew it. And he didn't seem to care.

And so she squeezed, until he finally felt fear, causing her to *increase* her grip on his throat.

Now, at last, he was getting the message.

As his eyes bulged, he knew she was going to kill him, and that was how it should be. St Sebastian looked down on him, glorying in his own pain. There was an inner calm and resignation about the boy that matched the martyr, but yet owed nothing to him, only to his inner being.

Because he knew his death would destroy the nun.

The accompanying nuns tried to warn her, 'Mother! Mother … please! … Stop!' She realised she had almost gone too far.

But that didn't actually stop her. Because it still had to be done. He had to be silenced. For the sake of the church.

It was the expression on David's near-blue face, as fear turned to resignation, and then to triumph. She wouldn't be able to hush up his murder as they had hushed up Konrad's.

If there was a word in Dave's brain as his young life slipped away, it would have been 'Gotcha'.

It was that final defiance that brought her to her senses and released her grip. Coughing and spluttering and sucking air into his empty lungs, Dave returned to the land of the living.

There was an inevitable gag reflex, with unfortunate consequences for Mother St Vincent standing directly in front of him. His school dinner was ejected in all its splendour over her black robes. Semolina: a pallid pink, after he had stirred in the little dollop of jam they put on top. Diced carrots, mashed potatoes and spam luncheon meat, all thoroughly consumed following the exhortations of the school dinner lady, and already partially digested. A second retch erupted unidentifiable vomit from even deeper in his guts, which also splattered across her robes and crucifix.

He caught a treasured memory of the horrified expression on her face before he blacked out.

He awoke to find the antiseptically-clean room was now septic. But the Sisters of Sorrow were prepared for such everyday situations. A galvanised bucket of hot water, billowing Dettol-laced clouds of steam, was brought into the office; sawdust was liberally scattered on the floor of the batcave. David was ordered to clean the tiled floor. Disappointingly, they didn't ask him to wipe down Vinegar Bottle herself.

The memory shook Dave with its significance. He had always thought he was afraid. Like when he received his fourpenny one every Saturday from Mr Cooper. Clearly this was not true.

In that moment, it occurred to Dave that kids needed to *personally* exercise their vengeance on adults. It was *their* right; why should it be passed to disbelieving, useless authorities? And they should do it in any way they could get away with. And his example showed there were many, many ways. He was destined for his role in this total war.

All super heroes have a seminal experience in their youth that they look back on and realise that the inciting incident – sometimes forgotten, yet secretly motivating their actions – is what makes the man.

So Dave, too, had an experience that confirmed the role destiny had chosen for him. He had vomited on a nun.

It was a seminal moment as well as a semolina moment. Cheered by this thought, Dave got off at White City.

CHAPTER FORTY-ONE

IT WAS STILL LIGHT as Dave strode across Wood Lane to the Centre. With his rediscovered courage, he was actually looking forward to going on *Tomorrow's Britain*. Coming face to face with the man he had tried to murder. He ignored his mother, who was now playing 'Paint it Black' and 'Here Comes The Night' in his head. Okay, he got the message, there was danger, but Keen couldn't possibly know he was the one. 'Call me Cool Dave from now on,' he chuckled to himself.

There was a Jaguar parked just outside the barriers to the Centre. A burly chauffeur strode across to Dave. 'Dave Maudling? Mr Keen asked me to pick you up, sir.'

'Oh. Where are we going?'

'He wants to film you on location, sir. Is that okay?'

'Sure,' said Dave, impressed as the chauffeur opened the car door for him.

They pulled away into the evening rush hour traffic. 'What is the location?'

'Near Wimbledon, sir,' said the chauffeur, taking off his hat.

'There's a new recycling plant there. Very futuristic. Everything's automated. Mr Keen thought it would be a good location for interviewing you about Dan Darwin.'

'Like the inside of a spaceship, is it?' asked Dave enthusiastically.

'It's state of the art, sir,' said the Inspector. 'Very efficient. Burns everything. Nothing's left behind.'

Dave passed the time thinking about what he was going to say on *Tomorrow's Britain* about Dan Darwin. He loved the original premise of the serial: whether alien life on other planets had evolved from the same original source as life on Earth. For the Reverend Julius Cambridge, the founder of *Homework*, the story was intended as a search for evidence of the existence of a Supreme Being that was responsible for evolution. He wanted the hero to find signs of the Deity's existence on other planets throughout the Galaxy, and suggested the first story should be called *The Footprint of God*.

But the creator took a more agnostic approach. He based his story on the original *Voyage of the Beagle*; his hero even looked like Charles Darwin, combining his youthful appearance with the dark, haunted eyes of Darwin in later life. He created the Martian equivalent of the famous voyage, with vivid descriptions of Martian alien biology. Darwin meets a terrifying, complex, warlike race that have evolved on the red planet. Wasp-faced, humanoid creatures, the Vroors, sting and paralyse a gentle, peace-loving race of Martians, the Micans, as live food for their eggs.

The Micans appeal to Dan to save them and this raises the first of many dilemmas for the hero. Sir William, the Space Controller, gives him the go-ahead to help, but this will mean killing the Vroors. He tells Dan that we mercilessly kill germs on Earth and the Vroors are nothing more than giant germs. But Dan is not convinced, he feels he does not have the right to interfere in the evolution of life on Mars and there must be another way.

The Vroors, especially their emotionless leader, the Apokrita, captured the imagination of the readers and the beautifully illustrated, full-colour strip carried the rest of the magazine.

Dan Darwin, Voyage of the Spaceship Beagle would be a hard act to follow. But the 1950s science fiction hardware would look dated now: he'd need to give the legendary *Beagle* spaceship a NASA look. And was Joy right? Did Commander Darwin really fit alongside the other 'punk' characters he was going to dream up for *Space Warp*? Could he have a more edgy, seventies character? Like who? Bowie? A Space Oddity? Would that bother the readers? They'd probably like it, but it might bother their dads. But their dads weren't buying the comic. But was there an artist who could actually make that work? Probably not.

Maybe it was asking too much; maybe he should stick to the NASA look, play it safe, even though playing it safe wasn't Dave's style, especially not after *Aaagh!*

He was still going through the different possibilities as the Jaguar pulled into the recycling plant's car park. It was empty, but for Fab's Jensen Interceptor and a handful of workers' cars.

The factory was a futuristic, silver, shark-like building, gleaming in the late setting sun. 'It really does look like a spaceship,' said Dave, impressed. 'Maybe we could do some filming out here?'

The chauffeur said nothing.

'It's very quiet,' noticed Dave as they passed through the grey, industrial interior lined with endless silver pipes and stainless steel cylinders, silent but for the humming of machinery.

'Night shift.' said the chauffeur.

'Wimbledon. Good location for a recycling factory,' said Dave conversationally. 'Near the Wombles. I always liked the Wombles. Those fur suits.'

The chauffeur shepherded him towards a control room, and a waiting Fabulous Keen. Keen was wearing plain white overalls, which Dave found disappointing. With all those futuristic control boards behind him, he should have worn something more sinister, like Doctor No.

'You got him here OK, Inspector?' said Keen, shaking hands with the "chauffeur".

'No problem,' said the Inspector.

'Inspector?' asked a startled Dave. 'What's going on? Where's the camera crew?'

'On their way,' said Keen.

'When will they get here?'

'Relax, Dave,' said Keen. 'Let me show you around.' They descended steel steps to the incinerators. 'I'm given the run of the facility at night. I have what they call "unprecedented access". No checks, no monitoring, no supervision.'

'What? You like it here?'

'I like the solitude, Dave. It helps me meditate on the meaning of life. And the meaning of death.'

He indicated the technology. 'I've learnt to operate the whole system. Forklift trucks. Cranes. Flame injectors.' He smiled at Dave. 'Combustion chambers.'

Keen indicated a thick glass with a sign above it, which read

CONFINED SPACE. ENTRY PERMIT REQUIRED.
INSPECTION WINDOW.

'Take a look, Dave. Go on.' Dave saw the flames roaring within. 'Like Dante's Inferno, eh? The temperature in there is 950 degrees Celsius.'

'It ain't half hot, mum,' agreed the Inspector.

'Look,' said Keen, 'here's one I incinerated earlier,' pointing to a conveyor belt of ash emerging from a furnace. 'That'll be smeared all over the M25, Dave.'

'Where is everyone?' asked Dave, as they escorted him away from the combustion chamber. He was now in pre-panic mode.

'They're good lads,' said Keen. 'There's a drink in it for them if they stay out of my way.'

Dave looked down at a massive bunker below them filled with residual rubbish with a giant grabber poised ominously above it. 'This looks a bit like Apokra, the Martians' city. Are we going to talk about Dan Darwin here?'

'No, Dave, we're not going to talk about Dan Darwin here.'

'Ah. You've got somewhere more impressive in mind?'

'Dave,' said Keen, 'I don't give a shit about Dan Darwin.'

'I don't understand.'

'Let's not waste time, shall we?'

Keen held up the liquorice pipe he had found in his apartment. 'I know.' Dave blanched.

'I remember when you were a mod on your trade-bike. You should have stuck to rockers.'

Keen indicated the vast pit of rubbish awaiting incineration.

'I've brought quite a few people down here. They don't always walk out.' He looked Dave. 'You're not walking out.'

It was only now that Dave realised just how loud the hum of the machinery reprocessing the gases was, and how it would drown out his cries for help. That's if anyone would listen.

'People know I'm meeting you,' he warned. 'Questions will be asked.'

'You never arrived at the studio,' said the Inspector. 'I picked you up outside.'

'You disappeared. Just like your mum. God rest her soul,' said Keen.

Normally, when Dave was afraid, he talked volubly and nervously. But now he was silent, just as he was silent when St Vincent was strangling him.

Because there was no way out.

'It's good to see recycling making a come-back,' said Keen. 'That's how it used to be in the war. Right, Inspector?'

'Waste not, want not.'

'Then the baby boomers came along,' said Keen bitterly. 'Ungrateful little shits like you, Dave, wanting more than one square of Izal germicide to wipe your arse. Whining about everything. Thinking you could change the world when you have no idea what the world is really like.'

'You murdered my mother.'

'I think you're letting your imagination as a comic book writer run away with you.'

'All those comics you write were rotting your brain,' agreed the Inspector.

'You were involved in her murder, Keen.'

Keen suddenly lashed out at Dave, punching him viciously in the face. 'You murdered the Canon.'

Blood poured down Dave's face and onto his shirt.

'Now look what you've done to yourself,' said the Inspector. 'You look just like *Carrie* on prom night. I hope you've got telekinetic powers, because you'll need them to get out of this, son.'

'He's got no powers. He's waste. Toxic fucking waste,' said Keen punching Dave in the stomach. He doubled up, mouth open, trying to suck in air.

Then Keen kicked him into the bunker below. The foul bed of

stinking rubbish, organic matter, household waste and unmentionable things at least broke his fall.

'And that's where he fucking belongs.'

As Dave looked around him he saw that much of the rubbish had actually come from Fleetpit's vaults. Old artwork, typeset pages and bound volumes of magazines and comics, including *Forces Sweetheart, Radiogram Fun, Pram and Oven, Tranny, Twinset, Homework, Two Pennorth, The Great War, Casino for the Man About Town, Stately Piles, Tally Ho!, Fags Army, Members Only* and, inevitably, *The Fourpenny One.*

They, like Dave, were scheduled for incineration.

Keen sneered down at him. 'An errand boy on his trade-bike. You were never going to amount to anything. You were always rubbish.'

He turned his attention to the crane, operating it so it dropped down, its tines digging deep, and picking up a giant claw full of debris, with Dave, squeezed and wriggling, at its core. Just like the claw in the seaside arcade games, only this one wasn't rigged: it was holding onto its prize.

The Inspector and Keen had considered interrogating him before killing him. The Inspector, particularly, wanted to know how Dave was shootered up, but they had decided not to waste time, especially as he was clearly a lone nutter. If he had talked, no-one would believe him.

The grabber started to swing the trash, including Dave, over, ready to drop it into the adjoining hopper.

'That's where the hydraulic rams go to work,' Keen explained to Dave below.

'Crushing everything before it goes into the incinerator.'

'It can turn Demis Roussos into Dudley Moore,' said the Inspector.

Dave's horrified face was visible through the Fleetpit garbage and the massive, industrial prongs.

'First of all, Dave,' said Keen, operating the control box, 'your ribs will crack, so you'll find it hard to breathe, then your lungs will be punctured. Sometimes I crush 'em and leave 'em for a while. So they're screaming and begging. Or trying to, anyway. But it's not so good if they can't talk and can only blink. Blinking's not the same. I get bored when they blink.'

'He chews *Sherlock's*. We choose *Sherlock's*. Everyone chooses *Sherlock's*. He chews *Sherlock's* ...'

'Then you're ready for the furnace.' The grabber was now directly over the hopper and ready to disgorge into it.

'So, unless you're wearing flameproof clothing, I suggest you start saying your prayers, son,' said the Inspector.

'Did you know, Dave,' said Keen, 'that the ear is one of the last organs in the body to shut down? So you'll still be able to hear the hiss of the flame jets as you go in.'

'May the curse of Mary Malone and her nine blind illegitimate children chase you so far over the Hills of Damnation that the Lord himself can't find you with a telescope!' Dave suddenly screamed in a strong Irish accent.

He had never talked in an Irish accent before, but then he had never been about to be crushed in an industrial incinerator before.

'You think you've got it all worked out in your credit and your debit ledgers, but let me tell you, Johnny Boy, the wine is sweet; the paying bitter.'

'Fuck. He sounds just like Jean,' said an open-mouthed Keen.

'Whoever burns his backside must himself sit upon it.'

It was the same subconscious force that had caused Dave to emit the primal scream that now drove him.

'I warned ye, didn't I? The bad deed returns on the bad deed doer.'

'Jesus, it is Jean,' said Keen. 'He couldn't know she told me that.'

'You can run a thousand marathons, have a convoy of ambulances take the sick to Lourdes, climb Croagh Patrick on your knees, buy yourself an entire beam of the One True Cross, and mortify your flesh to the bone, but it still won't save ye, Johnny Keen,' said Dave in a heavy brogue.

Fabulous had gone white. 'It's Jean, it's that mad bitch, all right.'

'When ye die, I'll be waiting for ye.'

'You're not taken in by this Scooby Doo doo?' scoffed the Inspector. But Keen was transfixed, unable to drop Dave into the hopper.

'We've got him bang to rights. He's just pissing us around' Insisted the Inspector.

Dave ranted on, possessed by his mother, or by his own fear, or by his demons, or all three. 'The Gates of Paradise will never open to you, Johnny Boy.'

'That's what she used to say to me in the club,' Keen whispered.

'Who does she think she is? The Purgatory police?' asked the Inspector.

'Maybe.'

'And what if she is, John? Look ... one more body's not gonna make much difference.'

'Your Stairway to Heaven is closed,' Dave warned.

'See? I told you he's faking it,' said the Inspector triumphantly. 'That's Led Zeppelin.'

'It's the American title for a *Matter of Life and Death*.' said a grim Keen. 'Jean would know that.'

'Just remember, rather than greasing your way to Heaven, a friend in court is better than a pound in the purse,' said Dave, his arms outstretched, Messiah-style.

A troubled Keen still looked undecided.

'John, listen to me,' the Inspector pleaded. 'I know we call on the Saints and Martyrs to intercede and put in a good word for us, but she's nothing. She's a fucking nightclub hostess. A whore. Like Mary Magdalene.'

'Are ye ready to suffer in Purgatory, Johnny? Flogging yourself with chains and hooks. Pressing a crown of thorns on your head. Pouring hot wax over your flesh. Licking the wounds of lepers.'

'Shit,' said Keen.

'But I will intercede with the Virgin Mother herself to take the harm of the years away from ye,' Dave promised.

Keen swung the grabful of garbage containing Dave back towards the bunker, depositing him in the trash and then carefully released the tines.

Dave clambered out and looked up at his erstwhile murderer. 'May ye live to be a hundred years, John, with one extra year to repent.'

* * *

'SO LET me hear it one more time,' said Keen, after they pointed Dave in the general direction of the nearest District Line station, the Inspector having declined to give him a lift in his Jag.

'I will obey,' said Dave. 'As a dead body obeys.'

'Or you will be a dead body,' warned the Inspector.

'Now that's a Jesuit warning, Dave,' said Keen pointing menacingly, 'and you do not mess with the Jesuits. *Perinde ac cadaver.*'

'So you're going to be as good as gold from now on? Right?' checked the Inspector.

'Yes, sir.'

'Or,' said the Inspector, 'we will use you as the plot for *Marathon Man 2.* Only we won't be drilling your teeth, son. We will be inserting a drill into your other cavities.'

Satisfied Dave was a busted flush, they let him go.

He remembered very little of the journey back across London to Farringdon Street, except that he always had the carriage to himself, even when he changed onto the busy Circle Line.

He didn't speculate on his 'possession' and what had inspired it.

He just assumed it was a result of that mental merger with his mother, the 'brain bypass' that enabled him to access hitherto hidden memories of Jean. The forgotten conversations he must have overheard when he was young, and she still had her Irish accent and Irish ways, that enabled him to recreate her.

It took him over an hour in the shower to get rid of the smell, which seemed to have impregnated his skin. Then he rocked himself to sleep in the foetal position. He was making a horrible whining, grizzling sound that, if he'd been awake, would have reminded him of the *Laarf!* editor Tom Morecambe's hideous whinnying laugh.

Meanwhile, before he climbed into his Jensen and sped away, Keen had turned in triumph to the rather more skeptical Inspector. 'I've a friend at court. You know, that's better than a plenary indulgence?'

The Inspector said nothing.

The policeman was familiar with the principle of intercession with the Divine. He knew millions passionately believed in it, not just in Christianity, but in other religions, too. That a mediator can intercede, so that sins are forgiven or waived on the Day of Judgment. It was not a belief the Inspector subscribed to, but he didn't want to rain on Keen's parade.

Keen exulted at the thought. He had already obtained a plenary indulgence and that was invaluable. It meant the remission of the entire punishment due for his sins, so that no further expiation was required in Purgatory.

But.

There were always those ifs and buts: riders and qualifications in the small print and he could never get a straight answer out of priests when he quizzed them about it, not even the Canon. They sounded more like lawyers than clerics when they tried explaining it to him, using so much convoluted gobbledygook, it made his head spin.

How can they talk about years off in Purgatory where they admitted there was no time? It was like a dodgy life insurance contract, designed from the off to get you to sign on the dotted line, but not actually paying out on claims. Only this was a death insurance contract, and, being no master of semantics, Keen was never quite sure if a plenary indulgence actually delivered what it promised.

It was all that had been available to him, until now. But this … *intercession* … it was a game-changer. Never mind faith, he had just had an *objective* – not subjective – spiritual experience. His days of firing up the comptometer were over.

'I have a "Get out of Purgatory free" card, Inspector.'

'Okay,' said the Inspector.

'I can do just what the fuck I like.'

'You normally do, John.'

'So you know what that means?'

'What?'

Keen smiled with anticipation. 'It's party time.'

CHAPTER FORTY-TWO

'I DID IT,' said Greg, as Dave entered the office of *The Spanker* and *Space Warp*.

'You saw Leni?'

'Yep. I handed in my notice. I'm going freelance.'

'That's fantastic news,' said Dave.

He was enjoying the trivia of normal life after his recent trauma, and also the thought of finally getting rid of Greg so he could produce *Space Warp* with Joy.

'That's a brave decision and the right one. I'm so pleased for you, mate.'

'I knew you'd be pleased,' said Greg.

'Yes, I really wish I had your courage.'

'But you have.'

'Oh, I wish, Greg.'

'I've handed in your notice as well.'

'What! What are you talking about?'

'I knew it's what you wanted, so I told her you wanted to go freelance, too.'

'No. No. No way. You had no right.'

'Yes. Yes. Yes. And Leni's accepted it.'

'But I'm a lifer,' said Dave. 'There would need to be a halfway house to help me adjust to life on the outside. It's out of the question.'

'Hear me out,' grinned Greg. 'The producer of the *Dan Darwin* movie has had several meetings with Leni, okay?'

'A *Dan Darwin* movie? That's great news. What's it about?'

'It's going to be set on Mars. And it'll have the *Beagle*, the Vroors and the Apokrita in it!'

'Brilliant. Why doesn't anyone tell me about these things?'

'Because we're just fucking cogs in the machine, mate. But now … *now* we get the chance to operate the machine. The producer wants to control the direction of *Dan Darwin*, so he wants to take over *Space Warp* and hire us to produce it as outside contractors.'

'Outside contractors?'

'We get a percentage of the profits. Fifteen percent. What do you say?'

'Our own comic? That *we* will own a slice of? Fuck the halfway house.'

'That's what I thought you'd say. You realise if it's a hit, we'll make a fortune? Think of how much money *Aaagh!* made for Fleetpit.'

'No shit, man. Dig that fucking swimming pool.'

'We could make so much money, we might even have to go into tax exile.'

'Life is tough, Greg. I think this calls for a liquorice pipe.' Dave took one from his confectionery box. 'You want one?'

'No, I'm not … oh, go on then. Just this once.'

They chewed on their pipes and considered their glittering futures.

'How did you persuade Leni to let us be outside contractors? Oh, Greg, you didn't go under the desk again? You're not back on the green snot, are you?'

'She said it would help her prepare for purification in the coming End Times.'

'How?'

'She gets a slice of the action, too.'

'Ah. A financial as well as a spiritual reason for her decision. That makes sense now.'

'She'll probably use the money to start a science fiction religion.'

'I think that's already been done, Greg.'

Then he had an afterthought. 'What about Joy? Where does this leave her?'

'The deal's just for us. Leni loathes her.'

'I thought she loved everyone.'

'She's made an exception with Joy.'

'She'll be gutted.'

'Joy's opposed to *Dan Darwin*. Leni can't have that.'

'We could talk Joy round.'

'She's not forgiven her for pulling that *Time Machine* stunt.'

'But working on a science fiction comic is her dream.'

'Leni sees her as a rival.'

'It's everything she's ever wanted.'

'She's out.'

Dave had been hoping to get Joy back, and *Space Warp* had looked like the perfect way. But, on the other hand, there was a huge amount of money to be made here. Megabucks. Based on sales of *Aaagh!*, *Space Warp* could sell 200,000 copies a week. He was already doing the maths. He could retire at 40. Joy, as a businesswoman, would understand his decision.

'I feel bad about it, Greg.'

'Me, too.'

'Maybe you can think of a good shitty way to justify this to ourselves?'

'It's my specialty.'

'Okay. Go for it.'

'Well, she's not exactly "all for one" when it comes to buying her round. "I think I forgot my purse".' Greg said with a Scottish accent. 'That's if she hasn't already rushed off to the loo. How's that?'

'That is a really pathetic justification, Greg.'

'There's more pathetic justifications where that came from.'

'That'll do. Thanks. I feel so much better now.'

Greg stretched out a hand. 'Put it there, buddy.'

They shook on the deal. 'The Two Musketeers,' said Greg.

'All for one and one for two.'

'But maybe we won't say anything to Joy for a little while?' suggested Greg nervously.

'Yes, she might overreact.'

Greg winced at the thought of Joy's likely response.

'It means we now have the rights to someone else's rights,' Dave pondered.

'That's the way of the world, Dave.'

'That's life.'

'It's tough on the *Dan Darwin* creator. According to Leni, he'll get zilch for our version,' sighed Greg, 'But what can we do?'

They continued silently chewing on their liquorice pipes. Finally Dave spoke.

'So is he getting any money for the movie?'

'He sold all rights, remember?' said Greg. 'Just some token fee as consultant.'

'Poor sod.'

'The usual film producer bullshit so they can say their hands are clean.'

'Still, at least our own hands are clean, Greg.'

He corrected himself. 'Well, fairly clean.'

He corrected himself again. 'Okay, just a bit grubby.'

There was a pause.

'Okay, we've sold out.'

CHAPTER FORTY-THREE

AS A STORM RAGED outside his turret, Dave looked out into the darkness and reflected on his forthcoming freelance existence. In a week's time, Fleetpit House would close its doors forever and he'd have to find new accommodation.

So he was moving in with his sister, Annie, for a while, which really didn't please her. The reason he was so hard up, despite living rent-free, was because he had just had his birthday and he'd celebrated by buying a vintage silver fox gilet for his mother. It was hanging up now, waiting for the next time she visited.

It certainly did look as though the Fabulous Keen business was over. He had meant it when he promised Keen and the Inspector that he would stay out of their way in future.

The Inspector had described graphically what would happen if he didn't.

He could carry on writing *Caning Commando* for *The Spanker* until Pete Sullivan had destroyed the comic, which was probably after he'd destroyed *Aaagh!*

One thing at a time.

And he could still put in his homicidal suggestions to readers, which a man who didn't know the difference between a Death Cap and a Field Mushroom would never notice. He was addicted to his sedition now; he couldn't let it go.

Perhaps he was always destined for a life of crime, he speculated.

He found his mind drifting back to that one time he had ended up in a police cell.

He had been taken as a boy to the police station by his mother for his youthful criminal activities. He had been going door-to-door, selling cloakroom tickets as fake raffle tickets to raise money for Doctor Barnado's. The first prize, Dave told his customers, was a parrot in a cage.

He made nearly five pounds before he was caught. A young Dixon of Dock Green-style policeman gave him a fourpenny one, and then let him stew in a cell for a couple of hours. There was no going through the courts and Social Services reports: it was instant justice in the 1950s. He was then returned to his mother, who came to collect him from the station.

'It's all right, Mrs Maudling. He'll be a good boy now. We'll beat the badness out of him and beat the goodness in. It's a long process, so you might need to bring him back a number of times. School holidays would be best.'

Mr Cooper was standing at the counter and watched, gloating, enjoying Dave's snivelling. He was gently warned by the same cop: 'So keep it indoors in future, Stan. If you hit the missus in the street again, we can't really turn a blind eye.'

'Neither can she,' grinned Mr Cooper.

The adult Dave reflected on the encounter. The young cop believed in the ubiquitous 'a good clip round the ear' method of dealing with delinquent kids, but Dave was born with the 'fuck you' gene.

He was alienated from his clergy, his school and the police. He was as Alien as any of Leni's 'Boys'.

He heard footsteps coming up the stairs and wondered if it was the phone killer. He had a foot-long spanner ready for him.

'So how are you, Dave?' grinned Mr Cooper. The adult Dave did a double take. His Nemesis was standing in front of him. Swaying from side to side, and – with the fumes emanating from him – clearly drunk.

'What the hell do you want?' Snapped Dave.

'Now that's no way to talk your old man. I thought I'd come and see you. You wanted more information about the nig-nog.'

'No. I know Ernie would never harm my mother. Unlike you.'

'I keep telling you, Dave. I'm not the one who topped her.'

'Oh, no? What happened to your wife then? I liked her. She tried to protect me from you.'

Cooper laughed a dirty, Sid James laugh. 'I remember now. Silly cow.'

'You practically admitted you killed her and buried her on your allotment. Is that what you did with my mum? Murdered her and buried her on the allotment?'

'I should have done. But I didn't. Now do you want this information or not?'

'No. It's worthless.'

'But I need money, Davey,' Cooper whined. 'They're making me redundant. When Fleetpit moves over the water, I'm gonna be out of a job.'

'My heart bleeds for you.'

'There must be something you want to know.'

'Yes. As a matter of fact, there is. Why would my mother have ever got involved with someone like you? It doesn't make any sense. What did you do? Drug her?'

His father grinned and gave that dirty Sid James laugh again.

'You didn't rape her, did you?' asked Dave, suddenly alarmed. ''Cos if you did…' He started to get out of his chair, ready to take a swing at Cooper.

'Relax, Davey. Relax. Nah. That's far too much effort. All that biting and scratching and struggling. No. I couldn't be doing with that anymore.' He shook his head and grimaced. 'I didn't need to. It was a doddle. I'll tell you if you really want to know.'

'Of course I want to know. I need to know how I ended up with someone like you as my dad.'

'It's gonna cost you, son.'

'How much?'

'A tenner.'

Dave handed it over. He had to know. How his beautiful, stylish mother – who had the pick of men at The Eight Veils, men with money, culture and status, like Peter Maudling – could have sunk so low as to form a relationship with Mr Cooper.

'Well, she was lonely when she came back from nig-nog land.

Missing Ernie. And hubby had the hump with her. He was like a fucking camel. So I'd take her dancing, she loved that. The movies. Music. Frank Sinatra, Duke Ellington. And I finally won her heart with poetry.'

Dave couldn't believe it. He had imagined any number of seduction scenarios but not that! The rain lashed menacingly against the windowpanes. 'You and … *poetry?*'

'Part of my technique, see? Find out what they want and give it to them. he perfect way to get them to drop their drawers. She told me how Ernie was happy-go-lucky, lighthearted, and read her poetry, so I just became Ernie.'

'You read her poetry?'

'I did better than that. I wrote her love poems, specially for her.'

'And she liked your "poems"?'

'Lapped them up.'

'What were they? Dirty limericks?'

'She couldn't get enough of them. I could do anything with her after I read her one. And I mean anything.' He looked meaningfully at Dave. 'Including wanting to have our love child.'

Dave stood up, repelled by this new level of loathsomeness. 'Who are you?' he asked.

'I'm whoever they want me to be.'

Dave could see it now. Cooper was able to soak up other people's personalities like a sponge. So he could be the perfect mirror to women's fantasies, because he had no character, no dreams, no personality of his own. There was no one really there. He modelled himself on the latest movie star or singer; anyone who had the charisma, the charm, the vitality he lacked.

He had modelled himself on Ernie Gambo. Because he was just a husk. A nobody. When he wasn't pretending to be someone else, his lack of identity created a raging emptiness inside him that he filled with meanness and rage and spite and violence.

'You don't know who you are, do you?'

For one moment, a sadness; a rare moment of vulnerable self-realisation, crossed Cooper's face as he acknowledged the terrible truth.

He quickly recovered, his face creasing once again into its habitual scowl. 'I'm your fucking father and don't you forget it.'

'So how could someone like you write love poems?' asked Dave. 'A nobody.'

'Copied them out of *Palgrave's Golden Treasury of Verse*,' Cooper grinned, then recited:

> *Nothing in the world is single;*
> *All things by a law divine*
> *In one spirit meet and mingle.*
> *Why not I with thine?*

'And we did a lot of … mingling, Dave,' leered Cooper, walking slowly towards him.

'Shut up!' said Dave, backing away from the awfulness of the truth. 'I don't want to know! I don't want to know!'

But Cooper continued his triumphant advance:

> *And the sunlight clasps the earth*
> *And the moonbeams kiss the sea:*
> *What is all this sweet work worth*
> *If thou kiss not me?*

'She gimme a gam after that one, Davey boy. I can still remember how good it felt.'

'I said shut up. Shut up! *Shut up*! I'm warning you!'

It was all a game to Cooper, just like the endless games he played on Dave when he came into the newsagents every Saturday for his *Fourpenny One*.

He had finally found a way to torment Dave again.

> *But a smooth and steadfast mind,*
> *Gentle thoughts, and calm desires,*
> *Hearts with equal love combined,*
> *Kindle never-dying fires :-*
> *Where these are not, I despise*
> *Lovely cheeks or lips or eyes.*

'Now that got her really hot, so she ...'

'Enough!' Dave smashed him in the face. The storeman recoiled, bashed his head against the wall, slid down it and slumped to the ground.

Dave stood over him. 'Get up! Come on! Get up, you bastard!' There was a trickle of blood from the side of his father's mouth.

'Come on! I said get up!'

Cooper flopped limply over to one side. Dave knelt down and felt his pulse. Casually at first, and then desperately. And then panic-stricken. There was nothing there. Nothing there! It couldn't be.

He looked at Cooper's blank, staring eyes.

It was.

The second one in a month. He was turning into a proper serial killer now. No murders by remote control anymore. He was the real thing. But no time to think about that now. Concentrate on the practicalities. Focus. What was he going to do with the body? Where was he going to hide it?

But he already knew the answer.

The lift slowly whirred and clanked and creaked its way down through the darkened, silent building to the basement. Pushing back the scissor gate, he dragged out Cooper's corpse and slowly made his way past endless rows and rows of empty Dexion shelves and over a few remaining soggy magazines and pages of art silently growing mushrooms in the darkness. Everything else had been incinerated.

At night, the vast, now empty basement was creepier than ever, even when he turned the lights back on, especially with the distant sound of the storm howling and thundering outside.

Puffing and panting, he manhandled Cooper towards the sewer pipe. He could hear the River Fleet within, in full turgid flow, thanks to the storm. Once, Sir Christopher Wren had tried to turn the Fleet into an elegant Venetian canal. But his plan failed miserably when a tanning factory released its chemicals into the water, setting the river on fire. Now it had found its true destiny as a sewer.

Dave unlatched the hinged square cover, raised the hatch, and the grill below, and threw them back with a clang that echoed in the deadly silence. Inside the huge pipe there was a steady stream of fast moving but recognisable sewage, seething and roaring as it sought an escape, smelling as disgusting as it looked. He dragged Cooper's body up onto the side of the pipe, feet first. Cooper was a dead weight, and he had to keep taking breaks, but he eventually managed to get his feet down into the opening.

With so much rain, the Fleet interceptor tunnels had come into their own. The usual system that carried the sewage to a treatment plant, couldn't cope, so the Fleet shared the load. It would result in the Fleet sewage flowing into the Thames. It was the perfect answer.

Sweating in the damp air, Dave hauled and pulled and dragged the rest of Cooper upwards, and then his corpse slowly dropped down through the hatch. Dave just had to shove his shoulders through and he'd be gone forever, along with the rest of the filth below.

Jonathan Swift had described the Fleet during such a storm:

'*Sweepings from Butchers Stalls, Dung, Guts and Blood, Drowned Puppies, stinking Sprats, all drenched in Mud, Dead Cats and Turnip-Tops come tumbling down the Flood.*'

And Mr Cooper.

Just one last push should do it and Cooper would be joining the flood. The stench was appalling and so was the thunderous sound of the furious river.

It was like the Fleet was a living creature, hating and resisting its humiliating incarceration in a pipe, desperately wanting to be free. It had once actually exploded, the sewage gasses ripping open the street above it, destroying houses and smashing boats into Blackfriars Bridge.

It didn't die easy, and neither did Mr Cooper.

Incredibly, he had regained consciousness and swung a fist at Dave, trying to land one last fourpenny one on his son.

The memory of so many past punches, so many humiliations, seethed within Dave and gave him the strength to deliver the ultimate fourpenny one in retaliation: slamming his fist into Cooper's twisted, snarling, vicious face.

Next moment, his father had dropped into the sewer, hit his head on the pipe wall with a resounding *bong!*, and was carried away in the raging brown torrent.

'It's all right,' Dave laughed manically into the void. 'It's only Dirty Barry!'

If the blows didn't kill him, then he would surely drown by the time the Fleet reached the Thames beneath Blackfriars Bridge.

It was fitting, Dave thought, that the ex-newsagent's departure down the sewer should coincide with the closing of the Fleetpit itself.

He knew from his days as an errand boy on the docks that many bodies are washed straight out to sea, and those that are recovered are often unrecognisable, so he was confident that he would get away with it.

He'd sometimes had to ride his trade-bike down to the U-bend at the Isle of Dogs where the dead bodies tended to collect. A chatty policeman explained to the fascinated teenager that forty bodies are generally pulled out of the river every year. He pointed out the police trawler gathering up one in a body bag, to be towed to Wapping.

'They've got to keep the bloated bodies in the water in case of possible infection, see?'

'What happens when they get to Wapping?'

'They're photographed straight away 'cos the corpses blacken in the air.'

'Who are they?' asked young Dave.

'Tramps. Deadbeats.' The cop shrugged indifferently. 'Nobodies.'

CHAPTER FORTY-FOUR

BACK IN THE TURRET, his mother was waiting for him, languidly smoking a Park Lane, dressed in yet another glamorous suit, with the silver fox gilet he'd bought her.

'Satisfied?' he said. 'Is he going to be joining you? Wherever you are?'

'Hasn't turned up yet,' she smiled. 'But then I'm not really expecting him. I think we both know where he's going.'

'Where's that?'

'That place near Wimbledon you visited?'

Dave looked across at her and shook his head sorrowfully.

'*Palgrave's Golden Treasury of Verse.*'

'We believe what we have to believe to get us through the night.'

'I know that one,' he agreed. 'On odd days, I believe you exist, for instance.'

'Thank you.'

'But on even days, I believe you're a figment of my imagination.' He stared at her. 'So, is my other dad there?'

'Peter? Where Cooper is?'

'Where you are.' She didn't reply.

'Do you see him? Is he all right? Could you give him my love?'

She went to the window and looked out at the rain beating down on Farringdon Street.

'And Ernie Gambo? He's not there, is he?'

'No,' she smiled, 'I haven't seen Ernie.'

'Good. I hope he's okay, wherever he is. I miss him, too. You see? Not all your lovers were bad guys. Ernie, dad, even Mr Peat wasn't all bad. Although I still hate him for giving me low chemistry marks. I had so much potential in chemistry. I could have gone far if it wasn't for him.'

'Yes, you could have been a pharmacist in Boots now,' she said. 'Instead of telling kids what poisons to use.'

He started packing his belongings, including his Viking beard and the moth-eaten fur boa. 'Seriously,' he said, 'I'd really like to know about dad. Is he all right?'

She slowly blew cigarette smoke into his face. 'You want to know about Peter?'

'Yes.'

'Are you sure?'

'Yes!'

'He was the worst of them all.' And she laughed a ghostly laugh.

He looked pained, but not distressed: after all it couldn't possibly be true. 'Don't say that.'

She looked up at him. 'I don't even know where or how to start explaining to you. I'd better warn you. It is not good.'

'Give me the Ladybird book version,' said Dave. 'After all, you were the perfect Ladybird mother.'

'He was a pig,' Jean reflected bitterly. 'He deserved everything that happened to him.'

That was too painful for Dave. 'Okay. Enough. I'm switching you off.'

But she was still there. She got to her feet and glowered in his face. 'You know why he agreed to having his brains fried? Because he wanted to forget me. He was trying to get me out of his head, but he never could. Not even with his mad-scientist-in-the-bath *bockbier*.' She smiled. 'Oh, I made sure of that. Reminding him about Africa. What he did to me in Africa.'

'What did he do that was so bad?'

'Humiliated me in front of everyone with his Paddy jokes. Spud jokes. Bog jokes. Famine jokes.'

'It was probably just affectionate teasing,' Dave placated.

'I lost my accent because he made me ashamed of it.'

'That doesn't sound like Dad.'

'Not the one you prefer to remember.'

'There's another one?'

'How does this sound? He'd quote Charles Kingsley on the Famine. "I am haunted by the human chimpanzees I saw along that hundred miles of horrible country…to see white chimpanzees is dreadful; if they were black, one would not see it so much." When Peter got drunk, he'd call me his "white chimpanzee".'

Dave was stunned.

'Would you like to hear more about Africa?'

'No.'

'He was as proud as a whitewashed pig mixing with the nobs in Government House. Celia Miles. The Honourable Celia, daughter of a Viscount with her *Woman's Hour* voice, skin like lumpy porridge, hands like cold clams and Mr Punch jaw and horsey face, but, because she'd gone to Cambridge, he just couldn't keep his hands off her.'

'I really don't want to know about dad's infidelities.'

'Why not?'

'Because yours are enough.'

He marched into the main attic to get away from her, but she pursued him.

'And Charlotte the Harlot. They could have been identical twins. Four eyes, plus fours, square jaws and jolly hockey sticks. I thought the Oxford bag was a dyke, so she wasn't a threat. How wrong could I be?'

'This is really more information than I need to know, mum.'

Dave realised how he must have blocked all this out as a kid: conversations he overheard or things she had actually told him. Her boundaries then and now were poor. Conversations he had access to after his mental merger with her. He picked up an old magazine from a pile to distract himself. It was a yellowing copy of *Stately Piles.*

'They're probably in there; Charlotte and Celia,' Jean noted. 'It was perfectly all right for him to have affairs, but, because I took a black lover, we were sent home in disgrace.'

She smiled grimly at the memory. 'So then I had a five-year headache.'

'But he still had his good points,' Dave said lamely. 'After you'd gone, he looked after me and Annie. He sent me to a good school.'

'Until he ran out of money, because he drank it all. So you had to leave school and become an errand boy, riding round on a trade-bike.'

'It didn't matter. I understood,' said Dave, trying to keep the peace. 'It was okay.'

She sat down in a broken Captain's chair; her phantom weight failing to upturn it. 'Well, I'm not so forgiving. I wanted my son to have a proper education, so he could get a decent job: a solicitor; a doctor; an accountant. A job I could be proud of. Not end up working on …' she waved her hand dismissively. '… *The Spanker.*'

He sat on the corner of an old 1940's office desk and confronted her. 'You're just the weird workings of my subconscious, mum. When I hear your music in my head, it's actually my intuition alerting me to danger. That's all. Nothing else. Freud probably has a name for you.'

'And how long have people paid attention to Freud?' she sneered. 'Less than a century. But from the beginning of time, people have called entities like me a phantom; a muse; a spirit; a guardian angel; a–'

'Demon?'

'So thousands of intelligent people, over millennia, were actually stupid, until Freud and co. came along and explained we're just an illusion of the subconscious, whatever that is.'

'He'd probably say it's a side effect of childhood trauma and having a narcissist mother.'

'I never touched narcotics.'

'Mum, writers have been having imaginary conversations with themselves since the ancient Greeks.'

'But we both know this is different, don't we?'

He went to the window. 'Storm's stopped.'

He turned round and confronted her. A curious mixture of nightclub hostess, glamour girl from *Photothrill,* Ruth Ellis, Diana Dors, and Mother.

'I believe in you, mum. But I don't want to believe in you anymore. When I leave this building, I need to make a new start. I can actually achieve something with *Space Warp.*'

'And I'd be in your way?'

'You know you would. I'll never stop thinking of you, but I have to do this.' She said nothing.

'I'm sorry. This is goodbye, mum.' This time, she faded away.

CHAPTER FORTY-FIVE

IT WAS their last day at Fleetpit House. Dave and Greg were packing their files and personal possessions into boxes and crates, ready for transporting to the Black Monolith and their new freelance careers as producers of *Space Warp*.

Dave felt a new lightness in his life, which was not even marred by Greg, who was endlessly talking about Trust, and had a glazed look in his eye.

Then Joy entered.

Dave eyed her with mixed emotions: so desirable and yet so deadly. Both he and Greg had been fearing this moment. 'All right, Judas and Quisling,' she snapped. 'How much did you sell out for?'

'I'm not sure I get your drift, Joy?' said Dave warily, playing for time, while Greg simply smiled inanely at her.

'On the science fiction comic we were meant to be working on together. *Together.*'

'Oh, yes.'

'Oh, yes. "All for one and one for all." '

'What's the problem, Joy?'

'I'm out.'

'Oh.'

'Finished.'

'I didn't know.'

'Don't come the fucking innocent with me, you turncoats. I've just heard it from the space cadet as she was dancing into work.'

'Dancing? Don't you mean jogging?' smiled Greg.

'I mean dancing. She doesn't jog. She's not like normal people, Benedict Arnold. She dances along the street listening to music from outer space she's channeling from "The Boys".'

'Maybe she's starting a new craze?' speculated Dave.

'Dancing and jogging: dogging?'

'Nah, that's when men spy on couples having sex in parks, so they know how to fuck properly,' explained Greg.

'I got you two out of The Hole.'

'And we are so grateful, Joy.'

'You would have rotted in there for the rest of your lives if it hadn't been for me.'

'We'll be forever in your debt. Right, Greg?'

'Right. Just like Britain and the IMF.'

'And we will repay you one day.'

'How?'

'A drink down the pub?'

'How much did she offer you to cut me out?'

'I'm afraid that's confidential,' said Dave.

'That much? What was the deal?'

Dave turned to Greg. 'We can't really discuss the details, can we, Greg?'

'You have to Trust, Joy,' said Greg agreeably. 'Trust that all is well with the world.'

'But all is not well with the world, Mr Smiley,' said Joy, upturning a crate. 'What are you two like? The Vatican? All hush-hush, sitting in secret conclave until white smoke comes out your arses? Did she make you sit in the keyhole chair to check you had testicles?'

'There was no need, Joy,' said Dave. 'She already knew we don't have any.'

'And you're going ahead with *Dan Darwin*, is that right?'

'Trust us, Joy,' said Greg. 'It'll be great.'

Joy stood on the crate. 'Have you any idea how you'll offend old fans, after Dave tore up *Dan Darwin* on TV?'

'Leni told me not to worry about the old fans,' said Dave. 'She says they're a niche audience.'

'Like the crack in your arse that I'm going to open up with one of those wing corkscrews. And if that works, I'm going to use it on your cock next. Come here,' she beckoned. 'Come on.'

'I'd rather not, Joy,' said Dave apprehensively.

'Oh, don't be so silly, come here, you fucking wimp. Look, what the fuck am I going to do to you, standing on a crate?'

'That's what I'm not sure about,' said Dave. 'This isn't some new kind of knee trembler you have in mind, because I understand the usual procedure is to stand on a brick.'

'It's in the same ball park, I promise,' said Joy seductively.

'We need to learn to Trust,' smiled Greg. He made a 'T' sign with his hands.

'Come on,' Joy encouraged Dave. 'See? Empty hands. I'm not going to glass you. You heard Greg. Trust me.'

He reluctantly moved forward, so she was slightly above him. She placed a hand on either shoulder, gave him a wide smile, then swiftly and expertly head butted him.

She stepped off the crate. 'See? I was right wasn't I? I gave you head.'

'It's all about Trust, Dave,' Greg smiled and made the 'T' sign again.

Joy glowered at Greg. 'I can think of two other signs for you. I'll deal with you later. I want it to be spontaneous. But I want you to think about it, and know it's coming. Clue: there's some unusual orifices in the human body that fur-boy's actually missed, that I'm gonna penetrate on you.'

She turned at the door and pointed menacingly at Greg.

'Trust me on this.' And made the 'T' sign.

'Well,' said Dave thickly after she'd gone, dabbing his bloody nose with a handkerchief. 'That went better than expected.'

'It was one of her better days,' agreed Greg.

'So what's all this Trust shit you're on about?' asked Dave.

Greg lowered his typewriter into a packing case. 'It's my new system. I read it in one of Leni's New Age books.'

'It wasn't in *Green Snot for the Soul*?'

'No. *The Me Me Me Generation: How to put Me first*. It says we have to trust what's right for us.'

'Like cutting Joy out?'

'That's what our instincts told us. Right?'

'Right.'

'So we have to Trust them. It works for Leni. I needed to figure out how she was so successful, so I could copy her.'

'At being a selfish bitch?'

'At self-fulfillment.'

'So no more self-sacrifice and doing our duty?'

'Are you kidding? That's for *old* people. Self-gratification is the way forward.'

'Do what you like and fuck everyone else.'

'It's an exciting new way of looking at life.'

'I doubt it. Aleister Crowley's "Do what thou wilt shall be the whole of the law," is from Rabelais in the sixteenth century.'

Greg looked thoughtfully down at his typewriter. 'On the subject of the law, I remember being round the back of Fleet Street and seeing journalists lowering their typewriters down on ropes to their mates in the street below, so they could go and flog them down the market.'

'They were self-gratifying themselves?'

'Achieving their full potential.'

'It's good to know the spirit of corruption and venality is universal in '70s Britain.'

'Trouble is,' said Greg, considering his ancient Imperial, 'I don't think we'd get much for ours. They're not even electric.'

'That's because they want us working through the next power cut. It's forward thinking of them,' observed Dave. 'We'll be creating *Space Warp*, the comic of the future, by candlelight.'

'I'm just not buying all these depressing strikes and the inflation shit anymore,' said Greg. 'The Black Monolith is a new beginning for us, Dave. A bright future of self-entitlement. Everything looks so ... *amazing* now.'

'You'll be waxing lyrical about Brotherhood of Man and the Worzels next,' Dave sighed. 'Well, I'm sorry to inform you, Greg, I don't have a combine harvester, I'm not a cider drinker and I hope you're not saving your kisses for me, because there is nothing ambivalent about my sexuality.'

'I know,' agreed Greg. 'You're armidextrous.'

'So enlighten me, Greg, as you throw your bone up into your Walt Disney-Julie Andrews-Hills are Alive-future: what is so amazing?'

'For a start, it's been a fantastic, long hot summer ...' Greg began.

'And?' pursued Dave relentlessly.

'Well, I don't know,' shrugged Greg.

'Come on. Apart from the drought and the standpipes and the shared baths? Just how much saccharin helps the medicine go down?'

'There's space hoppers, chopper bikes, 'Dancing Queen', Noel and Cheggers.' Greg said warmly.

'There are so many cynical responses to that, Greg,' said Dave, 'I'm salivating at the prospect. We'll put Noel and Cheggers to one side, shall we? Because I really don't want to drown in my own drool.'

'And it's not like when we – or you anyway – were growing up. Today, it's a safe world out there for kids to just be kids and have fun.'

'Is that what this *Me Me Me* book tells you? And you believe it?'

'It tells me how to set myself free. Look, I've got a chart that helps.' Greg unfurled a monthly calendar: each day had a box next to it with plus or minus signs marked on it. 'This is my Mancipation chart.'

Dave recoiled. 'A constipation chart? I thought you already kept a turd diary.' Greg shook his head.

'Oh, it's a masturbation chart, is it? I see. How often before you go blind? Or grow hair on the palms of your hands? Judging by all these plusses, you should be turning into a fucking werewolf just about now.'

'It follows my monthly emotional cycle,' Greg patiently explained. 'You see, men have a unique testosterone and hormonal cycle, just like women. So we can follow it and relate to those changes in our bodies, and it sets us free from them.'

'D'you mind if I check your arm for track marks?'

'Each day has an emotional value, positive or negative, no matter what's happened.'

'You mean if I won the pools on a misery day, I'd still feel miserable?'

'Probably,' said Greg guardedly. 'It's why we have to Trust our feelings.' He made the 'T' sign again.

Dave was lost for words. Greg pointed proudly to the chart.

'The Mancipation chart sets men free.'

'Have you shown it to Joy yet?' asked Dave, 'and could I please be there when you do?'

'Joy needs to know when we're having our emotional periods.'

'And what happens if I Trust my feelings and say you're talking shite?' asked Dave.

'I think you could be suffering from Irritable Male Syndrome.'

The phone rang. 'I think I'm just about to come on,' said Dave. 'Excuse me.'

He tensed, mentally preparing himself, in case it was the Major's killer on the other end of the phone.

His hand patted his foot-long spanner, dropped down through a hole into the lining of his jacket so it was suitably concealed. He could handle the killer: he was not afraid, now he had rediscovered that kid inside himself who had nearly been throttled to death by the Sister of Sorrow.

It was Scott on the phone. 'Dave …?'

'Hi, Scott. How are you doing?'

'Not good.'

Dave could feel the pain and anger in his voice.

'What's wrong?'

'The parties have started again.'

'I'm so sorry, man.'

'So are you still up for … you know? The Plan?' This was different. Scott was afraid.

'Dave …? Are you there?' He was very afraid.

'Dave …?'

It would mean risking his life. Keen had made it very clear that if he tried anything again, he was dead. And he would be risking his liberty. Not to mention his future career on *Space Warp*.

'Dave …?'

But who else was there for them? The law gave them zero protection. Keen, like his rich, important clients, was above the law.

Dave was their only hope.

'Let's do it, Scott.'

'You're sure?'

'Let's Carpet Bum the Hun.'

EPILOGUE

TRISTAN FOLLOWED the path of chivalry and courtly love. The true path, not the one that knights pretended to follow. Tristan knew that was just to fool the peasants. Chivalry, honesty, truth, honour and gallantry were qualities knights supposedly stood for, but it was a pretence; part of their carefully constructed armour.

He knew they stood for the exact opposite.

Knights had always lived by looting the poor and raping and abusing women. And he certainly had.

His father had explained to him who knights really were. Then and now. The only thing that the romantic version and the reality of knighthood had in common was their superiority over the peasants, who looked up to them and actually believed they were a force for good.

This unassailable truth, according to Tristan, was first expressed by William of Aquitaine, the original troubadour and great crusader, who his father told him to read when he was instructing his sons in the ways of the world. That valiant knight, grandfather of Eleanor of Aquitaine, was the very epitome of chivalry. William had got it so right: '*So I put my hands beneath her dress … Let others brag about love, but we have the bread and the knife.*'

Yes, Tristan had the knife, all right. He had found William's poetry a great comfort when he was on remand on that rape charge:

I'll tell how things look to me:
I hate a guarded cunt and a fish hole without fish
And the boasting of prats who never act.

Tristan could afford the best lawyer money could buy, and he got off on the rape charge.

His face had swelled up and he was in agony for a week after the Major had hit him with the typewriter, after he'd stabbed him through the ribs with the misericorde. But he was back at work at Fleetpit now.

He had begun his journalist career as an assistant editor of *Tally Ho!*, the hunting magazine. Then he was promoted to editor of *Diecast and Diorama*. His endless knowledge of knights was invaluable there. He used to collect them as a boy. He still had his display shelves of model knights from Castellan Collectibles.

Finally, he became editor of the highly prestigious *Chivalry and Livery*.

Both he and his brother had been inspired by their father, who had been knighted, and who explained to his sons about the natural order of predator and prey. He said it was the absolute *duty* of the rich to prey on the poor in order to cull the herd. He said that the rich knew this, but they had to pretend otherwise.

Not to prey on the poor was a betrayal of their function in life.

But it was very important to effectively disguise this fact, just as a predator in the wild camouflages itself with spots and stripes. Hence the fake Codes of Chivalry knights issue to reassure the prey that their predators actually cared for them.

Tristan had sought kindred spirits amongst the Knights of St Pancras, but, somehow, they'd found out he had been in a mental institution, and turned down his application.

It was after he had made his own Greek fire. He'd worked out the ingredients from reading medieval accounts. He had demonstrated the lost secrets of Byzantium by using it to set fire to a peasant's house. He'd loved watching it burn. He thought the other re-enactors would be impressed. But they were horrified. He'd tried to explain to them that war without fire is like sausages without mustard. They were no better than the rubber sworders. Weekend warriors. To be a true knight you have to live the life. They had reported his arson attack on the council house. It led to him being sectioned.

When he got out, he decided it was better to be a loner. Now, letting himself dry naturally after his cold shower, he started to dress. Natural fibre underwear. There was no polyester in the Crusades. Then the chainmail vest. Galvanised steel: 30,000 rings. It had taken him two weeks to knit. Always put it on with the pants. That was the rule. Then a linen shirt over the top, so no-one would know.

His thoughts turned to Dave Maudling.

It was time a knight put an end to his campaign of killing innocent people, hiding behind *The Caning Commando*. Killing was the job of a knight, not a peasant like Maudling.

When Giles had died after the power drill went through his head, Tristan had not been satisfied with the verdict of accidental death. He was merely suspicious at first. But then his sister-in-law and nephew, Sam, disappeared overnight without leaving a forwarding address. When they didn't turn up for Giles's funeral, Tristan knew he must investigate. They had to be involved in some way. Despite his best efforts, he was unable to track them down. Mother and son had gone to ground.

They had left in such a hurry there was still furniture and personal possessions lying around their house. He carefully went through his sister-in-law's drawers and files, checking her documents, but there was nothing that gave him a clue as to their current whereabouts.

Then he moved on to Sam's room. There was nothing there either: just a stack of board games like Monopoly and Totopoly, shelves of books, records, and piles of *The Spanker*.

Frustrated, he threw the board games across the room, tossed the books off their shelves, ripped football and pop posters off the wall, and kicked the comics over. Then he sat down in the silent room and pondered on his next move.

Looking at the newsprint comics strewn at his feet, he thought about his young nephew and why he would read garbage like *The Spanker*.

He thought about setting the comics alight and burning the whole damn house down. In fact, he actually struck a match and was close to igniting the comics. But then he remembered how he was sectioned the last time and realised he needed to calm down. He did this by reminding himself that burning the house was a poor substitute for what he actually wanted to do to Sam and his mother.

He noticed one of the comic strips was circled and asterisked in biro.

A comic was about the only thing he could read through the red mist in front of his eyes and the dull throbbing in his temples.

But when he read it, it only intensified the red mist in front of his eyes and the throbbing in his temples.

The strip that Sam had marked was a puerile story about someone called the Caning Commando, and it gave detailed instructions on how to sabotage an electric cane and make it look like an accident.

An accident?

That electric cane could easily have been an electric drill.

He looked at other issues of the comic. There were more examples where kids could carry out ingenious and secret vengeance on adults or on each other.

He turned to the indicia page and noted *The Spanker* was produced in the same building as his *Chivalry and Livery*.

Feeling a whole lot better, and with a new sense of purpose, he left the house.

A few discreet enquiries at Fleetpit, talking to the comic's art editor they called Deep Throat, and he discovered the Major and the editor Dave Maudling were responsible for *The Caning Commando* and these insidious, criminal ideas. He wasn't sure which one, but it didn't really matter.

They both had to die.

The Major had been dealt with. Now it was Maudling's turn.

Maudling was subverting the natural order of things. It would be Tristan's task, as a knight, to put a stop to that. To kill this man whose heart was not pure.

By not pure, he meant someone who was challenging the basis of a society that went back to at least the Middle Ages. This peasant had to pay the price for not knowing his place.

Like any true knight, he was always ready for the Quest.

The instrument he intended to use on his Quest was the Francisca throwing axe.

He went into his large, secluded garden, where there was a range of strategically-placed pumpkins and other targets for sword, axe and bow. Various four-legged foam beasts looked blankly across at him, dutifully awaiting their deaths. Again. Their vital organs were usefully displayed on the outside of their bodies so he knew exactly where he needed to cut and stab and pierce in order to kill them. He would regularly attack and kill this menagerie, striking at their visible organs. And then he would move on to the human foam targets, whose hearts, lungs, and intestines were also revealed externally.

It was his own personal *dieorama*.

Now he discovered – by attacking a human target – that the theory about the bounce on a throwing axe was correct. Thrown at the ground, in front of the target, like skipping a stone on water, it bounces and flies up into their testicles, guts, or face. However, it may also bypass them. It was satisfying to see his axe embedded deeply in his target's crotch, but, even after he'd adjusted the weapon's beard, it was too unpredictable, too random, to ensure it would end up there every time.

He would need to be up front and personal with Maudling to deliver that kind of blow.

Then finish him off with a blow to the head.

He got a length of rope and hung a pumpkin from a branch, then struck down at it, slicing cleanly through its fibrous orange flesh. The pumpkin moved as he struck, but that was okay. Maudling might also still be moving.

Then he tried a sideways swipe on another pumpkin. This time he split Maudling's face wide open.

He was pleased. He had cut through almost to the spinal column.

He carefully cleaned the orange flesh off the axe with a soft paper towel. Then he oiled the blade and polished it with a lint-free cloth, the kind used by opticians on glasses. He opened a black leather case, which had a foam cut-out in the shape of an axe, and the weapon fitted neatly within.

- The final battle between the Geek Detective and Fabulous Keen. But who is 'the other party' involved in his mother's murder?
- More kids' vigilante justice against adult abusers. Is kids' rule okay? Or is it *Lord of the Flies* mayhem?
- The dark secrets of a comic book artist revealed, with terrible consequences for Dave.
- The dark secrets of a comic book editor revealed, with terrible consequences for Dave.
- The dark secrets of a comic book publisher revealed with … yes, you guessed it.
- Which stories will make the number one issue of the famous SF comic *Space Warp*?
- The Caning Commando returns with three new stories: *Bum Rap, The Cane Mutiny* and *The Dark Arssassin.*
- Can Dave save Joy from the terrors of 'The House of Correction'?
- Why is Greg acting so strangely? And why won't he walk down Fleet Street with Dave and Joy?
- Psychopath Tristan Morgan catches up with the Geek Detective to avenge his brother's murder.

Don't miss our news and updates: join our mailing list at www.millsverse.com and we will send you two stories, completely free:

- *The Artists' Debt Collection Party*

- *Relieving Mr Mafeking*

CAN'T WAIT FOR THE NEXT BOOK?

The Grim Reader is a few months away, so why not join our mailing list and download a couple of stories from Pat while you're waiting?

Head over to www.millsverse.com to grab your stories, completely free.

THE ARTISTS' DEBT COLLECTION PARTY (Being an account of how the Toxic! artists, led by Pat Mills, did recover their unfairly withheld wages from the Publisher)

This true story short (just under 3000 words), written with Pat's trademark acerbic wit, is a companion piece to Pat's *Be Pure! Be Vigilant! Behave!* history of 2000AD, but it can definitely be enjoyed on its own.

RELIEVING MR MAFEKING

A longer short story (c. 7000 words) from the *Read Em And Weep* universe.

What is the dark secret of Mafeking and Jones? What is waiting for Dave Maudling in the basement of the famous caning emporium? And what does Mr Jones really mean when he tells Dave that Mr Mafeking is 'no longer with us'?

Dave's tough new comic *Aaagh!* – known to the press as the 'eightpenny nightmare' – is so controversial, questions are asked in Parliament. But Dave naively believes all publicity is good publicity.

Then Dave is invited to visit Mafeking and Jones of St James's, the famous cane-makers. Lured by the prospect of receiving a bottle of ten-year-old malt whisky, he accepts, and is shown an awesome array of swagger sticks, swordsticks, bullwhips, riding crops and school canes.

But there is a nightmare waiting for him in the basement.

This is a tale of revenge, treachery and treason, with even more blood and gore than *Aaagh!*

Also available from Millsverse Books

Serial Killer (Read Em And Weep 1)

By Pat Mills & Kevin O'Neill

Introducing the Geek Detective

Meet comic book editor Dave Maudling, the world's laziest serial killer.

The world's most cowardly serial killer.

Actually, he's never killed anyone himself – yet. His READERS do his killings for him.

Meet Jean, Dave's femme fatale mother.

She's glamorous. She's dangerous. She's dead.

She tells the 'lard-arse assassin' he needs to grow up, sort his life out, lose some weight.

And solve her murder.

Also available from Millsverse Books

Be Pure! Be Vigilant! Behave! 2000AD & Judge Dredd: The Secret History

By Pat Mills

As *2000AD* and *Judge Dredd* celebrate their 40th birthday, Pat at last writes the definitive history of the Galaxy's Greatest Comic, and the turbulent, extraordinary and exciting events that shaped it.

Everything you've always wanted to know about *Judge Dredd, Slaine, Nemesis, ABC Warriors, Flesh, Bill Savage* and more, is in this book.

The writers and artists who created them and the real-life people and events they drew on for inspiration. The scandals, back-stabbing and the shocking story that was too sensitive to ever see the light of day is finally told.

Funny, sad, angry, defiant, and outrageous: it's the Comic Book memoir of the year!

Also available from Millsverse Books

**Psychokiller, (Graphic Novel) by Pat Mills & Tony Skinner,
illustrated by Dave Kendall**

ARE YOU READY FOR YOUR DEMONIC IRRIGATION?

Doctor Morbus, the PsychoKiller, will see you now.

A Ouija board session to summon 1950s gangster Liquid Lenny goes horribly
right.

Lily the Fink starts acting weirder than usual.

Mary Anne's boyfriend is brutally murdered in his own bathroom, and she
develops a sudden penchant for doo-wop music and beehive hairdo's.

Timid Jamie Anderson saw something that night. He knows Mary Anne needs
urgent medical help. And there's only one doctor qualified to give it…

*56 pages of full colour stripart, and a bonus 9-page, beautifully gruesome art
gallery from Dave Kendall.*

Also available from Millsverse Books

Carlos Ezquerra's 2000AD & Judge Dredd Colouring Book

Colour like Carlos!

One of the best-loved and most successful sci-fi fantasy creators in the world collects 50 superb drawings of his top characters in a colouring book guaranteed to get your creative and law-giving juices flowing.

It's the Law!

Go wild with colour as Dredd arrests perps, chases mutants on his Lawmaster Bike, and fights zombies!

Strontium Dog, Durham Red, Judge Anderson, The Dark Judges, The Fatties, and many more beloved 2000AD characters join Dredd in this epic collection of Carlos's stunning creations. Unleash your creativity, relax, and lose yourself in the sci-fi world of Carlos Ezquerra!

Includes special introduction by John Wagner, Judge Dredd writer-creator!

ABOUT THE AUTHOR

PAT MILLS, famed as 'the Godfather of British comics', started his freelance career writing stories for *The Spanker, Aaagh!, Shandy* and *Laarf!*. He went on to create *2000AD*, featuring *Judge Dredd*, and wrote many of its key stories, such as *Judge Dredd, Slaine* and *Nemesis the Warlock*. His latest book *Be Pure! Be Vigilant! Behave!* is a *Secret History of 2000AD and Judge Dredd*.

Pat also co-created the anti-superhero character *Marshal Law*, with Kevin O'Neill, for Marvel Comics, and wrote the satirical French bestselling series *Requiem Vampire Knight*, with art by Olivier Ledroit, published by Editions Glenat.

His acclaimed anti-war series *Charley's War*, with artist Joe Colquhoun, has been the subject of major exhibitions in French war museums. His series *Accident Man*, co-created with Tony Skinner, has just been made into a movie starring Scott Adkins (Lucian in Marvel's *Doctor Strange*). He is currently working on volume three of the *Read Em and Weep* black comedy novel series: *The Grim Reader*.

You can find Pat on Facebook and Twitter
www.facebook.com/PatMillsComics @patmillscomics

Get in touch with Pat by email or social media. Don't forget to sign up to our mailing list – you'll get two fantastic free stories from Pat!

www.millsverse.com
pat@millsverse.com

Printed in Great Britain
by Amazon